McCa[...]
place th[...]
the hill. [...]
to the chest. Ignoring the bullets hitting all around
him, JD shifted his rifle to the second NVA and
pulled the trigger—the rifle clicked. There wouldn't
be enough time to reload. Dropping the CAR-15 to
the ground, he jerked the heavy .44 Magnum from
his shoulder holster. With AK rounds ricocheting off
the pipe, he fell to a prone position and sighted the
big handgun under the pipe. He pulled off the first
round, hitting the advancing man in the crotch. As
the man doubled over, a second round hit him in the
head. The sight of the exploding head caused the
third man to hesitate for only a second. That was all
the time McCall needed. Swinging the .44 over the
top of the pipe, he fired. The NVA soldier was blown
six feet backward, with a startled look on his face,
as he clutched the gaping hole in his chest.

STRIKER ONE DOWN

Soldier of Fortune books from Tor

NO. 7

SOLDIER OF FORTUNE
MAGAZINE PRESENTS:

STRIKER ONE DOWN

JAMES N. PRUITT

TOR

A TOM DOHERTY ASSOCIATES BOOK

STRIKER ONE DOWN

Copyright © 1987 by Omega Group, Ltd.

First printing: September 1987

A TOR Book

Published by Tom Doherty Associates, Inc.
49 West 24 Street
New York, N.Y. 10010

ISBN: 0-812-51217-0
CAN. ED.: 0-812-51218-9

Printed in the United States of America

0 9 8 7 6 5 4 3 2 1

STRIKER ONE DOWN

I.

⸻✦⸻✦⸻✦⸻✦⸻✦⸻✦⸻✦

0800 Hours
9 June 1967
MACV Headquarters
Saigon, South Vietnam

The bell on the teletype rang, signaling the end of the message. Colonel Jess Baron tore the hard copy off the machine and began to read.

"SITUATION REPORT—QUANG TRI PROVINCE
"SUBJECT: ENEMY SIGHTING—BIEN CAO VILLAGE
RELIABLE SOURCES REPORT NVA MAJOR AND TEN-MAN PATROL WERE IN VILLAGE OF BIEN CAO BETWEEN 0200 AND 0300 HOURS—EIGHT JUNE '67. ONE MEMBER OF THIS PATROL WAS IDENTIFIED AS CAUCASIAN AMERICAN DRESSED IN FULL NVA UNIFORM AND HEAVILY ARMED. A DOUBLE CHECK OF THIS SIGHTING THROUGH LEVEL-ONE SOURCES HAS CONFIRMED. NVA MAJOR IDENTIFIED AS NGO VAN THANH. FILE ON THIS INDIVIDUAL AT YOUR LOCATION. I.D. OF AMERICAN UNKNOWN. NORTHERN AGENTS REPORT THAT MAJOR THANH PLANS TO RETURN BIEN CAO IN NEXT THREE TO FOUR WEEKS. INFORMATION OBTAINED FROM SOURCES BELIEVED RELIABLE. . . . MAJOR COOPER SENDS. . . . . . ."

Baron signed for the message and, placing it in a classified folder, left the operations center and headed for the chief's office.

1

Major Thanh was no stranger to Baron, and he didn't need to pull any files to read up on the bastard. Thanh was one of Hanoi's top experts at interrogation and terrorist activities. Baron had seen firsthand what this man was capable of doing to a village that failed to support the NVA cause.

Jess Baron had led a Special Forces A Team across the DMZ to attempt the capture of Thanh. That had been two years ago, and the memory of that ill-fated mission would live with Baron forever. It had not been Thanh who was almost captured, but rather, Baron and the few survivors of the battle with Thanh and his forces. It had been a costly battle for the A Team. Of its twelve men, seven were killed and three wounded. The entire group would have been wiped out if it hadn't been for the timely arrival of a reinforced recon team that had been rushed to their aid. This message from Major Cooper was the first confirmed sighting of Thanh since that encounter.

Baron had already started forming a list of names in his mind as he opened the door marked CHIEF —MACV: STUDIES AND OPERATIONS GROUP. The colonel's new aide was a captain who had been in the country less than two weeks.

"Is the colonel in?"

"Yes, sir."

"Good. Can you hold all calls and interruptions for the next hour?"

The young captain looked up at the tall, stocky officer with the sandy-colored hair. The look he received from Baron's steel-blue eyes caused him to hesitate before replying.

"I don't know if I can do that, sir. The colonel has an important meeting this morning with . . ." He never got to finish his statement.

Curling his huge hands into fists, Baron muttered something under his breath and leaned forward with a devil's fire dancing in his eyes.

"It's really extremely urgent. Nobody for one hour. Okay?"

"Uh . . . yes, sir . . . I understand sir . . . one hour . . . nobody . . . got it, sir."

Baron felt the beginning of a smile force itself across his face. As he opened the door to the colonel's office, the smile broke free. Baron could still remember his early days as a captain and the times he had suffered intimidation at the hands of higher-ranking officers. The young man at the desk would survive.

Colonel Davis was pouring coffee as Baron shut the door.

"Morning, Jess, want some coffee?"

"That sounds great, sir. Just black, please." Baron sat down in one of the overstuffed chairs in front of Davis's desk and waited.

The colonel looked well for a man in his early fifties. He still had the broad shoulders to go along with his six-foot frame. There was no middle-age spread around this man's waist. Davis had taken good care of his body over the years and could still play one hell of a game of racquetball. Gray streaks had just begun to appear at the sides of his dark hair, but these only added a look of distinction to this man with sixteen years' experience in Special Forces.

Jess Baron had known Hap Davis for over ten years. They had met at Jump School in Fort Benning, Georgia. It was a friendship that had continued through tours of duty at Fort Bragg, Thailand, Vietnam, and back to Fort Bragg. When Davis had taken command of the Studies and Observation Group, he had requested that Baron be assigned to his command as his intelligence officer.

Handing the cup of coffee to Baron, the colonel moved to his desk and sat down.

"Well, Jess, you're looking mighty serious this morning. What's on your mind?"

"Sir, I've asked your aide to hold all your calls and

appointments for the next hour."

Davis set his coffee down and pulled out one of his favorite cigars.

"Jess, my boy, I sure as hell hope you have something important in that folder you got there. My first appointment this morning was supposed to be with the Vietnamese assistant chief of staff, and he doesn't like to be kept waiting."

Leaning forward, Baron placed the folder in front of the colonel, then sat back to drink his coffee and wait for the man's reaction. It wasn't long in coming.

"Damn! Bien Cao village has been a pain in the ass ever since I got here," the general said, shaking his head in disgust. "An American with the NVA? Shit! Ngo Van Thanh—isn't he that terrorist expert you almost nailed a couple of years ago?"

"Yes, sir, it's the same joker."

Davis read the message once more before placing it back into the folder on his desk.

"Jess, Major Cooper is one of the best intel officers we've got. He wouldn't send me a message like this unless he was convinced that the information was 100-percent accurate. Do you agree?"

"Yes, sir. I also found it interesting that Cooper referred to the Caucasian as an American both times, not a Russian, German, or anything else. He states that he's American personnel, period."

"You know, Jess, there's one thing I hate worse than these damn VC and NVA, and that's a son of a bitch that calls himself an American and then turns a weapon on his own country. You've been handling the reports out of the DMZ. Has this asshole been around awhile, or is he just coming into the ball game on the commie side?"

Baron lit a cigarette before answering. "I stopped by my office on the way up here, sir. The last confirmed reports of a Caucasian working with the enemy are dated 12 October 1966—that was when one of our recon teams waxed two Russian advisors outside of Quang Tri Province." Baron paused. Taking a long drag on his cigarette, he continued. "Of course, we still have that damn Salt and Pepper team working somewhere in the north, but they are strictly combat instructors for the North Vietnamese Army, and Hanoi keeps those boys well protected at all times."

Colonel Davis crushed his cigar out and slowly shook his head. "Goddamn Salt and Pepper! Jesus, how I'd love to get my hands on those two bastards. I'd personally blow their brains out and send the pictures to Hanoi."

Baron knew a long list of people who would like to have that honor, himself included.

Salt and Pepper were two American deserters—one white and one black. The reports started two years ago. At first it was thought that the two men were playing along with the NVA until they could get a chance to escape. But that idea was discounted seven months later when a Special Forces recon unit from Da Nang was captured north of the DMZ. There had been three Americans and five Montagnards on that team. In the initial contact, two of the Yards were killed and one of the Americans had been wounded. In a matter of minutes the team had been overrun by the NVA forces. The prisoners had been taken farther north for interrogation.

Their interrogators turned out to be Major Ngo Van Thanh, assisted by two Americans—one white, one black. An account of that interrogation was later provided by one of the Montagnards, who had escaped only moments before he was to be executed. The story he told had shocked and angered every Special Forces man in Vietnam.

According to the lone survivor, the team had been blindfolded and then pushed, dragged, and kicked through the jungle for two days and nights, finally arriving at an unknown village somewhere in the north.

A Major Thanh had removed the blindfolds and made a list of their names. He had asked a few questions of the Americans, but could not get any information other than name, rank, and serial number. The major had not been upset at their refusal to answer his questions; as a matter of fact, he had been very polite. Smiling, he had left the room and returned with the two Americans, whom he introduced as Salt and Pepper. They were to conduct the remainder of the interrogation for the major.

The black man, called Pepper, began the interrogation with the team leader, Sergeant Wathers. He made small talk at first, then leaned forward into Wathers's face and asked what unit he and his men were from. Wathers replied by spitting in Pepper's face. The huge black man only grinned. Slowly wiping his face with the back of his right hand, Pepper then quickly made a sudden downward motion with his left hand. Wathers screamed—his right cheek had been slashed to the bone. The wounded member of the team, Sergeant Todd, screamed, "You black ass bastard!" and tried to kick Pepper. This action only brought a sharp blow of a rifle butt to the back of his head, and he crumpled to the floor, unconscious.

The action distracted Pepper only for a few moments. Directing his attention back to Sergeant Wathers, he placed his knife on the table and tore the prisoner's shirt open. He then placed a small tube of bamboo, two inches long, over one of the fingers of his right hand. A razor blade was secured to the underside of the tube.

Pepper once again asked Wathers what unit he was from. Tuo, the Yard survivor, stated during the debriefing that the team leader could not have answered even if he had wanted to—his mouth had filled with blood. The black man had placed the bamboo tube against the right nipple of the sergeant's chest and pressed down hard. He drew his hand slowly through the nipple, across the chest, and through the left nipple. Wathers's screaming forced gushes of blood from the gash in his cheek. This seemed to excite the black interrogator, causing him to make three more quick slashes across the man's chest. There were no questions now, just more slashing and screaming, mixed with the haunting laughter of the interrogator and the NVA guards. Somewhere in the process, Sergeant Wathers passed out.

Major Thanh watched from a table in the corner of the room. He nodded his approval of Pepper's methods, then pointed to the white man, the one called Salt. It was now his turn.

Salt moved over to Sergeant Moore, a young buck sergeant who had been in Vietnam a month and was on his first mission. During Wathers's interrogation, Sergeant Moore had vomited all over the front of his shirt and pants. There were tears in his eyes as the white interrogator stepped in front of him with a knife in his hand. Showing no sympathy, Salt asked the same question that Pepper had asked earlier of Sergeant Wathers. The young sergeant, however, answered quickly—"Special Forces recon team out of Da Nang."

The knife flashed by so fast that Moore couldn't have known it was coming. There was a startled look of terror on the young sergeant's face, followed by a whimpering scream as he stared at his ear dangling from Salt's fingertips. Moore had answered too quickly. Therefore, Salt said, it must have been a lie. Moore began to plead, and begged them to ask him anything —he swore he would not lie to them. There were more questions, but each answer only brought another slash from the blade, until Sergeant Moore's face was nothing more than a mass of raw, bloody meat and gleaming white bone. As the torture progressed, Major Thanh made careful note of Moore's answers.

All attempts by the NVA guards to revive Sergeant Todd had failed. The rifle blow to the head had caused a concussion. Thanh moved to the center of the room and stared down at the helpless American. Calling Salt to his side, he informed him of Todd's condition and asked the proper procedure for this type of situation. Without saying a word, the white soldier stepped over the body of the Green Beret, and pulling a .38-caliber pistol from his shoulder holster, blew the top of Todd's head off. Replacing the pistol, Salt turned to the major and smiled. Thanh placed his arm around the American deserter and remarked that the action had been correct, but that in the future such things should be done outside—it would be less messy that way. Both men laughed at the remark.

Tuo and the team's remaining two Montagnards stood helplessly by in silence as they watched the sadistic killing of their American leaders. After the killing of Sergeant Todd, the major ordered one of the NVA officers to take the Montagnards out into the jungle and execute them. That was the last Tuo had seen of Wathers and Moore.

As the three Yards were escorted to the edge of the compound, a light rain began to fall. The guards started to complain, wanting to get the executions over with immediately. The NVA officer asked if they wanted to dig the graves or let the condemned men do it. The complaining stopped.

The group had traveled 50 yards into the jungle when the officer stopped them, handed one of the Montagnards a shovel, and ordered him to start digging. Two of the Yards had resigned themselves to their fate, but not Tuo. He had worked with the Green Berets since the early days of their arrival in Vietnam, and one thing he had learned from his new American friends was that you never quit or give up, no matter how bad the situation may appear.

The rain began to fall harder as the first man finished digging and passed the shovel to the second Yard. The prisoner automatically began to dig. The graves would be shallow—there was no need to bury deep in these jungles; within a week they would be overgrown and impossible to find.

The intensity of the rain had made the NVA officer impatient. Cursing, he grabbed the shovel from the second man and threw it at Tuo's feet, ordering him to start digging. Tuo realized that time was running out. He knew he had to make his move soon.

The officer forced the first Montagnard to kneel in front of the grave he had just finished digging. Placing the Chicom pistol to the back of the man's head, he fired. The sound of the shot was barely audible over the heavy pounding rain. The man's body jerked forward and fell face-first into the grave.

The guards cheered wildly; then, grabbing the second man, they forced him to his knees, too. The officer walked up behind him, placed the pistol to the back of his head, and pulled the trigger. But this time the gun didn't fire. The prisoner fainted at the sound of the misfire and fell into the grave. The officer screamed at the others to get the man up, shoved his pistol back into his holster, and grabbed a guard's rifle.

Watching, Tuo realized this would be his only chance to escape. Three of the guards were struggling to get the man out of the hole; but the mud caused them to slip and slide and drop the man in the grave once more. Tuo picked the exact moment when all attention was on the confusion around the hole. He swung the shovel with all his strength, the edge catching the NVA guard to his right square in the face. The officer saw the move and brought his rifle halfway up before Tuo swung the shovel back to his left; its edge sunk deep into the man's throat. Snatching the rifle from the dying officer's hands, Tuo fired full automatic into the hole, killing the remaining three guards, as well as his Montagnard teammate.

Wasting no time, Tuo grabbed three magazines for the weapon and ran off into the jungle. It took him five days to work his way back to the south. He was found half-conscious by a patrol from one of the southern-based A camps. After Tuo's report, Salt and Pepper became two of the most wanted men in Vietnam.

Jess Baron's thoughts of that after-action report were interrupted by a voice in the distance.

"Jess, Jess boy. Are you still with me?" Davis had refilled the coffee cup and was trying to hand it to Baron.

"Sorry, sir. The discussion about Salt and Pepper brought back memories of Sergeant Wathers's team and the lone survivor's debriefing. I suppose I'm like everybody else. I'd love to get my hands on those two bastards for just five minutes."

"Hell, Jess. You and half of Fort Bragg would like that chance."

For the next few minutes each man sat silently sipping his coffee, each involved in his own private thoughts. Davis was the first to speak.

"Jess, do you think there's a chance that this American with Thanh could be our boy, Salt?"

"Well, sir, I would really like to believe it is, but I find it hard to picture Thanh running around the DMZ with one of Hanoi's hottest propaganda properties."

Davis leaned back in his chair and stared out the window of his office as he said, "Of course you're right, Jess. One thing this guy Thanh isn't and that's a fool. Hell, he has a better intelligence net throughout South Vietnam than the CIA. How many people have we lost chasing this son of a bitch?"

Baron was obviously uncomfortable with the question as he spoke.

"Sir, in the past three years we have lost three complete recon teams, one from CC South and two from CC Central. To this date not one member of any of those teams has ever been found. It's as if they disappeared or never existed. Of course, you already know about Sergeant Wathers's team from CC North. They were Thanh's last victims. We've also lost two of our best agents in the North. We believe Thanh is involved in their disappearance." Baron paused for a moment, shifted his position in the chair, then continued, "I know you're aware that I lost seven good men from an A Team trying to nail this asshole. We were so damn close to having him in our hands that I got careless, and he burnt us good."

Swinging his chair around to face Baron, Davis spoke in a low, but firm, voice. "That's bullshit, Jess. I read all the reports on that action. You did the same damn thing I would have done. Hell, why do you think I requested you be assigned to my staff? You're a damn good officer, mister—that's why you're here. Now, what do you suggest we do about this Bien Cao business?"

Davis's remarks rekindled something inside Baron. For a long time he had blamed himself for the loss of the seven men from the A Team. Now, he felt as if a heavy burden had been lifted from his shoulders. Before he could answer the colonel's question, there was a knock at the door and the aide came into the room.

"Excuse me, sir. I know what the colonel's orders were, but the Vietnamese assistant chief of staff is out there and he's throwing a fit. He's been waiting for over an hour, sir. Says he's going to report this inconvenience to General Westmoreland if he doesn't get some action right away."

Neither officer had noticed the time. Davis stood and handed the file to Baron.

"Jess, see what you can work up on this thing and meet me back here tonight with your plan. You can have anything and anybody you want for this one, Jess."

"Yes, sir . . . 1900 tonight."

Saluting smartly, Baron turned and headed for

the door as Davis turned to his aide. "Tell that asshole out there to come in. I can't wait to hear what damn Vietnamese unit he wants to pull out of combat today."

"Yes, sir." The aide held the door open for the Vietnamese general. As the man stormed past, the aide closed the door as Davis was saying, "General Ky, my friend, what can we do for you today?"

Baron smiled at the young officer, "I appreciate the stall job you did on that guy, Captain."

"Oh, it was my pleasure, sir."

The colonel turned and walked down the hall. He had a lot of planning to do, and he had a gut feeling that no matter what he came up with, 1900 hours tonight was going to be anything but a happy hour.

Arriving at his office, Baron called in his new S-1 officer, Captain Taylor, and issued the following order.

"Captain, I want you and your staff to drop whatever you're doing and move down to classified. I want the records of every Special Forces man we have working Special Ops for us or the CIA."

The captain had a pained look on his face. He paused for a moment before saying, "My God, sir, that's got to be more than eight hundred records!"

"More like nine hundred, Captain. Let me give you some guidelines that will help you out. First, I want the files on personnel that have more than eighteen months' experience and are still hard at it today. Second, after you've pulled those files, I want you to pull records on all personnel that have been in the business for a year and have extended for an additional six months. That should cut it down for you."

The captain looked exasperated as he said, "It'll help, sir, but it's still going to take a while."

Baron's expression didn't change as he coolly said, "You've got a total of four hours, captain. I want the first of those files hitting my desk in the next thirty minutes."

Taylor hadn't been assigned to the command long enough to familiarize himself with the colonel's personality. His first thought was that the colonel was joking. But from the tone of voice and the cold stare he was getting, he knew the man was dead serious.

"Yes, sir. You'll have the first batch in thirty minutes. Is there anything else, sir?"

Baron paused, then as if suddenly remembering, he said, "Yes, Captain. The first two files I want you to pull are those for JD McCall and Abraham L. Richardson."

Taylor wrote the names down on his pad. With a slight grin and intending only to remove the tension from the air, he said, "Abraham *L.* Richardson, sir? Don't tell me this guy's middle name is Lincoln!"

Baron found no humor in the remark.

"Captain, if I were you, I'd wipe that shit-eating grin off your face and get those damn people busy downstairs. I expect McCall and Richardson's files on my desk in fifteen minutes, or you're gonna find your ass burning shit barrels in Nha Trang before the sun goes down!"

"Sorry, sir. You'll have those two records immediately."

As he left Baron's office, closing the door behind him, the young S-1 officer took a deep breath and wiped the sweat from his forehead. He was still looking a little pale when the admin sergeant came up to him.

"Damn, sir. You look like you just saw the devil himself. What's going on?"

Taylor knew the sergeant wasn't too far off with that statement. In the three weeks he had been in Vietnam, nothing tightened his stomach as fast as the man in that room.

Waiting for an answer to his question, the sergeant wondered if the captain were daydreaming.

"Sir, would you care to enlighten me as to exactly what we're supposed to be doing today?"

The question got Taylor's attention. Grabbing the sergeant's arm and pulling him in the direction of the basement door, he said, "Burning shit in Nha Trang if we don't get moving!"

"What?"

"Never mind, Sergeant! Just get everybody downstairs. We've got a lot of work to do."

It was 1800 hours by the time Baron closed the last file. Leaning back in his chair, he lit a cigarette and rubbed his bloodshot eyes. The selection of the first two people had been easy. McCall and Richardson. It had been JD McCall's team that had saved Baron's ass from Major Thanh that day. Baron remembered how he had tried to thank the tall, lanky sergeant from Oklahoma, but had been told to forget the thanks and just keep him in mind when something hot came along. This operation was going to be right up McCall's alley.

Richardson was an easy choice, too. He was McCall's assistant team leader and of the same high caliber. However, the rest of the selection process had been hard for Baron. He had begun by separating the married men from the single men. More than likely a married man was still here for the additional money that gave him a chance to pay off the mortgage back home, but possessed too much damn pride to quit running with Special Operations. He separated these from the others and laid them aside to go back to them if he couldn't find enough single men. That hadn't been necessary: he had found the ten men he wanted—all single.

Pulling the bottom drawer of his desk open, Baron reached in, grabbed a bottle of Jim Beam, and poured himself a drink. Leaning back once more, he stared at the list of names before him. Sipping the bourbon, he began to ask questions in his mind: Could ten people pull it off? How many of these men would finally have to face the oddsmaker to pay up for past favors long overdue?

He lit a cigarette and thought of all the plans that still had to be made. Maps, aerial photos, intel updates, unit coordination, air support, and a dozen other things he hadn't even thought of yet. Major Cooper's message had said Thanh would be in the area in three or four weeks. Baron would have to reach the men's units and get them together as soon as possible. They had to be isolated, briefed, and trained as a team. Three weeks was not very long.

Reaching for the bottle again, Baron noticed it was 1830 hours. He still had to meet the colonel at 1900 hours to report his progress. Placing the bottle back in the drawer, he locked his desk, folded the paper with the ten names, placed it in his shirt pocket, and headed for the door. It had started now. If the colonel approved Baron's plan, there would be no turning back. Special Forces didn't work that way.

II.

CCN— Command and Control North
Da Nang, South Vietnam
0700 Hours, 10 June 1967

Colonel Bob Howard had been with Special Forces
for 10 years and had just taken command of CCN a few
weeks ago. He was a big man, solidly built, with broad
shoulders and a trim waist. He kept his dark brown hair
cropped short, Ranger-style. His experience with Special Forces had made him more than familiar with the
types of operations run by CCN.

Howard had just finished reading the message from
Saigon when Ted Jackson, Howard's executive officer,
walked into his office.

"Morning, sir."

"Morning, Ted, have a seat. I've got something here
I want you to see."

Howard handed the message to Jackson and sat
down behind his desk to wait for the man to finish
reading. Ted Jackson didn't match the normal percep-
tion of what a Special Forces man should look like. He
was only five foot eight, and might weigh a hundred and
fifty pounds, soaking wet. The slim facial features were
offset by the large black eyes. They reminded Howard
of paintings he had seen of little kids with the big black
eyes. Jackson had been at CCN for 13 months and had
just extended for six more. Colonel Howard valued the
man's knowledge and experience and had relied

16

heavily on Jackson's advice regarding the men of CCN.

Jackson had just finished reading when Howard said, "Looks like they got another good deal going out of Saigon, Ted."

"Hell, sir, you'd think those people down there would be satisfied trying to get these guys killed with normal operations without throwing in this kinda shit."

"You got any ideas about this thing, Ted?"

Jackson shook his head. "No telling, sir. They do this every time they have a really hot mission going on. And this one's going to be a real ballbuster."

Howard arched his eyebrows as he asked, "What makes you think that?"

"The names on the list, sir. JD McCall—he's one of the best in the business. Been running missions out of here for close to three years now and is still alive to talk about it. Richardson—he's McCall's assistant team leader. He's been here about two years, but he'll be the first one to tell you that the only reason he's survived this long is because of McCall. The two guys are like brothers."

Howard leaned back in his chair. "JD McCall . . . I heard a lot about the man but had never had a chance to meet him until I got here. Come to think of it, I've only seen him once in the three weeks I've been here."

Jackson grinned as he said, "He stays pretty active, sir. I believe he was out on an operation when you got here."

"That's right, Ted. I remember you briefing me on the missions we had out at the time, and by the time he came back in I was at that conference in Saigon."

"That's right, sir. You say you've only seen him once, sir?"

"Yes. As a matter of fact, it was just a few nights ago, at the club. He didn't really talk that much."

Jackson grinned. "Don't let that bother you, sir. JD doesn't talk a whole lot to anybody except maybe Richardson."

Picking up the message, Howard continued, "Well, what about these other two men they want down there? Ah . . . Barnes and Hotujec."

"That's Ed Barnes, sir. The guys call him Cowboy. He's been running operations for over seventeen months and has the next-best team in the compound. Barnes and McCall are kinda like the old hands around here. Hotujec's been with Barnes for a little over a year. Barnes says the kid's pretty good and learning fast. So you see, sir, whoever picked these people spent a good deal of time checking them out."

"You know, Ted, I heard some pretty wild stories about McCall when I was back in Bragg. Some people say the guy's got a death wish. You got any theory on why McCall's been here so damn long?"

"I don't think anybody could give you a definite answer to that question, sir. I did a little background check into JD's records. He's been in the Army for twelve years now. He came in right after his marriage went down the tubes in 1956; applied for Special Forces in 1962. That was the same year his mother and father were killed in a car wreck outside of Tulsa. The only other survivor of the McCall family was a brother, Roger McCall. The kid was a sophomore in high school when the accident happened. JD brought the kid back to Fort Bragg with him and put him in school. But things didn't work out. You know how tough the SF course is. Well, JD was gone a lot and didn't really have that much time to spend with his brother. The kid was pretty much on his own. JD came back from a field exercise one day and the kid was gone. He had left a note saying he felt like he was a burden on JD and joined the Army. Of course, he forged JD's signature on the consent form. JD didn't stop him from joining up, but did make him promise to finish school at the first opportunity. Roger McCall never got the chance to keep that promise. His first assignment was with Military Advisory Command, Saigon. He was a doorgun-

ner on a chopper that was shot down outside of Vung
Tau. JD left for Vietnam right after the funeral, and
he's been here ever since."

Howard was more than impressed with his executive
officer as he said, "Damn, Ted, you found out all this
information just going through McCall's records?"

Jackson gave a slight laugh as he replied, "Well, his
records and . . . ah . . . a complete background report
from my brother-in-law, who just happens to work for
the FBI in Washington."

Howard was smiling as he said, "You're a sneaky
bastard, Major. So tell me, do you think McCall stays
to avenge the lost brother?"

"No, sir. From the talks I've had with JD, I believe
he just doesn't feel like there's anything left to go back
to."

"There's no girlfriend, children from the first marriage, distant relatives?"

"No, sir. Nobody."

Howard sat quietly in his chair, his face a mirror
reflecting heavy concentration. Finally he said, "Ted,
hasn't McCall ever asked to go back to the States on
leave? I mean, how can a normal person do this shit for
three years and never need a break? It's not healthy,
Major."

Jackson lit a cigarette and paused a moment before
answering.

"You know, sir, now that you mention it, McCall did
talk about going home for a break once. We even flew
to Saigon that day. I went to a staff meeting and McCall
headed for headquarters command to see about his
leave. When I saw him later that day, he was in the
American Hotel bar getting half smashed. He wasn't
talking much, but from what I could gather, headquarters had told him in no uncertain terms that a leave
outside of South Vietnam was out of the question."

Howard straightened up in his chair. He found this to
be more than interesting. Here was a man who had

spent more time in Vietnam running high-risk missions than anyone involved in Special Projects, yet he couldn't get approval for leave from the same people that continued to send him on deadly operations.

"Did you check headquarters' reasons for turning down McCall?"

"Yes, sir. I should say, I tried to. But I was politely told to fuck off and stay out of it. JD met me at the airport the next morning and never said any more about it. Hell, sir, that was over ten months ago, and he's never said another word about it."

Howard had made a lot of friends in his ten years with Special Forces. He made a mental note to check into the incident over McCall's leave the next time he was in Saigon. They might tell a major to fuck off, but if they told this colonel that, they better be ready to explain the reason why.

Picking up the message once more, Howard said, "They say they want these guys in Saigon as soon as possible. I take that to mean right now. Can we round them up that fast, Ted?"

Jackson moved to the large map of Southeast Asia that covered one wall of the colonel's office. "Well, sir, Barnes and Hotujec are on stand-down right now. They should still be in the rack this morning; they closed down the club last night. They'll be feeling a little rough today, but they'll survive. Now, McCall and Richardson were inserted into target, Hotel Five, two days ago. Their mission is to locate and destroy a reported pipeline that Charlie's been building in the northern section of the DMZ. As of this morning, the team hadn't spotted anything but a few scattered NVA patrols. JD relayed back that he was going to be heading farther north to widen the search for the pipeline.

Howard stood up and proceeded over to the map. Viewing the area marked off to designate the DMZ,

Howard asked, "Where do you think that team is right now?"

Major Jackson pointed out a grid square ten miles inside North Vietnam.

"Dammit, Ted, he's gone out of the range of our artillery support!"

"McCall knows that, sir. His FAC rider reminded him of that this morning."

"What the hell did McCall say?"

"McCall told him to make sure the club didn't run out of Jack Daniels before he got back, because oil fires make him thirsty." Jackson grinned. "JD's got a hell of a sense of humor, sir."

"Undoubtedly, Major. I want you to have someone shake Barnes and Hotujec outta the sack and get them ready for the trip to Saigon. We'll put them on the first flight out this afternoon. Then get our Quang Tri launch site on the radio and have them relay extraction orders to McCall before the man decides to go all the way to Hanoi. If they haven't found that line by now, I doubt they will."

"Yes, sir. But we'll have to scramble if we're going to get them out before dark."

"Well, let's get with it, then, Major. I want that team in Quang Tri before last light."

"Roger, sir," said Jackson as he left the office and headed for the Operations Center.

Howard pulled a grease pencil from the box hanging beside the map and drew a large, red circle around the grid square that Jackson had pointed out. Tapping the pencil against the map, the colonel muttered softly to himself, "Where are you, JD McCall, and just what the hell are you doing right now?"

Richardson hit the ground just in time, as the grenade fragments tore wood and bark from the tree trunk above his head. There were two more explosions to his left—dirt and tree limbs rained down all around him. Crawling through a slight depression in the ground, he reached a small pile of rocks. They weren't big rocks, but they were a hell of a lot better than a sinkhole in the ground.

Richardson's strategic move had not gone unnoticed by the NVA. They shifted their fire to the rockpile. Bullets ricocheted left and right, over and around the stones like a thousand mad hornets. From Richardson's right came an increase in the volume of fire from McCall's position. JD was trying to take some of the heat off his partner. The incoming fire on the rockpile slacked off. For the time being, anyway. . . .

McCall rolled to his left, dropping the empty magazine from the rifle and locking another one in place. The remaining four members of his Chinese team were laying down a steady field of fire in three directions, and the NVA were coming right back with some impressive firepower of their own. McCall had started this operation with an eight-man team. Now, two of the men lay dead among the trees. They had been caught in the initial burst of machine-gun fire from an NVA position just above the pipeline. Richardson had worked his way up the hillside and knocked out the machine gunner with a grenade, but the gunfire and explosion had drawn a crowd of NVA troops from the hilltop. They had flanked the team, and now the battle was on.

Leaping to his feet, McCall broke for the pile of rocks around Richardson, bullets tearing up the ground only inches behind him. Taking a dive, he rolled into the cover of the stones . . . and into Rich. Spitting dirt and grass from his mouth, McCall looked up into the black face of his American teammate.

A grin surrounded the perfect set of white teeth. "Whatcha trying to do, JD? Tunnel your way out?"

"Fuck you, Rich."

The firing had dropped off to only a few sporadic rounds as McCall leaned back against the rocks. The Chinese had stopped firing, and two of them had worked their way over to the bodies of their dead comrades and were stripping them of all grenades and ammunition while the other two covered them. They had been with McCall for a long time and knew that the action of the past five minutes had only been round one.

Flipping his Zippo lighter open, McCall lit a cigarette and inhaled deeply.

At the sound of the lighter clicking open, Richardson had flinched; he shot a fierce look at McCall and said, "Goddammit, JD, you almost gave me a fuckin' heart attack! Besides, you know you ain't supposed to be smokin' on a recon patrol."

McCall laughed. "You know, Rich, I gotta funny feeling they already know we're here."

Their laughter dissolved into the eerie quiet that surrounded the hill where only minutes ago there had been deafening explosions and rifle fire. Now there was only perfect silence.

McCall sat quietly smoking his cigarette as he watched the Chinese improve their positions. They knew things were going to get a lot worse before they got better. McCall liked working with Chinese. They never complained, were loyal as hell, and loved a good fight. MACV Command had offered him a Montagnard team when he had first arrived, but he had turned them down. He had nothing against the Yards. It was just that the Chinese were bigger and could carry more.

McCall was just about to put his smoke out when he heard the sound. It came from behind him and to his right—the unmistakable sound of material brushing against foliage. Rich had heard it, too. Charlie was about to make his move on the team again. Without a word being exchanged, both men slid down into the prone position and began to crawl slowly away from the rockpile and into a small group of trees.

The move had alerted the Chinese, and all weapons went to automatic. There were more sounds now. To the left a stick snapped. A Chinese shifted his rifle in that direction. Behind them, dry leaves echoed a crunching sound. Another rifle shifted to the new noise. It would come at any moment now.

Suddenly the tan satchel flew through the air like a lopsided balloon full of water, and landed in the center of the rockpile. McCall yelled, "Satchel charge!"

The whole team pushed themselves hard against the ground. The explosion shook the earth around them, turning chunks of rock into deadly missiles that amputated limbs and leaves from the trees.

McCall slowly raised his head. He heard a loud ringing in his ears and saw blood dripping onto his sleeve—his nose was bleeding. He hadn't left his mouth open when the concussion from the explosion swept over the team. But there was no time to worry about that now.

Eight NVA came charging through the smoke and dust of the explosion. They held their weapons at hip level and fired, rounds spattering in the ground all around McCall and Richardson. The two Green Berets opened up at the same time. Starting from the center of the line of NVA, McCall fired left, Richardson to the right; in less than 10 seconds, all eight NVA lay dead or dying. The rest of the team was receiving fire from three directions. The Chinese had broken up one charge by two lines of NVA with grenades, and were pouring a wicked volume of automatic-weapons fire into the trees to their right.

In a matter of minutes it was over. Silence now covered the hillside. McCall rose slowly to his feet and surveyed the scene of death that lay all around the team. There were 23 dead NVA that he could see, and no telling how many wounded had either crawled or been dragged back into the jungle, but from the number of visible blood trails, he knew they had put a hurt on them. One thing for sure, Charlie was going to think twice before he tried another on-line attack against this team.

Richardson had just reloaded his CAR-15 when he noticed the blood on McCall's sleeve. "Hey, boss man, you hit?"

McCall lit another cigarette before he answered. "Naw, just concussion from that charge." Taking a long drag on the smoke, he continued, "We nailed 'em pretty damn good that time, Rich. They'll back up and regroup before they try again. Now'd be the time to blow the pipe. What'd ya think?"

Richardson shook his head, "Man, you never know when to quit, do ya? Hell, here we sit, low on ammo, it's comin' up dark city real soon and ol' Charlie's not even close to calling this game off. He's got us pinned in and ain't about to let us out of here. And you wanna go up this little hill and piss him off some more. McCall, you're fuckin' unreal!"

"Hell, Rich. I know all that shit, but we came up here to blow that line and I figure since we're just sittin' here on our ass with no place to go . . . well, what the fuck, let's go for it!"

"Ho, you silver-tongued devil. I don't know why I always let you talk me into doing crazy shit." Reaching for his rucksack, Rich pulled the straps and opened it up. "Damn stuff was gettin' too heavy to carry anyway."

Richardson began unloading the one-pound blocks of C-4 plastic explosives he had been carrying for the last two days. Peeling the wrappers from two blocks, he pressed them together and wrapped a piece of tape around them; then pulling a pen from his shirt pocket, he made a hole between the two blocks. "You got the caps?" he asked.

McCall pulled out a small box enclosed in foam rubber. Slowly opening the box, he handed it over to Richardson. The five, long, silver blasting caps lay encased in a soft sponge pad.

Removing the first cap, Rich placed it gently into the hole. Then, cutting a piece of fuse six inches long, he glanced at his watch and lit the cord. Counting to himself, he watched the fuse burn down, and then said, "Hell boss, we just like downtown. How many holes you want in that little ol' pipe?"

McCall didn't bother to look up as he began to work with the explosives. "We'll go with five. That should be enough to blow the fuckin' thing back to Hanoi."

While Rich finished off the last charge, McCall moved around the perimeter checking the Chinese positions. As he came up to his interpreter, Sang, he noticed the man trying to hide his left hand. Kneeling next to the old man, he said, "Let me see that hand, Sang." The man shook his head as he answered, "It is nothing, Chung Se."

"I'll be the judge of that. Now, let's see it."

Without looking at his team leader, Sang slowly brought the bloody hand up.

There were two fingers missing. The old man had not said a word. This was one more reason McCall only worked with Chinese mercenaries. They never complained. For them, this was just a job. Working with the Green Berets, they made more money in two months than they could make in Taiwan in a year. Some were married, and others planned to marry after their contracts were up. The risks were high, but the advantages outweighed the risks. With this money they could return to Taiwan, buy homes and land, and raise their children in comfort.

McCall gently wrapped the bandage around Sang's hand. Looking into the old man's eyes, he growled, "Dammit, Sang, why didn't you say something, you ol' fart! Jesus, you're almost fifty years old—I figure you've earned the right to say ouch!" McCall pulled a tube of morphine from his pocket.

Sang looked at McCall, and through broken, brownish teeth said, "No drug, Chung Se, it make me sleepy, no can fight. You know I one tough mutter, maybe take shot when choppers come, take us all home."

McCall's reply was cut off by the crackling of the radio.

"Midnight Rider. Midnight Rider, this is Eagle One, Eagle One, over."

Eagle One was the code name for McCall's Forward Air Controller, Master Sergeant Pappy Grant. He was flying somewhere above the team in his OV-10 aircraft. It was equipped with the latest high-speed communications gear. This gave Grant the capability to contact rescue choppers, request air support, and contact artillery bases. Grant had the responsibility of watching over three recon teams in a 60-square-mile area. It all came down to one thing: no FAC—no choppers to get you out.

McCall keyed the handset. "Eagle One, this is Midnight Rider, over."

"Midnight Rider, I have orders for immediate extraction of your unit. The order came from the top man, Rider. Over."

"Eagle, this is Rider. Good to hear from ya, ol' buddy. We've got a situation going on down here. I'm requesting a Prairie Fire emergency at this time, over."

Grant's reply was immediate. "Rider, this is Eagle. Roger, understand you are declaring Prairie Fire at 1635 hours. Assets are being scrambled. Are you in contact at this time, over?"

"Negative, Eagle. Last contact ten minutes ago. Estimate enemy force at company strength. We have two good guys KIA, enemy losses so far, twenty-three confirmed. We have located the pipeline and will destroy before extraction. Anticipate another attack within fifteen to twenty minutes. Do you roger, Pappy?"

Grant had been recording the conversation with McCall. That was standard procedure on every mission. Pressing his throat mike, Grant answered, "Roger, Rider. I've got the picture. Eagle Two says that TAC Air and choppers are en route. ETA your position, twenty-five minutes. Can you hang on that long, Rider?"

"Hell, Eagle. We've been hanging for years. Thanks for the comforting words, Pappy. Just hearing that sexy voice of yours makes me feel better. Let me know when Eagle Two is five minutes out. . . . Well, Pappy, hate to hang up on ya, but it looks like things are going to be getting pretty hectic around here in a few minutes. See ya' later. Rider out."

Grant was yelling into his mike. "Rider, Rider, come in. What the hell are you talking about? What's happening down there, Rider? Answer me, dammit!" His only reply was a steady hissing in his headset. . . .

Richardson had waved to get McCall's attention. He raised six fingers and pointed to the left, then signaled with eight more and pointed to JD's far right. The NVA were moving into position for another attack.

McCall acknowledged the signal before turning back to Sang. "Are you sure about the morphine, ol' friend?"

Sang smiled. "I sure, Chung Se. You need worry more 'bout, how they say, your honky ass."

McCall stared at the bandage around Sang's hand. The old man's blood dripped slowly to the ground. He placed his hand on Sang's shoulder, and with a grin he said, "You've been pickin' up some bad words from that Alabama colored-type person over there, haven't you?"

"You both honkies to Chinese. Don't worry 'bout us, Chung Se. We tough mutter fuckers, remember."

McCall winked at his longtime friend before grabbing the radio and running back over to Richardson's position. Dropping beside Rich, he asked, "Well, tiger, you ready to set the world on fire?"

Richardson stared at him in disbelief. "Wait a minute, man! I was all for it when we had a little time, but those mothers are gonna hit us any second now, and that fuckin' pipe's a good fifty yards up that damn hill. We'll get our ass caught right out in the open when the blitz comes."

McCall didn't answer as he looked up the hill at the pipe. He placed the selector switch on his CAR-15 to full automatic. Laying the rifle down, he picked up two of the charges and flipped them to Rich. Placing the other three next to his rifle, he looked over at his partner.

"Now look, Rich. We been searching for that fuckin' piece of metal up there for two damn days. Those pricks have blown away two of our people and shot Sang's hand half off. Yeah, we might get our balls handed to us out there, but goddamn if I'm gonna let Charlie shoot the shit out of us and keep that fuckin' pipe, too. Now . . . you comin' or not?"

Richardson glanced up the hill as he said, "You dickhead! You're gonna get me killed yet! Then, who the hell is gonna be the first black governor of Alabama?"

Richardson was still mumbling to himself as McCall came up on one knee, clutching the charges in one hand and the rifle in the other. "Hell, man, you wanna live forever?" With those parting words, McCall got to his feet and began the long run for the pipe.

Rich paused for a moment as he watched JD scramble up the hill. With a low "Ah, what the fuck," Rich jumped up and began closing fast on McCall.

McCall was already taking fire. Bullets tore at the ground around his feet and through the trees above his head.

Two NVA broke into the open in front of Richardson and opened fire, full automatic. They would have had a better chance on single fire. They had fired wild, the rounds going over the American's head. Rich did a forward flip and, rolling to his right, he cut both men down. Back on his feet, he saw JD at the pipe placing the charges.

McCall had two in place and was moving up to place the third when three NVA came charging down the hill. He took out the first man with four rounds to the chest. Ignoring the bullets hitting all around him, JD shifted his rifle to the second NVA and pulled the trigger—the rifle clicked. There wouldn't be enough time to reload. Dropping the CAR-15 to the ground, he jerked the heavy .44 Magnum from his shoulder holster. With AK rounds ricocheting off the pipe, he fell to a prone position and sighted the big handgun under the pipe. He pulled off the first round, hitting the advancing man in the crotch. As the man doubled over, a second round hit him in the head. The sight of the exploding head caused the third man to hesitate for only a second. That was all the time McCall needed. Swinging the .44 over the top of the pipe, he fired. The NVA soldier was blown six feet backward, with a startled look on his face, as he clutched the gaping hole in his chest.

Richardson had closed the distance to McCall and fell by his side. His breathing was coming in short gasps.

McCall reloaded the .44 as he said, "Hi, Rich, what took you so long? I thought you black folks were supposed to be fast on your feet."

Between gasps Rich said, "Fuck you, McCall."

Snapping the Magnum back into his holster, McCall grinned and said, "Get your charges in place fast, Rich. I'll cover. Pappy's working a Prairie Fire for us. ETA in about ten minutes. Fast movers, the whole works, so shake it up."

"You bastard! You knew we were gettin' out of here before we came up this hill. Shit, man! The fast movers could have took out the damn pipe."

"Maybe they could, maybe they couldn't. This way we know for sure, Rich."

Richardson's face was strained as he said, "That's it, brother! You're gettin' too damn nuts for this ol' boy. Soon as we get back, I'm askin' to be assigned to another team and, man, this time I mean it!"

McCall didn't bother to answer. He'd heard it all before. Taking the charges from Rich, he moved farther up the pipe and placed them on the heavy metal. Two NVA came out of the jungle brush behind McCall. Richardson cut them down with two short bursts and yelled up the hill, "You ready yet, hero?"

McCall waved for Rich to head back down the hill. Rich nodded and ran down the slope. Diving into the circle of Chinese, he came up facing Sang.

"Chung Se Mac going to blow pipe now, yes?"

"Hell, Sang. I wouldn't be surprised if the son of a bitch put his balls on top of those friggin' charges just to see how hard they really are."

Sang gave a short laugh. "You good bullshitter, Chung Se Rich. I know you care what happen to boss man, same as me."

Slamming a fresh magazine into his rifle, Richardson swore, "Ah shit, the mother humper probably belongs to the fuckin' Oklahoma KKK, but let's give him some cover fire anyway."

Sang had a grin on his face as he swung his rifle in the direction of the pipeline.

McCall went down the line of charges, pulling the igniters, then began the run down the slope. He sensed the NVA before he saw them. There were four to his right front, no more than 15 yards away. Richardson switched from automatic to single fire and fired two quick rounds, dropping two of them. McCall and the two remaining soldiers fired simultaneously. Bullets flew back and forth.

McCall fired five feet in front of one of the NVA and walked the rounds up the man's leg, chest, and head. A lesson learned the hard way by the NVA trooper: On full automatic, start firing in front of your target, and the rifle will ride up on its own.

The second NVA had already learned that lesson. One of his rounds caught McCall in the lower leg, spinning him like a corkscrew into the dirt. The CAR-15 flew out of his hands as he hit the ground. The red-orange blur flashing through McCall's eyes was followed immediately by burning pain shooting up his leg. In the distance, McCall could hear the explosions; he could feel the ground vibrate with each blast. The heat from the pipeline fire warmed his face. To JD, the whole thing was happening in slow motion. The flashes from the rifle barrel, the impact, the spinning, hitting the ground with teeth-jarring force. . . . Strange the ground should feel so cold . . . the feeling of emptiness in his hands.

McCall watched helplessly as the CAR-15 tumbled out of reach. He groped for the Magnum, but his hands seemed to weigh a ton. The fingers refused to work. He gazed up at the gun barrel lowered to his face.

The NVA behind the rifle grinned the biggest smile McCall had ever seen on a Vietnamese. The guy had JD cold, and he wanted to drag it out. McCall wasn't about to give the NVA soldier the pleasure. In perfect Vietnamese, McCall said, "Your fuckin' mother is known as the best cocksucker in Hanoi, asshole."

The look of anger on the soldier's face was instantly replaced by one of pain and disbelief, as Richardson withdrew the knife from between the NVA's shoulder blades. Wiping the bloody blade on the dead man's pants, he knelt by McCall and said, "Ya' know, boss, you really shouldn't talk 'bout a guy's mother like that.

You're liable to piss 'im off. . . . Ya' know what I mean?" Seeing the blood just above the boot of McCall's leg, he asked, "You hit bad?"

"Naw, just the leg. Not as bad now. Thanks, Rich, I owe you one."

"No thanks needed, boss. Hell, that leaves me owin' you about fifty anyway."

"Come on, Rich. I'll bet Pappy Grant's havin' a baby by now."

Rich helped his team leader to his feet and the two men moved down the slope to the radio. Sure enough, Grant was screaming, loud and clear. "Goddammit, JD! What the fuck's going on down there?"

McCall took the handset and said, "Hey, Pappy, that a new radio procedure or what?"

There was a moment of silence. When Grant came back over the radio, JD could hear the relief in the voice. "Well, at least you ain't dead. I'm glad you could find the time to talk to me. Judging from that black smoke, I'd say you got your oil line. Over."

McCall talked to Grant while Rich bandaged his wounded leg.

"Sorry 'bout that, Pappy. Things got a little busy around here. Since we've paid the phone bill now, do you think it would be too much to ask to go home?"

"Roger, Rider. Choppers are less than ten minutes out. Have your people in position and ready. We'll be working the AIEs and fast movers around the LZ, so watch yourself an' try to keep somebody on that fuckin' radio, okay?"

"You got it, Eagle. This is Rider standing by. Out."

Passing the handset to Richardson, McCall pulled a tube of morphine from his shirt pocket. Pushing the pin inward to break the seal, he moved over to Sang.

"How's the hand, you tough ol' water buffalo?"

Sang managed a smile, but JD could tell it was an effort.

"Hurt some, Chung Se. Same, same your leg."

"Well, old friend, Doctor McCall has something for that." Pushing Sang's sleeve up, he gently held the old man's arm out and injected the painkiller. "Now, you rest awhile, Sang. The battle's over; we're going home."

Sang nodded in acceptance of the fact and leaned back against his rucksack.

McCall walked back over to the radio. He could hear the distant sound of the choppers. Grant was on the radio again. "Rider, this is Eagle. We have inbound at this time. Give us a smoke."

Richardson pulled the pin on a canister and flipped it into a small clearing. There was a pop, a few sparks, then violet smoke began a twisting ascent skyward.

"Pappy, we've popped smoke. Can you identify? Over," said McCall.

"Okay, Rider. We've got a violet smoke. Eagle Two says it's going to be too tight down there for a sitdown. We're going to have to go with the stabo rigs. You copy, Rider?"

"Roger, Eagle. I have two KIAs that will be going out with two survivors on the first chopper. Over."

Grant paused a moment before coming back with, "Rider, you sure you want the dead to come out first?"

"You know how I work, Pappy. They came in here with me and, by God, they've earned the right to come out first."

"Okay, JD. It's your show. We'll keep an eye out for the bad guys during extraction. Good luck, buddy. Eagle, out."

Turning to Richardson, McCall yelled, "Get 'em ready for stabo. I'll take care of the two dead." Rich waved and moved over to get Sang ready.

McCall knelt beside the bodies of the two dead Chinese. Closing their lifeless eyes, he felt a deep, inner sense of loss. Sadness was in his voice as he said, "You have found everlasting peace, my friends. Sleep well."

The first chopper hovered above the trees. The weighted ammo can broke through the limbs and hit the ground. The snap links on the can were attached to a hundred-foot rope anchored to the floor of the chopper. Unhooking the links from the can's handle, McCall attached the snap links to the links that were sewn into the dead men's web gear.

A second can crashed through the treetops. Richardson hooked Sang and one other Chinese to the ropes. Double-checking the connections, McCall gave the crew chief the thumbs-up. The chief acknowledged and relayed the word to the pilot. The chopper slowly lifted its precious cargo a thousand feet into the sky before it swung for home.

As the second chopper came in, JD waved for Rich and the rest of the team to get hooked up. Each man kept his rifle at the ready—more than one team had been blown away just when they thought they were safe. Ironically, what made the extraction so dangerous was the rescue chopper itself. The downdraft of the blades could cause the tree limbs and bamboo to slap together with such force that it was hard to distinguish the noise from rifle fire—hard, that is, until that neat little hole appeared in your uniform.

McCall made one last check of the area, then reached into his rucksack, pulled out three Russian AK-47 magazines loaded with ammo, and threw them among the dead NVA. Charlie would make a sweep of the AO after the team had been extracted. Some inexperienced young NVA soldier would find the loaded magazines and think he'd really lucked out. He would add them to his arsenal for future battles. That future would be a short one. The fifth round of each magazine contained a small but effective amount of C-4 plastic explosive. When the firing pin hit the casing, the bullet would go off like a grenade, taking the NVA's head with it.

Hobbling to the last rope, McCall snapped himself in and waved the chopper off. The pilot lifted straight up for 2,000 feet, then began moving fast over the thick jungle carpet below. In less than two minutes, the team was flying through the sky at 80 miles an hour, 2,000 feet up, hanging a hundred feet below a helicopter by a one-inch-thick rope. It was a hell of a way to get home. But at least it would be home.

III.

——✕——✕———✕———✕———✕——✕———✕———✕

Doc Lawton handed McCall a tall glass of Jack Daniels before he started working on the bullet hole in his leg. As JD tipped the glass up, the door opened and Major Jackson and Colonel Howard entered. Doc nodded to the two men and continued probing the perfect round hole in McCall's leg.

"One hell of a fine job you pulled off out there, Sergeant McCall," said Colonel Howard. "We've got forty-two confirmed body count from the aerial photos and the TAC Air boys reported three secondary explosions from the top of that hill you were on."

McCall downed half the glass of Jack before he answered. "Not that good, sir. I lost two of my best men and my number-one boy lost two fingers."

Major Jackson had moved over to the doctor's side. Watching Lawton work on the wound, he said, "What's the word, Doc?"

"Clean shot, Major. I don't see any real muscle damage, but it'll be sore as hell for a few days."

Finishing off the Jack Daniels, McCall grinned slightly and said, "Hell, Doc, you mean we may be lookin' at a chance for a seven-day R an' R for medical reasons."

Howard answered the question. "Afraid not, McCall. We received a message from Saigon this morning. They want you and Richardson down there as soon as possible. They've asked for Hotujec and Barnes, too. We sent them down this morning, and they'll pick you up at the airport upon arrival."

McCall shook his head. "Damn! Barnes and Hotujec? Now, what would Saigon want with a crazy Pole and a short John Wayne?"

"We informed Saigon of your situation," the colonel continued, "and that you had been slightly wounded. But Colonel Baron says he wants you there, regardless. He said you'd understand once he had a chance to brief you. Sorry, JD."

"Hell, that's okay, sir." McCall sighed. "If Jess Baron wants me, even with a hole in my leg, it must be something pretty damn important. Has anybody told Rich?"

Jackson poured another shot of bourbon in McCall's glass as he said, "I gave him the word before we came over. He said he'd get everything packed up and ready to go. We have you guys on the 0530 flight out of Da Nang. Are you gonna be able to make it with that leg, McCall?"

JD winked at the major. "Sir, if you and the colonel could leave me alone with Doc for a few minutes, I think we could work out a deal on some of those feel-good pills he keeps in that safe over there. Of course, we couldn't do that in front of a commanding officer. I'm sure there's some fucked-up regulation about that somewhere in the books."

Howard smiled and turned to his XO. "Come on, Major," he said. "I'll buy you a drink. Hell, maybe five or six." Both men left the room and headed for the club.

It was still dark when Colonel Howard and Major Jackson watched McCall and Richardson disappear into the C-130. Within minutes the rear ramp was up, and the huge aircraft taxiing down the secondary runway, vanishing into the darkness at the far end of the field. Jackson lit a cigar as the two officers headed for their jeep. They could hear the pilot testing his engines at the end of the runway.

"Major, do you think we'll ever see either one of those men again?" asked Howard.

Major Jackson slid in behind the steering wheel of the jeep and stared into the warm, humid darkness. "God only knows, Colonel. I've been here for what seems a lifetime, and asked myself that question at least a hundred times. But, one thing I know for sure: Wherever those two guys are going, you can bet Charlie's gonna be in for one hell of a bad day."

Both men watched in silence as the C-130 roared down the runway and disappeared into the night.

Hotujec and Barnes met the plane at the off-load ramp. Greetings and insults were exchanged as the gear was loaded into the jeep. Heading for the downtown area, Barnes reached under the seat, pulled out a bottle of Jack Daniels, and handed it back to McCall.

"Here you go, asshole. Thought you might need this. We heard you tripped over your big feet and shot yourself in the leg comin' out of a whorehouse."

Taking a hefty shot from the bottle, McCall passed it over to Richardson. Pushing Barnes's beret down over his head, JD laughed. "Sure. Pick on a poor ol' wounded veteran."

All four Green Berets were laughing as they passed an MP jeep going in the other direction. The younger of the two MPs saw the bottle of Jack Daniels being passed around.

"Hey, Sarge. Those guys were drinking the hard stuff in that jeep. Shouldn't we go after 'em? That shit's a major violation!"

The old sarge didn't even slow down as he glanced over at his young partner.

"Kid, you only been here a couple of weeks, so let me clue you in. First, all four of those dudes were wearing green berets. Second, they all had on shoulder holsters, and you can bet your sweet ass they're carrying some of the biggest Magnums you ever saw. Third and finally, if they happen to be carrying little pink cards from an outfit called SOG, then they can pretty well do anything they damn well please. Now, I don't know if that includes shootin' the shit out of a couple of MPs, but I ain't too damn crazy 'bout findin' out. Especially over a fuckin' bottle of booze."

The kid didn't say anything more as the jeep swung onto the main drag of the Saigon Strip.

After moving the gear into their rooms, the four men reported to Colonel Baron's office at SOG headquarters. There had been a lot of speculation about this hush-hush operation, but nobody was sure of anything. They figured they'd find out soon enough.

Colonel Baron's aide escorted them into a combination office and lounge. Baron had left word that he would be with them soon and that the bar was open. If they needed anything, they only had to let the aide know.

As the door closed behind the aide, Hotujec smiled and said, "Ah yes, gentlemen, it is now a few minutes past ten and the man said the bar was open. I believe it's rum-and-coke time." They all agreed heartily.

Drinks had been poured all around when the door opened again. It was the aide followed by three men wearing green berets. Someone at the bar howled, "Jesus, I don't believe it! They even got the Three Stooges for this one. How in the hell did they ever get you guys to leave that vacation resort down at CC Central?"

The three new arrivals glanced at each other and then back at the bar before they all cracked smiles.

"They called us up here to protect the fuckin' bar from you dickheads from CC North. Now we see why. Thought you girls had to go to AA meetings on the weekends."

The room erupted in laughter as old friends shook hands.

The three new arrivals were from SOG's Command and Control Central team, located outside the city of Kontum in the central highlands. The crack about the resort vacation came from the long-standing feud about who took on the toughest missions, CCC or CCN. But to the men present, it was only a joke. Each man knew the others' reputations.

There was Sergeant Don Hayes, a huge black man from Macon, Georgia. He had 12 years with Special Forces and had been running SOG operations for a year and a half. His ability with a knife was well known.

Sergeant Johnnie Bowman stood five foot eight and was built like a bull. He had been in Vietnam for two years and was planning to extend for another six months if he could. Bowman was from Waco, Texas, and hated any jokes about the Lone Star State. He loved to fight, be it in the jungle or the nearest bar.

The third and final member of the group was an old-time friend of JD McCall's. He was on his third tour of duty in Vietnam and was the oldest man in the room. His name was Charlie "Hawkeye" Hawkins. He stood six foot three and had wide shoulders and rippling arms that could break a man's back like a twig. Yet this giant of a man was best known for his gentle compassion as a Special Forces medic. McCall had seen this man use his skills on friendly and enemy troops alike. To Hawkins, a wounded man was just that, a wounded human being—no matter what uniform he wore.

McCall had warned Hawkins time and again that his trusting attitude and compassion were one day going to get him killed. Hawkins brushed the warnings off by saying, "When it's your time, ol' horse, it's your time. Ain't gonna make no difference what you're doin' at the moment."

Twenty minutes and three drinks later, all seven men were exchanging their latest exploits against Charlie.

Don Hayes was describing his last trip to the hospital. Refilling his glass with a double shot of scotch, he continued with his story.

"So, me and Patterson are movin' the team up this ridge line. Man, we been four days searchin' for this NVA hospital that's supposed to be located underground in this one area. We were duckin' and dodgin' NVA patrols every day. Well about noon on the fourth day we take a break on the side of this one hill, pull out some chow and kick back. After about five minutes, Patterson suddenly sits up real quick and gets real quiet—hell, he scared the shit out of all of us. My damn Yards had guns pointin' in every fuckin' direction. Pat leans over to me and whispers real low, 'Hey, Don. Can ya hear it?' Now, hell man, the kid's been with me for almost a year, right? So I figure he's learned somethin' by now. But I don't hear shit, see. Pat keeps swearing up and down he hears a generator hummin' away someplace close. So I put my ear down to the ground, playin' like ol' Tonto, and sure as hell I hear this low hummin' sound. 'Fore I can say anything, Pat's crawlin' off about fifteen yards. The next thing I know he's givin' us the signal to hit the deck and flippin' the handle off a grenade. He tosses it a couple of yards in front of him and runs like hell—divin' over my ass before the thing blows. Well, man, let me tell ya, that little hummin' sound turned into one helluva roar in about two seconds!"

Hayes paused and took a drink of his scotch. The room was quiet. All eyes were on Hayes.

"Well, finish it, mother!" yelled Barnes.

A wide grin appeared on Hayes's face. "Man, it was one of those fuckin' mammoth beehives built underground. They stung the shit out of everybody in less than a minute. We must've run a mile before the little bastards gave it up. Had to medevac the whole damn team."

Everyone was cracking up over Hayes's story when

Colonels Baron and Davis entered the room.

The aide yelled "Attention!" but no one at the bar moved. With a helpless look on his face, the aide turned and left.

Silence fell over the room. The NCOs knew Baron, but only a few had met Colonel Davis. McCall grabbed two glasses and headed for the bar. "Colonel Baron, Colonel Davis. Y'all still drinkin' scotch?"

The two officers walked up to the bar. Colonel Davis was the first to speak, "Hell yes, Sergeant McCall. They make anything else?"

The moment of tension had been broken. Baron introduced everyone. Davis had met McCall, Richardson, Hotujec, and Barnes on one of his inspection tours of CCN, and he had heard or read the names of the others on after-action reports since taking command of MACV SOG. He knew Baron had picked the best for this mission.

Within the next hour, the final three members of the team arrived from CC South. Baron introduced Davis to Sergeants Jim Brady, Bob Taber, and Larry Murphy. All three men were team leaders from SOG's southern base, located at Ban Me Thuot. Brady was on his second tour and had worked with McCall before. Bob Taber had just taken over a team of his own and had proven he knew his business in the area of recon. The newest guy on the block was Larry Murphy. He only had ten months in-country, but Baron had been impressed with the man's record. He had been an instructor at the Airborne school in Fort Benning for a couple of years before he applied for Special Forces. He had been the honor grad of his class and, within his first six months in Vietnam, had been awarded the Silver Star twice and the Bronze Star for valor. It was an impressive record.

After an hour of small talk and a few more drinks, Baron announced it was time to start the initial briefing. "All right, gentlemen, and I use the term loosely, if you will follow me, we'll move into the other room and I'll let you know why you're here. This will be an informal briefing, so if you have a drink, take it with you."

The men refilled their glasses before filing into the conference room. A slide projector was set up in the center of a table facing a screen hung on a wall.

Baron dimmed the lights and began, "Gentlemen, your mission will be to capture or, if necessary, assassinate this man." The slide projector clicked and the screen filled with the face of a Vietnamese. "This is Major Ngo Van Thanh. Some of you may have heard of him; he's Hanoi's number-one terrorist, interrogator and all-around hellraiser. He may only be a major, but he has high-ranking friends in Hanoi. He does pretty much what he pleases."

The picture changed to a detailed map of the northern area of South Vietnam on the DMZ. Placing a pointer on the screen, Baron continued. "This is Bien Cao village, in Quang Tri Province. It is located ten miles south of the DMZ. On eight June, Major Thanh was in this village. This is the first confirmed sighting of him south of the DMZ in over two years. Our intelligence people firmly believe Thanh will return to this village sometime between the twenty-fifth of June and the first of July. Additional intel has indicated that Thanh's headquarters is located somewhere in this area." The pointer moved past the DMZ and into North Vietnam. "We figure about thirty-five to forty miles into the general vicinity of Dong Hoi province. We're trying to confirm that information at this time. For now, we'll go with the probability that the information is correct."

Baron took a sip of his scotch before he continued. "As I said, the mission will be to capture or kill Thanh. Hopefully you can snatch him in Bien Cao. But if not, and he should escape our trap at Bien Cao, you will be inserted into the area between Dong Hoi and the DMZ to block Thanh's escape to his headquarters."

This last statement brought some low whistles from the audience.

"I realize this will put you guys right in the middle of Charlie's backyard, but that's why we've picked who we believe are the ten best men in the business to pull this thing off."

McCall stood and asked, "Sir, I've been sittin' here thinking about where I've heard this guy's name before. Isn't he the same joker who made the papers by showin' up at a press conference with two fuckin' American deserters a couple of years ago?"

Baron nodded, "You got it, JD. This is the same guy. As a matter of fact, on the night he was in Bien Cao he had a white American with him. The guy was dressed in NVA uniform and carrying an AK-47 and a Chicom pistol."

This information brought the room alive. Hotujec was on his feet now.

"Damn, Colonel! You think that asshole could've been the white half of that fuckin' Salt and Pepper team?" The room went quiet as the team waited for Baron's answer.

"We're not sure, Jeff, but it's possible. If it was Salt, then this black guy they call Pepper had to be somewhere around the edge of that village with a back-up mob of NVA in case of trouble."

Hotujec sat back down as McCall said, "No wonder you wanted me here, bullet hole or no bullet hole in the leg. I appreciate you letting me in on this one, sir. I think we all do. We all knew Sergeant Wathers and his team."

Everyone in the room agreed with McCall.

Baron cleared his throat and said, "JD, you and Rich were my first choices for this operation, and I tried to pick eight people with a hell of a lot of talent to work with you."

"To work with me, sir?"

"Yes, McCall. You're the team leader. Doc Hawkins will be the second in command. Are there any objections, gentlemen?" There were none.

McCall sat down and looked over at Hawkins, who winked at him and whispered, "It's gonna be a hot time in the old town on this one, JD."

McCall agreed, "Ya got that shit right, Doc."

Richardson asked, "Sir, do we have any idea how many troops Thanh has with him on these little expeditions across the Z?"

"From what we can tell, Rich, he moves around with at least a platoon."

Bowman asked the next question. "Sir, I know you said to either capture or kill this Thanh character, but what if we can get our hands on this damn Salt and Pepper team? Do we waste 'em or what?"

The answer came from the back of the room. "Dead will be perfectly acceptable with this command," said Colonel Davis. "Sorry I butted in there, Jess. Go ahead."

"That's fine, sir. I wasn't quite sure how to answer that one. Okay, let's say that Salt and Pepper are out there with Thanh. The ideal situation would be to nail all three targets in Bien Cao when the thing goes down, but we'll just have to play it the way it falls."

Switching off the projector and turning the lights back up, Baron said, "JD, Doc, I want you to work me up two operations plans. One for Bien Cao and another one for the Dong Hoi area if you have to go north. Anything you want, you get, just ask us. If we don't have it, we'll find it. Gentlemen, today is the tenth. In two weeks I want this team ready to go into position at Bien Cao. Are there any questions?"

Baron paused for a moment. The ten men in front of him looked at one another. There were no questions.

"Okay. Since there are no questions—Colonel Davis, would you like to say a few words?"

Colonel Davis moved to the front of the room.

"Gentlemen, Colonel Baron has assembled ten of the best people we have in Special Forces for this mission. I want to say that if there is any force in the world that could pull this off, it's you men here right now. And God have mercy on anybody that gets in your way." This brought a few cheers and grunts from the team.

Turning to Colonel Baron, Davis said, "Colonel, since half the day is already gone, I think we should adjourn from this briefing and head back to the bar. We can start the training tomorrow. What d'you say?"

"It's fine with me, sir. But it's up to the team leader. What about it, JD?"

McCall looked around at the other NCOs. "Hell, sir. That's like askin' a wino if he'd like a job as cashier in a liquor store! Why not. Tomorrow we start to work, but today is party time."

The team rushed out of the room and for the bar. McCall stayed behind for a moment and stared at the blank screen in front of him. He had a strange feeling about this mission. He had been killing NVA for almost four years now, but this time he would be trying to kill two Americans. Granted they were two sorry sons of bitches, but they were still Americans. Somewhere in the States there was a mother and father worrying and praying for a son who had been listed as missing. Could that son be Salt or Pepper? All McCall knew was that they were somebody's sons, and that a Green Beret from Oklahoma was going to kill them. . . .

IV.

Training began each morning at 0600 hours. PT was the first order of business with 20 repetitions of 10 different exercises followed by a 10-mile run. After this came showers, breakfast, and then down to the ranges for weapons firing. McCall had asked for, and received, two M1 Springfield match-grade rifles with scopes and specially designed silencers. The range had been marked off in distances of two hundred yards, with the final targets at 1,000 yards.

McCall had told Baron that the 1,000-yard marker would separate the regular shooters from the experts. Even with match-grade weapons, a man had to calculate wind direction and make adjustments for the false sight picture caused by the heat mirage drifting up from the sunbaked sands of the range. Today's training had turned into a contest among the team members, with each man putting up 100 dollars, winner take all.

Cowboy Barnes had started the show. He did well until he came up to the 800-yard target. As he squeezed off the tenth and final round, he rose to his feet, dusted off his uniform, and said, "Shit, there went a hundred bucks downrange."

Hotujec and Bowman were tearing up the targets at 600 and 800 yards, but when it came to the 1,000-yard mark, both men were out of the running. A total of 20 rounds went downrange at the final target, but only five hit the paper, and those weren't even close to the bull's-eye. Bowman jumped up and smiled at McCall.

"Hell, JD, I might not've killed the son of a bitch, but I sure as hell scared the fuck out of him."

Hayes and Brady were up next. Hayes made it to the 800 line, then he blew it. Brady had passed the eight but could only put four shots in the last target . . . out of the bull's-eye.

Hawkins, Taber, and Murphy had all taken their turns. Taber didn't make it to the 800 mark, but said he liked working in close anyway. Murphy put seven rounds in at 1000, with two of them in the black. Doc Hawkins hit for 10 at the 600, but after two rounds at the 800, he got up and told McCall he was going to have to change his nickname from "Hawkeye" to "Four-eyes." He couldn't even see the target at 800 yards.

Richardson and McCall were the last shooters. Rich lay down on the firing line, wrapped the sling of the rifle tight around his arm and took up a solid prone position. Sighting the weapon a couple of times, he raised his head, looked over at McCall, and said, "Ya wanna make this thing more interestin', JD?"

McCall was checking his sights as he answered, "What ya got in mind, partner?"

"Well, let's say 100 bucks for every round in the bull at 1,000 yards."

This brought a string of low mutters from the rest of the team. Hotujec said, "Damn, JD. Sounds like ol' Rich here knows something you don't."

"Yeah," said Bowman. "He must have some of that Alvin York blood in him."

Everyone was laughing as McCall said, "Okay, partner, if you'll throw a case of Chivas Regal in the pot, ya got a deal."

Richardson's eyes went wide. "You dickhead," he yelled, "you don't drink Chivas Regal. You drink that god-awful Jack Daniels—hell, you know what a case of that shit costs?"

Now McCall was grinning. "Hell yes, I know what it costs. That's why I don't drink the stuff unless somebody else is gonna buy it . . . so what d'ya say, man?"

"Okay, Boss, you wanna shoot first or last?"

"Go ahead, Rich. I'd like to see what I'm up against."

Richardson rechecked the sling and tightened it a little more around his arm, while JD called down to the pit and told the Vietnamese corporal in charge of the detail to pull and mark the target after each shot.

Doc Hawkins told Rich that if he tightened that sling any more, he was going to have to amputate his arm. Richardson didn't answer; he was concentrating on the small black spot 1,000 yards away.

Red flags had been placed every 200 yards along the left edge of the range. Richardson sighted in on the target with his right eye, then opened his left to watch the flags. At 400 yards, the flag hung perfectly still, at 600 it fluttered every few seconds, but the one at 800 would blow almost straight out for five to 10 seconds, then flutter and hang straight down for a few seconds, only to be blown back out again.

Richardson watched the red cloth perform its little dance for a full two minutes. Hayes said, "Hey man, we'd like to see you shoot before the sun goes down."

Richardson ignored the remark. With the front sight setting a little high of center, and opening his left eye every few seconds to watch the flag at 800 yards, he began a slow squeeze on the trigger. The flag was in the flutter stage.

Waiting patiently for the flag to stop blowing, he slightly increased the pressure on the trigger. A trickle of sweat worked its way down his forehead. Wait . . . wait . . . now. . . . The M1 cracked once. Rocking with the recoil, Richardson brought the rifle back into position. His left eye caught the flag moving out and upward again.

Releasing his finger from the trigger, he rolled on his side and wiped his forehead, then his eyes. McCall said, "What d'you call the shot?"

Richardson thought about it for a moment, then said, "In the black . . . a little high and to the right."

In the pit, the Vietnamese heard the whistle of the round as it passed over their heads and into the target. Pulling the heavy frame down into the hole, they searched for evidence of a hit. The crew had been in the pit for over three hours now, and Murphy had been the only man to hit the bull's-eye.

The Vietnamese corporal shouted "Choei Hoi" as he pointed to the bullet hole. It was in the black, a little high and to the right. Grabbing a white spotter's disk and a marker peg, he placed them in the target and yelled for the crew to take the target back up.

As the target went back up into position, five sets of binoculars were sighting downrange. Hotujec said, "I'll be damned, JD, he called it right on the money!"

There was a cocky smile on Richardson's face as he looked over at his team leader. "That's one," he said.

McCall lowered his binoculars and replied, "Could've been dumb luck!"

Rolling back into position for his second shot, Rich muttered, "Don't you wish." As he lined up, he could hear side bets being made behind him. Watching the flags once more, he placed the sight high-center, a little more to the left this time, and fired. The target disappeared into the pit and came back up within seconds. The white disk was sitting dead-center of the black ring.

There were whoops and cheers from the men behind Richardson as the winners held out open hands to take their money from the doubting Thomases.

The pit crew called back to the firing line and said they had two targets operational and asked if Rich and McCall would like to use them. They could alternate shots.

Doc Hawkins asked the corporal if they were in a hurry to get out of the pit. The corporal shook his head and explained that the crew was also making bets in the pit, and it would be easier to keep track of the money that way.

McCall said, "Would it bother you if we alternated shots?"

Richardson answered, "No, I was about to suggest the same thing anyway. It'll add a little more pressure to the game."

McCall nodded to Doc, who called the pit and told them to run up both targets.

JD rolled his sleeves down, wrapped the sling tight around his arm, and shifted to the prone position. The amounts of the bets had dropped off for the moment. The rest of the team was waiting to see how well the boss did.

McCall watched the 800-yard marker as he took up the slack in the trigger. As the red cloth began to go lifeless, JD took a deep breath and exhaled half of it. The flag was still. . . . The M1 bucked as McCall fired, the recoil driving the stock of the heavy weapon into his shoulder.

There was silence on the line as the target was pulled into the pit. Rich said, "Call it."

Still looking downrange, McCall said, "Center . . . at about eight o'clock."

The target came back up.

"Jesus! JD called his shot, too. It's in the black at eight o'clock. You two fuckers must have been related to Buffalo Bill," said Barnes.

The betting was back to normal. McCall glanced at Rich. "Whatcha think, partner?"

Richardson was lying on his side and holding a pair of binoculars. "Could've been dumb luck," he answered.

"Not hardly," replied McCall.

JD's second shot was dead-center. This brought a renewed air of excitement from the crowd in the background, and that's what it was—a crowd. A platoon of straight-leg infantry had driven up halfway through the contest and Doc Hawkins had explained to the platoon leader what was going on, and invited the men to get in on the betting. They had. Now Doc had most of their money.

Richardson and McCall were even shot for shot as the tenth and final rounds were locked into place. Richardson looked over at JD and said, "Hell, man, we ain't winnin' nothin'. Those guys behind us are cleanin' up."

"Looks that way. You got somethin' in mind, Rich?"

The crowd was quiet now, as they listened for Richardson's new proposal, and a chance to raise the stakes on the last shot.

"Well, boss man, why don't we have 'em pull the targets down an' put a white disk in the center of the bull? Closest to the marker wins."

McCall thought it over for a few seconds, then said, "Sounds good to me, Rich. But if I'm gonna have to show off, it's gonna cost you two cases of Regal."

"You sure make it hard on a guy, JD. Now, what happens if I win?"

"Hell, that's easy. If you beat me, I'll take you down to Mama Foue's and pay for all the pussy you can screw until we leave."

This offer brought wild cheers from the crowd. Hawkins gazed skyward as he said, "Oh Lord, couldn't you give me supervision for just one shot?"

Rich was rubbing his crotch as he smiled and said, "That could get pretty damn expensive, JD. Ya know how I like that pussy."

McCall laughed as he patted Richardson's rifle. "Yeah, but you got to shoot this gun before you get to shoot the one you're playin' with. An' I'm bettin' they both have the same effect—a lotta noise, but not much action."

Richardson rolled into position and said, "We'll see, JD. We'll see."

Rich waited for the target to come up. When it did, the disk was no more than a speck of white surrounded by black.

The leg lieutenant shook his head as he lowered his field glasses. Doc stepped up to him and asked, "What's the matter, sir?"

"Sergeant, there is no way those two men can hit that marker from this distance. Hell, I can hardly see the thing with these glasses."

Doc pulled a wad of bills from his pants pocket and grinned at the young lieutenant. "Well, sir. I got five hundred dollars here that says one of our boys is gonna hit that disk down there."

The officer called his platoon sergeant over and they talked in low whispers for a moment, with the sergeant looking downrange and shaking his head. Hawkins heard the man say, "No fuckin' way, sir! Hell, I'll take half the bet if you want to cover the other half."

The lieutenant agreed and the two men handed Doc their money.

Rich waited for all transactions to be completed before he sighted in on the target. Straining his eyes at the tiny speck, Rich fired.

Glasses went to faces as the target went down into the pit and came back up. He had missed; the round hit at the far edge of the black at about one o'clock.

"Good try, Rich," said JD.

Doc yelled, "Okay, gents. That only leaves one shooter with one shot. I'm still coverin' all bets. Now, who wants to take some of this easy money off my hands?"

With McCall left with one shot, the infantry guys pooled their money and bet it all that McCall would miss.

Doc covered the $1000-dollar wager. Turning to JD, he said, "Bang away, boss."

McCall sighted in on the target, took a deep breath, let it out, and squeezed off the final shot. The target went down, then came back up. People were yelling, "Where's the marker? Where'd the round hit?"

The crackling of the radio brought instant quiet. It was the pit calling. The Vietnamese corporal was bringing the disk to the firing line. All eyes were on the jeep that raced up the left side of the range.

The lieutenant was the first one to the jeep when it stopped. The corporal jumped out and saluted. "Good afternoon, Dai Uy."

The officer returned the salute. There was excitement in his voice as he said, "Come on, man! Where did that last round hit?"

McCall and Richardson had joined the crowd that surrounded the little man.

The officer's voice almost cracked as he screamed, "Dammit, Corporal. I asked a fuckin' question. Where did that last round go?"

Reaching into the jeep, the man turned around and held the disk in the air above his head. The lieutenant turned pale for a moment. A hush had fallen over the crowd as someone said, "Jesus Christ, he only missed the damn center of the disk by an inch."

The whole team let out a wild yell, and rushing over to McCall, picked him up and put him on their shoulders. The infantry guys were looking a little green around the gills as they slowly walked off. The lieutenant was the last to leave. Looking up at McCall, he said, "Thanks for the shooting lesson, Sarge."

McCall nodded and, removing his beret, made a sweeping gesture with it. "My pleasure, sir."

JD was lowered back to the ground and walked up to Hawkins. "How'd we do, Doc?" he asked.

Hawkins finished counting and, with a grin from ear to ear, he said, "One-thousand-seven-hundred-and-sixty bucks. Not bad, JD."

Richardson was still staring at the disk and shaking his head. "Man, I really didn't know you could shoot like this, JD."

The corporal broke out laughing. Doc and JD joined in.

Richardson looked around at the rest of the group and asked, "You guys got any idea what's so fuckin' funny?"

Barnes answered with, "I'm not sure, Rich, but I got a feelin' there's a turd in the soup somewhere."

McCall was laughing so hard he had tears in his eyes. Putting his arm around the little corporal, he said, "Gentlemen, I'd like you to meet Nhu Vai Foue. He's Mama Foue's number-one son."

Rich looked a little confused as he said, "What the hell you talkin' about, man?"

"Hell, Rich, you don't really think I could hit that little piece of shit at a thousand yards, do you?"

Rich's face went blank. "You mean . . ."

"That's right, ol' buddy. Nhu, Doc, and I set the whole thing up this morning while we were down in the pit helping the crew get the targets ready. Remember that shot you heard before we came back up to the line? Well, that was Doc, shootin' a hole in that disk. Ya see, partner, I remembered you telling me once that you fired on the 1st Army Rifle Team. I figured you'd get a little cocky when we came up on the line, so I wanted to be ready for ya."

Rich yelled, "You sorry motherfucker! You would've made me buy that Chivas Regal, too, wouldn't ya?"

"I don't know, Rich. I'd have had to think about it. But hell, when those infantry guys came along with all that money, Doc and I just expanded on the plan a little bit. It worked, too."

The thought of pulling one over on the legs brought a smile to Rich's face for a second. Then he said, "Well, did I really beat your ass or not?"

Corporal Foue shook his head, "No, Chung Se Richardson. In first five shots you hit black circle four times. When other soldiers show up, Chung Se Hawkins call me on radio and say to mark all shots in black.

He say we make lots of money from other soldiers. Your last five shots, you hit black only two times, but I mark them good. Chung Se Mac hit seven times ir black for real. He beat you fair an' square."

"You sure, you little sawed-off runt?" said Rich.

"For sure, Chung Se."

Doc was moving around to the team members and giving them back the money they had lost on the rigged match. Paying the last man, he turned to McCall and said, "Well, boss. What d'we do with all this newfound money?"

JD glanced at his watch, then down the firing line, where the Infantry unit had started firing. "Well, since it's after 1500 hours, we'll call it a day. I think we better get our asses out of here before that platoon sergeant figures out how we screwed 'em. How much money did you say we had, Doc?"

"One-thousand-seven-hundred-and-sixty bucks."

"Give Nhu five hundred and sixty to spread out among the boys in the pits. Nhu, tell the boys they did a number-one job for us today. As for the rest of you, we're gonna get the weapons back to the compound, then we're gonna get a case of Chivas Regal and head for Mama Foue's. We're gonna put the rest of the money on the bar and drink and fuck till it's all gone."

There were wild whoops and howls from the team as they picked up their weapons and equipment and loaded the truck for the ride back to the compound.

As they passed the infantry officer, McCall waved. The team was cracking up as they passed the platoon sergeant in the uncovered deuce and a half. Barnes couldn't help himself. He yelled, "Hey, top! You know why they call the Infantry the queen of battle, don't you?"

The truck was too far down the road for the sergeant to hear the final remark, but he didn't have to hear what was said. He already knew.

The lieutenant walked up to him and said, "What the hell were they yellin' about?"

With a disheartening look on his face, the platoon sergeant simply said, "They were just telling us we just got fucked, sir. That's all."

The following morning the team began its PT as usual, but to anyone watching the small group, it would have looked more like an aerobics class in a retirement home. The party at Mama Foue's had been a classic. When they performed the side-straddle hop, there were low, painful groans as their feet slammed into the dirt, sending shock waves to alcohol-soaked nerves in the head. The four-count pushup looked more like a band of Arabs praying to Allah. All but a few of the men were on their knees, and as McCall counted the cadence, they would slowly lower their heads, then raise them. Hotujec had lowered his head on the first cadence call and simply stayed that way until the exercise was over.

"Recover!" shouted McCall, louder than even he had intended, the word vibrating through his hangover.

JD watched the men struggle to their feet and sway haphazardly as he said, "Shake it out, guys. We still got the ten-mile run to go."

A silence fell over the group and, from the looks on their faces, McCall could see that a 10-mile run would be nothing short of a death sentence. Some of them already looked dead.

Doc Hawkins dropped to his knees, placed his hands together, and looked up at the early-morning sky. "Oh, great Ranger in the sky, strike down this tormentor of alcohol-crazed bodies and set your people free!"

As the group jogged out the front gate, Murphy moved in next to Doc.

"Don't look like your prayer of desperation worked, Doc."

"No shit. Can't figure it out either—it worked for Charlton Heston."

When McCall reached the four-mile mark he turned around and saw he was running by himself. The team was strung out along both sides of the road. A couple of them were on their knees, heaving the night's entertainment onto the ground. McCall wasn't feeling so hot himself. He walked back to the compound, picking up the stragglers as he went. Once inside the wire, he reminded the group of the old saying, "If you're gonna party with the big dogs, you better be able to piss on the tall trees."

Any further attempt at PT was out of the question. McCall said, "Okay, girls, that's it until 1300. We're gonna be working on extractions this afternoon. I strongly suggest you all get some rest this morning —we're gonna be workin' late tonight. Any questions?"

If anybody had one, he wasn't about to waste time asking it. All anyone wanted to do was lie down.

"Okay, dismissed."

Everyone headed for the showers, the Alka-Seltzer, and bed.

By 1400 hours the team was standing in the middle of a jungle clearing waiting for the UH1H helicopters to come on station. A light drizzle had begun to fall. It was a welcome relief from the day's oppressive heat. McCall divided the personnel into two teams of five: one would work on the ladder extraction, while the second would be pulled out with stabo rigs. The choppers would lift them up to 1,000 feet, fly around for about five minutes, then set them back down in the clearing. The teams would then switch duty and go through the routine again. This would go on until McCall was satisfied with their time.

Although the members of this handpicked group

were experts in the business, they had never worked together as a team. Each man had a certain way he did things, and his way might be different enough to throw the whole team out of sync. This was what McCall wanted to find out.

On the first attempt, he let each man do his own thing—it turned out to be a gang-bang for the ladder crew. Sergeants Brady and Taber chose the side ladder climb. As the chopper came down they each grabbed a side of the ladder and began to work their way up the main side cables. This wasn't a bad method unless there were three other people trying to take the thing head-on. Between the down-blast of the rotor blades and the continuous swaying in and out of the ladder caused by each man's weight applied to the different rungs, the exercise was a fiasco. One of the front men would start to place his foot on the next rung, only to have the man on the side move up, pulling the main cable outward with his hands and inward with his feet. The front man would miss the rung and be left hanging by his hands while his feet searched desperately for support.

McCall told them they were going to have to do it again. They all agreed. The stabo extraction went smoothly; after all, it only required the man going up to hook two snap links to the two he wore on his web gear.

McCall watched as the five men scrambled to the dangling ladder. This time they all went at it from the front. Three men moving in unison went up four steps and waited for the other two to begin moving up. Once all five were on the ladder they moved as one until they were halfway up. Then they leaned forward and hooked their snap links to the rungs as a precaution.

McCall thought it went a hell of a lot smoother this time, but they were still taking too long. It was going to be a long afternoon.

By 1800, the team had practiced extractions, insertions, and link-up procedures on the LZ. The light rain had stopped by 1600, and the steamy heat and sticky humidity enveloped them. They were all tired when JD finally called it a day. The choppers landed and the weary soldiers climbed aboard for the ride home.

The wind blowing through the choppers was instant relief to the men in their sweat-soaked tiger stripes. Sergeant Matt Brady sat in the seat by the door's edge and watched the lush green jungle below. He thought of how war had spoiled the true beauty of Asia. The doorgunner had just lit a cigarette when the loud pop of lead hitting metal echoed through the chopper. As the gunner screamed into his mike, there were two more hits in rapid succession. Both aircraft were taking fire.

The helicopters climbed out of rifle range. The crew chiefs checked for damage and called the results to the pilots. McCall requested a report on his people in the second chopper. Doc Hawkins got the thumbs-up from Murphy, Taber, and Bowman. Yelling to Brady, he waited for the okay signal. It never came. Brady was dead. The bullet had entered his left side and traveled upward to the heart. It was a one-in-a-million shot, and Matt Brady had been in the right place at the right time.

It was a sad-hearted group that went to bed that night. They had lost one of their number to a stray bullet from an unseen enemy. They all felt remorse for Brady, but deep down, each man was grateful it had not been him. . . .

V.

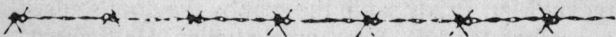

A memorial service was held for Sergeant Brady before the body was shipped home; a solemn service conducted in the Special Forces manner. Two candles were lit and placed at each end of a small table. In the middle sat a pair of Brady's spit-shined jump boots, neatly laced. Resting atop the boots was his green beret. Less than 48 hours ago, they had all been drinking and laughing together, and now Brady was gone. The chaplain's words had touched each of them. McCall didn't like funerals; they allowed feelings to creep through the wall of hardness he projected to others, and made him realize how vulnerable JD McCall really was. . . .

The operation had been codenamed Operation Dispatch, and the team designated Striker One.

As the days passed, hours were spent studying photos of both Bien Cao village and Dong Hoi Province. Every map that contained any part of the target areas was put at the team's disposal. Prominent mountain ranges, roads, villages, streams, and rivers were studied by each member of the team. McCall and Doc Hawkins gathered the group in the conference room to discuss the operation's plans. They would need to prepare for two different operations, one in Bien Cao and another in Dong Hoi Province.

So many different thoughts and ideas had been brought up at the meeting that McCall finally suggested that since they were all experienced recon people, each man work up his own plan of operation. Once this had been accomplished, McCall, Hawkins, and Baron would go over each of them and select one or use a combination of all the plans to formulate the operation.

Tactical support in South Vietnam would be no problem. TAC Air and Artillery were in easy reach of Bien Cao. The problem would be the northern area. If they had to chase Thanh across the DMZ, they would be limited to TAC air in the form of F-4 Phantoms, and that would be risky at best for the pilots. If the weather turned bad, you could eliminate the Phantoms, and choppers wouldn't last five minutes that far north. Between the heat-seeking missiles and 37mm cannon fire, they'd be blown out of the sky. Striker would have to make it back to the DMZ to have any chance of getting out. Each man realized this fact, but it didn't change anything. They were going, no matter what the odds. If nothing else, for Brady.

With only four days left, another briefing was scheduled. This time there was only coffee, no wisecracks or jokes. Striker One was all business. Colonel Baron shifted the projector screen a few inches and pushed the remote-control switch he held in his hand. As a brightly colored map of Vietnam appeared on the screen, Baron said, "Men, I want to thank you all for the time and extensive effort you put forward in developing your individual op plans. They were all detailed and highly professional. It was interesting to note that they were similar—with only a few variations. I would like you to hold all questions until both plans have been fully briefed."

Turning to the map, he placed the tip of the pointer on Bien Cao village.

"First, we'll go over the operation in the south. At approximately 0500 hours on the morning of the twenty-fourth, Striker One will depart Tan Son Nhut airfield by C-130 for Da Nang. Upon arrival, the aircraft will taxi to a closed, high security off-loading ramp. You will be transferred to a security van and taken to an isolation area in the immediate vicinity of the 101st Tactical Air Support Command. The team will remain at this location overnight. The following morning at 0530 hours, you will be transported to the chopper pad and loaded onto two UH1H helicopters for insertion into an area outside Bien Cao. Now, due to the fact that we have had to plan for two operations, each man will pack two rucksacks. One for the Bien Cao area and another for the more extensive area to the north. Everything that the team has requested will be waiting at the isolation area in Da Nang. The rucksacks for the southern area, of course, will go in with you. The second rucksack will be loaded on the extraction choppers at Firebase Carol, located about fifteen miles south of Bien Cao. Hopefully you won't need them. But if our boy Thanh and his sidekicks don't show, or should somehow escape, the team will be extracted from Bien Cao and flown north. You will change over rucks in flight. We will be getting continuous updates from our agents regarding Thanh's movements. Hopefully, he will show up in Bien Cao, but if he doesn't, we'll radio the situation to you while you are flying north." Baron paused for a moment, a serious look on his face. "Gentlemen, if Major Thanh doesn't come to us, you are going to go to him. We are determined to eliminate this man, once and for all."

The room was perfectly quiet. There was nothing to say; it was going to be an all-or-nothing operation, and the men in the room knew it.

Baron continued. "Our choppers will get you as far north as possible. Your team leaders and I have gone over all the possible routes Thanh could take out of Bien Cao, should he escape and scramble for the north. But I wouldn't insult the intelligence of any man in this

STRIKER ONE DOWN   65

room by saying Thanh will show up where we think he
will. It's strictly guesswork. If he does, that's great; if
he doesn't, you're going to have to hunt him down.
Sergeant McCall and I have agreed that, since each
member is going to be carrying the URC-10 emergency
radio, you will each carry three extra batteries per
radio. One man will activate the emergency beep for
five minutes each hour. That way, we can keep track of
your movements in the north. Of course, you will also
have the PRC-25s. After completion of your mission in
the north, Striker One will escape and evade to an area
in this general vicinity, five miles northeast of the
DMZ. This specific area will be monitored for thirty
days after insertion. Should you become separated,
each man will try to link up in this area. Should your
radio go out or be lost, find some way of placing the
day-letter code on the ground in an open area. A copy
of the thirty-day code will be passed out after this
briefing. We will also have daily overflights covering
your progress. Once we receive a signal, either by radio
or through the day-letter code, we will scramble choppers and TAC Air into the pickup point. Estimated time
on target is twenty minutes. Well, guys, that's about it.
Now, what are your questions?"

Cowboy Barnes had the first one.

"Sir, would it be possible for you to have a Mike
Force on standby just this side of the DMZ? I mean,
since you're gonna be monitoring our progress, you'll
have a pretty good idea about when we should be
nearing that pickup point at the Z. And it sure would
be nice to see a friendly face in the area."

Baron looked to the back of the room. "Colonel, I
think we can handle that, can't we?"

Davis nodded as he said, "Roger that, Jess. I'll set it
up myself."

Hayes stood up next. "What about weather projections, sir?"

"You will receive an up-to-the-minute briefing prior to departing Saigon and another one prior to insertion into Bien Cao."

"Thank you, sir."

McCall and Hawkins looked at each other. McCall said, "Go ahead, Doc, you ask him."

Doc asked, "Sir, what about the Striker dead? Do you want us to try to bring them out?"

It was the one question that Baron did not want to answer.

"Doc, I wish there was a way to do it, but to be honest with you, I believe it's going to be hard enough for a live man to get to that pickup point from the north, let alone carry a dead man with him. Therefore, all Striker personnel killed in action will be buried and the coordinates logged. Any chance for body recovery will have to come after this war's over."

The question had obviously made Baron uncomfortable. The men could detect the slight tone of sadness in his voice as he asked, "Are there any more questions?" There were none. "That concludes this briefing, gentlemen. Thank you."

The following three days were spent checking weapons and studying further the terrain around Bien Cao and Dong Hoi Province. Messages were sent out to all unit commanders around the Bien Cao area. They were instructed to halt any and all operations within the general vicinity of the village. Units along the DMZ were informed to limit their patrols to the immediate areas of their bases.

Colonel Davis didn't want Major Thanh to have a chance encounter with anyone but Striker One. Davis had also coordinated with the Air Force and Navy in reference to the team's plan to activate the emergency beeper five minutes each hour. All intelligence reports and references to Striker One were to be confined to U.S. personnel. No Vietnamese personnel, regardless of rank, were to know of the existence of Striker One.

It was well known throughout Special Forces that the mission of more than one special-operations team had been compromised before it ever got out of the compound. These mysterious leaks of information had often resulted in the recon team being wiped out on insertion. The colonel knew this was going to be a tough mission and wanted to give Striker every chance possible. If the Vietnamese didn't like it, fuck 'em.

The flight from Saigon to Da Nang proceeded as planned. Striker One was in the isolation area. Each member of the team ran a final check of his weapons and equipment. There was nothing to do now but wait.

McCall and Hawkins were going over the latest weather projections for the next seven days. The first three didn't look bad, but after that, the weather would start going downhill fast. A squall would be moving in from the east, followed by another storm that was expected to remain in the area for at least 72 hours. Bad weather meant no air support.

Doc poured himself a cup of coffee as he said, "Gonna be a real bitch if we have to head north, JD."

McCall lit a cigar. "I know, Doc. But if we get a shot at that fuckin' Salt and Pepper, I don't really give a shit. I'll worry about the rest of the shit after I have those two guys' balls in my pocket."

Doc cracked a smile. "Well hell, JD, you got more to lose on this operation than I do."

"How you figure that, Doc?"

"Hell, man, you got a chance of losin' three pairs of balls to my one."

The sound of laughter carried out into the room where the rest of the team were either playing cards or sharpening knives.

Bowman looked through the doorway to McCall's room. "Now, what the hell do you suppose those two found so damn funny?" he wondered aloud.

Murphy finished shuffling the cards and said, "From

what I've heard about JD, he's more than likely convinced Doc that we ought to run on up to Hanoi and grab ol' uncle Ho since we're gonna be in the area anyway."

Hayes pulled three cards from his hand and threw them in the center of the table. "Give me three, Larry. Hey, Rich, you been with JD a long time. Do you think he'll try any off-the-wall shit on this operation?"

Richardson sat on the edge of his bunk, slowly and smoothly moving his huge Bowie knife back and forth across the sharpening stone. He stopped and looked at Hayes.

"I'll tell ya what, Don. Any crazy white boy that would climb up on a rock surrounded by a hard-core platoon of NVA and ask the sons of bitches if they wanted to surrender before he had to hurt 'em is capable of any damn thing."

Bob Taber threw in his cards. "Hell, I heard about that! Did McCall really ask them to surrender?"

The game had come to a halt as the men in the room waited for Richardson's answer. Placing the knife back in the upside-down scabbard taped to his web gear, Rich grinned. "He sure as hell did. Those bastards had been chasing us all morning. We had reached the crest of this one hill when McCall just stopped and said, 'Fuck it, we ain't runnin' no more.' So we set up a defensive position right there. It wasn't long before ol' Charlie started movin' all around us. We could hear 'em crawlin' up through the bush and gettin' into position to open up on us. JD had called our FAC for an extraction, but was told it was gonna take close to an hour to scramble everything and get to us. All the time them NVA were comin' closer and closer. I'll tell ya the truth, man, my asshole was so tight you couldn't have driven a broom straw up the damn thing with a sledgehammer. It wasn't just me either, brother. That was the first time I ever saw our Chinese get uptight, and we had been in some pretty damn tight spots before this one. Well, JD picked up on the situation real fast. He moves into the center of our little ol' defensive circle and tells the Chinese not to worry—he has a surefire way out of this mess. Now, ya could tell from the look in those boys' eyes that they had some serious doubts that brother McCall had all the answers this time. Hell, the next thing we know, JD jumps up on top of this big-ass rock in the center of the circle, and in perfect Vietnamese, tells the NVA he's only gonna give 'em this one chance to surrender, then we're gonna kick ass. It was the damnedest thing you ever saw. The whole mountain was quiet as a churchyard. We must have stood there for a full minute with our mouths open staring up at this insane person. He just grinned down at us and said, 'Well, at least they're considering it.' Man, that cracked us up. Now, ol' Charlie had to be pretty confused by all this shit. I mean, hell, here he had us outnumbered and completely surrounded and we're askin' him if he wants to surrender and laughin' our asses off. We didn't hear a thing movin' around that hill for a full ten minutes after that. So, ya can call the guy nuts or fucked up maybe, but I'll tell you one thing: when he stepped down off that rock, the Chinese would have followed him straight into hell to pinch the devil's ass!"

The team looked around at one another and shook their heads. Hotujec slapped the poker table and said, "Hell, fellows, I got a feelin' we're gonna have a real blast on this one. . . . Shit, I ain't had so much fun since . . ."

Barnes cut him off before he could finish. "Yeah, we know, Jeff, you ain't had so much fun since the pigs ate your sister!"

The security guards on duty at the gate of the isolation area turned and looked back at the team house, the source of all that laughter. "Hey, man, ain't those guys supposed to be movin' out in the morning on some hotshot secret mission?"

The other guard shifted his rifle to light a cigarette. "Yeah," he replied, "but from the sound of that shit, there can't be much to it. Those Special Forces dudes are always makin' a big deal out of nothin'."

"Hell yeah, you're right. We could probably do the damn job better ourselves. I always thought those mothers were overrated anyway."

By 0430, the team had finished a light breakfast, and the weapons and equipment had been loaded into the van for the short trip to the chopper pad. Nobody was talking much this morning. That was to be expected. Every man, no matter how tough he seemed, experienced that moment when the realization of what he was about to do reached deep into his stomach and made his mouth go dry. It was the feeling of fear in its rawest form, knowing that outside that room death walked the jungle floor, patiently waiting to claim the losers of this deadly game. Each member of the team knew the feeling well; they had felt it before, and this morning was no exception. The feeling would pass—that was what made these men what they were. They would give ol' man death proper respect, then do what they had to.

Rucksacks were pulled onto broad shoulders, weapons were double-checked and put on safe. The huge blades of the UH1H helicopters rotated slowly at first, each turn picking up momentum.

Colonels Davis and Baron gave McCall the latest weather and intel updates. The weather was the same and agents reported that Major Thanh had departed Dong Hoi Province, heading south. The two officers stood at the edge of the chopper pad and watched as the nine men of Striker One loaded the helicopters. Both were well aware that this could be the last time they ever saw these men.

The blades reached maximum RPMs. The pilot glanced back at McCall and gave the thumbs-up. McCall nodded. They were ready for lift-off. The pilot lifted the chopper straight up, then tilted the nose down slightly. The aircraft shot out across the rice paddies, the second chopper close behind.

Davis and Baron watched the choppers until they were out of sight. Turning to leave, Baron noticed Davis still staring across the open fields. For a moment he thought he saw tears welling up in the old man's eyes.

"Is something wrong, sir?"

"You know, Jess, tonight, back in the States, some guy will turn on his new color TV, plop his ass down in a new recliner, and yell for his wife to bring him a beer. When the news comes on, he'll switch the channel because he's tired of hearing about this fuckin' war. It doesn't concern him. Someplace else a group of college kids will be glued to the news station, hanging on every word being said by some so-called foreign correspondent who doesn't know his ass from a hole in the ground about this war. But every word he speaks will be taken for truth by those kids, and they'll run out and try to burn down their school in protest of something they don't understand. All that will be happening in our country tonight, Jess. I honestly believe half the country would like to see Striker die and the other half could give a damn one way or the other. It's times like this that I ask myself why in God's name we keep sending the few good people we have left out to die for a bunch of assholes that don't even give a fuck."

Baron looked out at the fields as he stood next to Davis.

"Colonel, I wish I could give you an answer, but I can't. But I will tell you what scares the hell out of me. What's going to happen when we don't have any more McCalls, Richardsons, and the rest to do these dirty fuckin' jobs. Those kids back in the States won't have to burn their schools—it'll be done for 'em. No, sir, I can't give you an answer; I don't think anyone can. We can only hope that years from now somebody will look back and say they were terrible times, but thank God there were those few who cared, and risked it all to save the rest."

Davis slowly wiped his hand across his eyes and said, "Thanks, Jess, for listening to the ramblings of an old man. I hope you're right. Maybe someday men like these will get the respect they deserve. Let's get over to the operations shed. I want to hear everything that comes out of that area once Striker's on the ground."

The jeep pulled away and headed for the operations center. The dust from the road settled onto the steel of the helicopter pad—a silent witness to the courage of nine men flying to their fate.

VI.

━━━✳━━━✳━━━✳━━━✳━━━━━✳━━━✳

Striker One moved off the LZ and covered the three miles to the outskirts of Bien Cao in good time. Setting up in a concealed position 500 yards off the main road into the village, the team would wait until nightfall before moving into ambush positions. The plan was simple: Doc Hawkins, Hotujec, and Hayes would swing around to the far end of the village and set up along a trail that came in from the left. McCall, Barnes, and Murphy would work their way to the right and set up an ambush site along a trail that paralleled the main road. Richardson, Bowman, and Taber would take a position directly to the rear of the village on a slight knoll that ran along the tree line. Using a starlite scope for night vision, they would have a clear view of the entire area. If Thanh came into the village from an unguarded direction, Rich would be able to spot him and radio the rest of the team to move in. They would wait out the night. If Thanh didn't show, Striker would fall back before first light and regroup a safe distance from Bien Cao. The entire operation would depend on the team's ability to go undetected during the daylight hours. The team was aware that if they gave the slightest hint of their presence, Thanh would know about them before he ever crossed the DMZ.

The first night had passed without a sign of anything. It was well known throughout Vietnam that once darkness fell, people disappeared into their homes and remained there until dawn. To wander around after dark was suicide. If Charlie didn't get them, the Americans would. Once the team regrouped, they all reported the same thing. Nothing had moved anywhere in Bien Cao during the night. McCall radioed the report back to Colonel Davis. Davis rogered the message and informed McCall that their agents in the North had confirmed Thanh's departure from Dong Hoi Province. The major was heading south.

Having found a safe area for the team to wait for nightfall, McCall worked out a schedule for daytime security. Each man would pull two hours. The team would be awakened at the first sound of anyone approaching their position. All encounters would be handled with knives—no shots were to be fired. Hayes took the first shift. The remainder of the team formed a circle on the ground, and, within minutes, were sound asleep.

The security shift had changed three times when Barnes woke McCall. "JD, it's your turn in the barrel, ol' boy."

McCall sat up and rubbed the stiffness out of his legs. "Anything happening out there, Cowboy?"

"Naw, heard some arty and a couple of aircraft off to the east 'bout half an hour ago. Other than that, it's been quiet as a coffin."

McCall glanced up. "Nice fuckin' terminology, Cowboy."

"Hell, man, you gotta admit, that's pretty damn quiet."

"Ya gotta point there, Cowboy. You better get some more sleep. It's gonna be another long night."

Barnes dropped down next to McCall. "You think he'll show tonight, JD?"

"I sure as hell hope so, Cowboy. God, how I hate playin' this waitin' shit."

Barnes offered McCall a piece of gum.

"No, thanks, Ed. I got burnt out on the stuff 'bout a

year ago when I tried to quit smokin'. Everybody kept tellin' me I was gonna die of cancer if I didn't get off the weed. So I gave it a shot. I started chewin' gum and candy all the damn time. That went on for 'bout three months, but it didn't work out." McCall paused, his face suddenly serious. He looked Barnes straight in the eye and said, "You know what happened, Cowboy?"

Barnes shook his head, "No idea, JD."

McCall smiled. "Now I got cancer and bad fuckin' teeth."

Barnes grinned. "You know, JD, Richardson's right. You're fuckin' nuts. But I'm sure as hell glad you're on my side. I'm gonna grab a few winks and think about your bad teeth."

Barnes shifted around on the hard ground until he finally found a comfortable position and slowly drifted off to sleep. JD liked Cowboy. As far as that went, McCall figured he couldn't be in any better company than he was right now. Of the team members, he had known Charlie Hawkins the longest. They had worked together back at Fort Bragg in the early sixties before the war really started heating up. They drank together, were in more barroom fights than he could count, and chased the same women. Those were the good ol' days. Both came to Vietnam in 1963—long before the big American buildup—when an advisor was just an advisor.

They had been treated well by the Vietnamese people in those early days. They understood the people and were always respectful of their ways and beliefs, but after the buildup began in '65, things began to change. It was no longer just a few Americans, it was thousands, and wherever there are thousands of GIs, you'll find thousands of dollars. The Vietnamese were not used to having much as far as luxuries or the money to even think about buying them. That is, until GI Joe came rolling in with his pockets full of money. It didn't take Mama San long to figure out what the American soldier wanted to spend his money on. Whorehouses and steam-an'-cream joints appeared overnight throughout Vietnam. Drugs were as easy to get as a case of the clap, and money flowed like water. We had brought the good life to Vietnam.

Like anywhere else, money, women, booze, and drugs brought trouble with them. There were rapes, muggings, murders, and more damn gunfights than the OK Corral. Suddenly the Green Beret Advisor was considered no different from any other American soldier with a hard-on and a pocket full of money.

It was in the first few months of the buildup that Hawkins and McCall found out just how fucked up this war was going to get. They were sitting in a Saigon bar when a doped-up American soldier threw a grenade into the bar to kill a guy he thought was his old drill sergeant from Fort Dix. Of course, the drill sergeant was still in New Jersey. Doc Hawkins had been wounded badly enough to earn a medevac back to the States. McCall received frag wounds in both legs, but they weren't that serious. McCall hadn't gone to another bar, with the exception of Mama Foue's, since. It wasn't that he was afraid, but he'd made up his mind he'd kill the next crazy son of a bitch that tried anything like that again, and he didn't give a damn if the guy was an American or not. By the time Hawkins returned to Vietnam, the NVA and the Green Berets had reached an understanding: no quarter given, none expected. Doc didn't follow that rule all the time. But then, he was a medic.

Command and Control North had the highest kill ratio of any outfit in Vietnam. But that reputation didn't come easily—it also had the highest casualty count of any unit its size. Hawkins left CCN for Ban Me Thuot and CCS; they had requested some experienced recon team leaders to help train the new boys arriving each month from Fort Bragg, and Doc said he was ready for a change of scenery. This was the first time

McCall had seen him since he left.

No, it wasn't hard to work with people like these. McCall knew that every man on this team would drive himself to the limit of his endurance, then reach down and pull that extra mile that few men possess.

As the final glimmers of light faded beyond the mountains, the members of Striker went over their plan of operation once more. The only change would be a test of their emergency beepers on the URC-10s. The Air Force wanted one turned on at midnight so they could check it out on their aircraft tracking-and-monitoring equipment. This job had been passed to Bowman. If everything was working right, the Air Force would be able to pinpoint Bowman's position within 25 feet.

By one in the morning, Bowman had done his thing with the radio and the Air Force relayed to Colonel Davis that they had a go on all systems.

Activating the starlite scope, Richardson placed it to his eyes and began a slow sweep of the village. The scope provided clear images of each hut and ramshackle house in Bien Cao. The objects appeared to be covered in a soft, hazy, green fog, caused by the filter in the scope. Starlite was like a cat's eye in the night. The scope was moving from left to right. Nothing. Not even the dogs were moving around tonight. Turning to Bowman, Richardson handed him the scope and whispered, "Here, man, take this thing for a while. I'm startin' to get green-eye. Everything's lookin' the same."

Bowman took the scope and continued the sweep of the village.

Hayes knew he was going to have to change positions soon. His right leg was starting to cramp up on him. They had been lying motionless for over five hours now. He began to inch the leg outward, but suddenly stopped—he thought he had heard voices in the darkness. Looking to his right, he saw Doc place a finger to

his lips. Hotujec had heard it, too. The sound came
from up the trail, maybe 15 yards away—the cramped
legs would have to wait. All three men lay perfectly
still, their breathing short and silent. Seconds passed
into minutes, and those minutes seemed like hours to
the three men. Hayes began to wonder if the jungle was
playing tricks on them. As if in answer to his thoughts,
there was the click of metal against metal. There was
definitely someone out there. More whispers came
from the darkness.

The first NVA soldier emerged from the jungle cover
onto the trail and knelt down, his head moving slowly
left then right, the eyes searching each side of the trail.
The man stayed in this position for a full minute,
listening for any sound out of place. Satisfied that all
was as it should be, he rose to his feet, moved a few
more yards down the trail, and repeated the process.

The three Green Berets pressed themselves hard
against the ground. The NVA soldier knelt less than 10
feet in front of Hotujec. They could hear the man's
shallow labored breathing. Once again the man moved
farther down and knelt, only this time he raised his arm
and slowly waved it in the air above his head. The
signal brought seven heavily armed NVA troops down
the trail. They were spread out, four on one side of the
trail and three on the other. They passed Hawkins's
position and disappeared into the darkness. Moving his
hand quietly to the radio hanging from his web gear,
Hawkins pressed the talk switch twice. The sound of
the radio breaking squelch had taken less than a
second. Doc could only hope the rest of the team heard
it—he couldn't chance it again. The trail was clogged
with NVA regulars filing past him. Detection now
would ruin the whole ball game, not to mention the fact
that they'd be dead within seconds.

A total of 35 NVA had passed their position. Five
minutes had gone by since the last man passed them.
Hawkins told the other two to stay down. Looking over

to Hawkins, Hotujec asked, "What'd you think, Doc? Are we clear?"

Doc shook his head and whispered, "Don't think so, Jeff. You notice, not one of them thirty-five guys turned around to look back up this trail. That's because they know they're covered back there . . . rear-security team."

Hayes leaned over and said, "Well, where the fuck they at?"

"Patience, brother Hayes. They'll be comin' along anytime now, and when they do—" Hawkins paused, and reaching up to his web gear, unsnapped the 12-inch knife from its scabbard and continued "—we're gonna ruin their friggin' nightlife for 'em."

"Well, that's fine with me, Doc. I like workin' in close."

Moving their rifles off to the side, all three shifted to the prone position and waited. Doc had figured right. Four more NVA were moving slowly down the trail. Each time they stopped, the last three would turn and listen for any sound coming from behind them, then move a little farther and stop again. This was the rear-security team. They wouldn't go into the village. Their job was simply to keep the trail secure and give early warning if anyone approached. If anything went wrong in the village, the others would break contact and scramble back up the trail while the rear-security team provided cover fire. Tactically, it was a well-planned operation, but there was always the chance of the unexpected—as they were about to find out.

Hawkins slowly and quietly raised himself into a kneeling position, placing all of his weight on his left foot. Hayes and Hotujec did the same. Doc tapped Hayes on the arm and held up three fingers, then four. Hayes acknowledged the signal. He would take out the third and fourth men while Hawkins did the first and Hotujec the second.

Gripping their knives tightly in sweating palms, the

three men waited. The NVA began to move—four steps . . . six . . . ten . . . finally stopping directly in front of Hawkins. The number-one NVA had just begun to kneel when Doc pushed off on his left foot; Hayes and Hotujec moved at the same time.

Doc grabbed his man by the hair, jerked his head back, and drove the blade into the man's throat and downward. The razor-edge blade severed the man's jugular, sending spurts of blood into Doc's face. Hayes sprung forward with such force that he almost knocked the number-three man out on impact. At the same time he smashed the heel of his boot into the fourth man's face, sending the NVA sprawling backward into the brush. Hayes straddled the third man's back, pulling his head back, and, in one powerful slashing movement, almost cut the man's head off. Doc and Hayes both leaped onto the fourth man. Both knives went through the man's body, pinning him to the ground. Hotujec kicked the second NVA's rifle from his hands and drove his knife into the man's chest. The NVA's body slid slowly down Hotujec's leg to the ground.

The action had taken less than 10 seconds, and not one shot had been fired. Moving quickly, Doc grabbed a body and whispered, "Okay, get the bodies off the trail and let's get set up. This party is about to get underway."

The rest of Striker had heard Doc's signal. McCall, Barnes, and Murphy moved up the side trail to the tree line at the edge of the village. Bowman swung the starlite scope to the left edge of the village. The scope was worth its weight in gold at this minute.

Richardson and Taber inched up next to Bowman. "Whatcha got, man?" Rich asked.

Bowman moved the scope slightly left, then right. "I'm not sure . . . I think . . . hold it! There they are, by God!" Passing the scope to Richardson, he said, "Center on the trail, then move ten yards left and right."

Rich stared through the eyepiece. Hazy green figures were kneeling on-line at the edge of the trees. Lowering the scope, Rich pulled out his radio and pressed the switch. Speaking just above a whisper, he said, "Striker, we have thirty to forty bad guys to our left front just at the tree line; they're on-line and holding. Do you roger, leader?"

McCall replied, "Roger, Starlite. We're just to your right at the edge of the village. Hold your fire until we have all of them in the open. Doc, you copy Starlite's last?"

Hawkins came back over the air, "Roger, leader. We've taken out the rear security and are placing the last of the charges at this time. We'll be ready to start this show whenever you are. Over."

"Our two runaway boys didn't happen to be with the rear security by any chance, did they?"

"No such luck, leader. Hell, I'm not even sure Thanh's with that bunch in the trees."

There was a pause, then, "No sweat, we'll be finding out soon anyway. Leader out."

Richardson, Bowman, and Murphy left the scope on the knoll, and moved silently down the hill and took up positions at the rear of the village.

Hawkins and Hotujec finished placing the blocks of C-4 explosives on each side of the trail when Hayes appeared unrolling the wire for the last claymore mine that he had placed in the center of the trail. The claymore was what McCall had tagged "the granddaddy of all shotguns." It contained 1000 steel ball bearings that could cut a path 15 yards wide. Removing the safety wire from the firing mechanism, Hayes placed the detonator next to the other two already on the ground and said, "We're all set, Doc. What now?"

Hawkins switched the selector on his rifle to full automatic. "Now we wait for JD to start the ball rolling."

McCall watched as the NVA spread out in a half-circle around Bien Cao. He had to admit these guys were good at this business, but then again, these were hard-core NVA, not local-yokel VC.

Barnes lightly tapped JD's arm and pointed to the left. Five NVA were moving out of the trees and heading for the village-chief's hut.

McCall was on the radio. "Striker, this is leader. Stand by, they're bringing the head man out any minute now. Stay alert, it's gonna be gettin' pretty fuckin' hairy around here real quick. Try to pick your targets, but don't take any chances. If you ain't sure, blow it away. Leader out."

The old chief was led to the center of the village, a soldier poking him in the back with an AK-47. Words were exchanged. The chief began yelling for the people to come out of their homes and welcome their brave Vietnamese brothers. To make sure everyone complied, the remainder of the NVA moved into the ville and went from house to house, dragging, pushing, or kicking people into the square.

McCall unhooked a grenade from his belt. Pulling the pin, he gripped on the release lever tightly. Barnes and Murphy did the same. McCall watched as the last of the villagers were pushed into a tight-knit circle.

The NVA officer in charge asked his NCO if all were present. The answer was affirmative. Before the political speeches started, the officer ordered men to search the homes for food and to gather it in the center of the village.

This was what McCall was waiting for. It would get the mass of NVA troops away from the civilians. All the NVA but the officer and three men fanned out through the village. Turning to Barnes and Murphy, McCall said, "Well, boys, looks like it's dance time. Shall we start the music?"

Barnes grinned and said, "Hell, yes. Let's give 'em a little thunder and lightning played in 'Frag Flat.'"

McCall's arm was already in motion. Barnes and

Murphy let fly with their grenades at the same time. One of them bounced and rolled into the doorway of a hut just as two NVA were coming out with their arms full of chickens. The explosions sounded as one. Dirt, bamboo, and pieces of raw meat rained down on Bien Cao. Chicken feathers drifted down around McCall like large snowflakes.

At the sound of the grenades, Richardson, Bowman, and Taber opened up on four soldiers that were passing 10 yards in front of them, firing full auto. They cut the four in half before the sound of the grenades faded.

The officer and three soldiers who had been guarding the people dropped to the ground and fired wildly in all directions. The screaming civilians scattered in mass confusion for any cover they could find.

Murphy and Cowboy were now laying down a steady stream of fire into the huts to their left. At least five NVA dove into shacks after the grenades went off. Grabbing his radio, McCall yelled, "Rich, you guys split up and try to drive 'em in Doc's direction. We'll close in from this side. Leader out."

The starlite team heard the order. Nothing was said as Richardson moved off toward a shack to his left front. Bowman dropped the empty magazine from his rifle, pushed another 30-round clip into place, and moved off to his right. Taber gave Bowman a thumbs-up and sprinted for the center of the ville.

The NVA officer was screaming, trying to restore some type of order among his troops. He had to get them regrouped in order to mount an effective counter-attack. Two more explosions lit up the sky as Richardson and Bowman lobbed grenades on the far side of the village.

McCall, Murphy, and Barnes broke from cover and ran to the first row of huts. Breathing heavily, JD yelled above the gunfire, "We'll split up here, Cowboy. You guys watch your ass, you hear?" With that, McCall spun away from Barnes and into the doorway of the first hut, his CAR-15 unleashing 30 rounds of death. In the psychedelic flashes from the gun barrel, McCall could see the surprise and pain in one young NVA soldier's face as the rounds tore through his chest. Reloading, McCall was out the door, heading for another hut.

Barnes stood with his back pressed hard against the side of one of the shacks. He inched his way to the doorway, not sure if there were one or two NVA inside. Pulling the pin on a grenade, he was about to toss it through the door when he heard the whimpering of a child. Blowing the hell out of Charlie was one thing, but kids were a different ballgame. There had to be a better way. Kneeling beside the door, he placed the pin back in the grenade and hooked it back on his belt. Placing his rifle against the side of the hut, he pulled his .357 Magnum from its shoulder holster. He picked up a rock, took a deep breath, and let it out slowly—it was now or never. Yelling "grenade" in Vietnamese, he threw the rock into the darkness of the small room. There were screams of panic as the word was repeated in the tiny room.

Barnes stood to the side of the doorway, waiting. A figure flashed by him. It was an old Vietnamese woman. She had been shoved through the doorway and landed hard on her face. An NVA soldier followed close behind her. Barnes let the man take three steps past him before the heavy Magnum roared. The slug hit the NVA between the shoulder blades, driving his lung out the front of his chest.

A second NVA appeared in the doorway holding a small girl in front of him. Seeing Barnes, he dropped the child and swung his rifle upward. The two men were no more than eight feet apart. With his free hand, Barnes knocked the rifle barrel to one side as the man fired, the AK-47 rounds hitting only inches from the little girl. Springing forward, Barnes placed the barrel of the Magnum against the man's forehead and pulled the trigger. The NVA's head exploded, showering Cowboy with bones, brains, and blood. Wiping the mess from his face, Barnes picked up the little girl and, holding her small, shaking body close to him, said, "Don't cry, little angel, it'll be over soon." Helping the old woman to her feet, he gently handed the girl to her and told her to go back in and stay on the floor of the hut. The old woman nodded, and for a fleeting second, Barnes thought he saw a glimmer of gratitude in her eyes as she disappeared back inside.

Murphy busted into a shack firing waist-high. There was a scream and an NVA clutched his chest and fell over. A Vietnamese family lay huddled in the far corner, their eyes closed, waiting for Murphy's bullets to rip through their bodies. Murphy paused for only a moment and shook his head. When were these people going to understand that he was in this country to help them, not kill them? Speaking in a quiet, reassuring voice, Murphy told them to stay inside, then rushed back outside. There was plenty of work still to do.

On the far side of the village, Richardson caught an NVA making a break for the trees. Dropping to one knee, he switched the CAR-15 from automatic to single fire and squeezed off three quick rounds. The NVA grabbed his side and spun to the ground. Switching back over to full automatic, Rich walked up to the wounded soldier. The NVA began screaming, "Chew hoi, chew hoi, G.I." The man wanted to surrender. Richardson stared at the man for only a second before he fired. The automatic fire jerked the man's body all over the ground. Dropping the empty magazine from the smoking rifle, Richardson reloaded as he said, "We're playin' by your rules, motherfucker, remember!"

Bowman dove for a pile of wood as the bullets tore up the ground behind him. One round caught the heel of his jungle boot, sending stinging pain up his leg and spinning him down behind the logs. Crawling to one end of the pile, he leaned back and wiped the sweat from his face. There was no feeling in the foot. A quick check found no blood, but the heel of the boot was gone.

He had run into three NVA as he was crossing between two huts. It had come down to a quick-draw contest between the four men. Bowman nailed one of them, but the other two dove for cover just in time. Now they were putting the heat on him. To make matters worse, he wasn't sure where the two NVA were now. Moving to the center of the woodpile, he swung his rifle over the top and fired a quick burst, then dove back to the end of the logs to watch for the flashes he knew would be coming. It didn't take long. The AK rounds ripped apart the center of the wood. One NVA was lying in the doorway of a hut to his right and the other one was flat on the ground to his left front.

Leaning back against the pile once again, Bowman rubbed his tingling left leg and said, "Good goin', dickhead—ya got your ass in a crossfire, no other cover for 20 fuckin' yards and those AK rounds are gonna eat this woodpile to pieces. Yes, sir, Bowman, you really are the elite . . . an elite asshole." Slapping his rifle, he muttered, "Where the fuck's Clark Kent when ya need him?"

His answer came in the form of a loud explosion to his right. Taking a quick glance around the end of the pile, he saw the remains of both the hut and the NVA scattered over the ground. He saw a figure jump to its feet. It was Richardson. He paused for just a moment, waved to Bowman, and was gone again.

Bowman laughed out loud as he said, "Well, what the hell do ya know? A black fuckin' Clark Kent! Wonder how Lois is gonna take the news."

Pulling the pin on a grenade, Bowman tossed it over the woodpile in the direction of the NVA on the ground. The man scrambled to his feet and tried to run, but Bowman cut him down before he made five yards, the bullets knocking him sideways and on top of the grenade just as it exploded. Moving past what was left of the NVA, Bowman looked down and said, "Man, this just ain't your day."

Richardson linked up with McCall and Barnes. Bowman came limping up with his arm around Murphy for support. The firing had stopped. McCall asked about Bowman's foot. Bowman told him it was nothing and would be all right in a little while.

JD's eyes searched the open area of the village. "Anybody seen Taber?" he asked.

Murphy answered. "Saw him clearing a place on the west side of the ville about five minutes ago. Haven't seen him since. He could be layin' low right now, waitin' to see what's gonna happen next."

"You're probably right," replied McCall.

Switching on his radio, JD spoke quietly. "Doc, this is leader. The show's over on our end; we nailed 'em pretty good. I'm not sure how many are heading your way, but it couldn't be more than ten or fifteen. Do you roger, over?"

"Roger, leader. Copy, ten to fifteen possible. We got enough stuff laid out to handle three times that many." There was a moment of silence before Doc came back over the radio, "Can't talk anymore, boss. We got company comin'. Out."

The surviving members of the NVA unit had regrouped at the end of the trail they had come in on earlier and were now moving back to the safety of the DMZ. The last remaining NCO of the unit moved up next to the commanding officer. "Sir, do you think it wise for us to return back up this trail?"

The young NVA officer was obviously still shaken from the village firefight, but was quick to remind the sergeant of his rank and position. "Sergeant, during our glorious battle, did you hear any gunfire from our rear security force? Of course you didn't, because they were doing their job. They only await our arrival so they may cover our retreat. Now stop acting like an old woman and more like the NCO you are supposed to be."

The NCO listened to his commander, but his mind kept repeating the warning given by one of his American instructors in Hanoi: the black man had said, "Never go out the way you come in. It will cost you your life." Further argument with this officer was useless. The sergeant moved up the trail.

Hayes held a detonator in each hand. He had placed one of the claymores in the center of the trail and another 10 yards farther down on the side of it. A third had been placed off to the side in reserve, but if JD's count was right, they wouldn't need that one.

Five NVA appeared at the bend of the trail, followed by what was left of the shot-up NVA unit. Hayes would wait until the mass of them were in the kill zone.

The NVA stopped for a moment. Two of them seemed to be arguing about something. Hayes whispered under his breath, "Come on, mother, just 20 more feet, and mama's little boy Hayes has somethin' for your ass."

The argument ended and the NVA moved up the trail once more. The last thing the NVA sergeant saw before he departed this earth was a bright flashing light in front of him. There was no pain; there hadn't been time for that. The ball bearings had disintegrated the NCO and five other members of the unit. One second they were there, the next they were gone. Depressing the handle on the second detonator, Hayes watched the flash as the second claymore on the side of the trail caught five more NVA broadside. The NVA that had somehow escaped the two deadly blasts dove off to the side of the trail into the relative safety of the jungle brush. Doc and Hotujec gave them a few seconds to feel secure before they squeezed their detonators. The two-pound blocks of C-4 they had planted earlier at the edges of the trail lit up the sky. Trees, dirt, rocks, and body parts were scattered everywhere.

Through the ringing in his ears, Hawkins could hear JD calling on the radio.

"Doc, this is leader—come in. Over."

"Roger, leader. You can turn out the lights. The party's over."

"Good copy, Doc. Any chance any of those bastards got away? Over."

Hawkins glanced over at Hayes and Hotujec, "What d'ya think, guys?"

Both men shook their heads. "Ain't no fuckin' way, Doc!"

"That's a negative, leader. Nobody got out. We're fine. How about the rest of the team? Over."

"We're missing one, but he could be stayin' down and waiting for daylight. I suggest we do the same. It'll be light soon. We'll check out the bodies at first light. I'm going to advise the ol' man of the situation right now. Anything you want to pass on? Over."

"Negative, leader. Agree with your plan to wait for first light. We'll be standing by. Out."

Colonels Davis and Baron stood silently in the Tactical Operations Center listening to McCall finish his report. "Are there any further instructions for Striker at this time? Over."

The two officers conferred for a moment before Baron took the mike. "Striker One, you will have your choppers inbound at first light. Conduct a search and identification of the dead as soon as possible and confirm or deny that primary targets have been hit. If they are not among the dead, you will prepare to execute Plan Two. Do you roger? Over."

Striker acknowledged the message and signed off. Baron passed the mike back to the radio operator and looked at Davis. "You look worried, sir."

Davis walked over to the map of North Vietnam. Tapping the large red area that had been drawn around Dong Hoi Province, he said, "Jess, that son of a bitch wasn't in that bunch McCall tangled with this morning. Don't ask me how I know. I just have that damn gut feeling. I can't believe that Thanh, with all his experience, would make it that easy for Striker to kick his ass. I'm betting McCall and the boys took on some NVA platoon that was infiltrating to the south. It was just their bad luck to have picked Bien Cao as a stopover point."

Baron stood next to Davis and stared at the map. "That's highly possible, sir. We'll know for sure within the next two hours. McCall said they got all of them."

"I'm sure they did, Jess. But if I'm right and it wasn't Thanh, there's a damn good chance he wasn't far from that village when the firefight started. That'll turn him around and the bastard will be running for home right now."

"Damn, sir. That's not gonna leave us much time to try to cut him off."

"Exactly. I want you to make sure those backup rucks are on the exfil choppers when they go into Bien Cao."

"Roger, sir. I'll take care of it personally."

"We'll have two things working against us now, Jess. Time and weather."

"Yes, sir. I hope your feeling about Thanh is wrong."

"You and me both, Jess. Now, go ahead and see to those choppers."

"Yes, sir."

Baron left the center as Davis returned to a desk next to the radio operator. The room was perfectly quiet except for the steady hissing coming from the speaker that hung on the wall above the radios.

* * *

Predawn gray broke on the horizon. Hawkins's radio crackled to life. "Doc, this is leader. Check out your end of the action, but be damn careful. You know how the little bastards love to fake it. If you find any of the targets, let me know right away. After you've checked them out, head on into the ville. Leader out."

Doc turned to Hayes and Hotujec. "Well, you heard the man. Let's go check 'em out. Or should I say, what's left of 'em."

The three men stepped out onto the trail and began to head toward Bien Cao. After about 10 yards they started spotting parts of the NVA bodies littering the area. The dirt on the trail had turned a dull rust color from the blood. There were no survivors. Doc estimated they had killed at least 16, but it was hard to tell. There was an arm here, a leg there; one guy was lying at a strange angle against a tree, missing everything from his waist down. Judging from the parts available, 16 was a good guess. More important was the fact that all the dead were North Vietnamese; not a black or white man was in the bunch.

In the village, McCall and the rest of the team found Taber. He was dead. From the looks of the dead NVA around him, he had put up one hell of a fight, the end coming when he ran out of ammo and had to use his knife. The body of one of the NVA lay across Taber's legs, with the knife protruding from the back of his head. Taber had been shot seven times in the chest and face.

The sadness was noticeable in McCall's voice as he said, "Rich, you and Murphy cover him up and move him out to the chopper LZ. The rest of you go on with the body count and let me know if you find any of our targets. Now, move out."

They all knew JD felt responsible for Taber. No one said anything as they went about their assigned task. Watching Taber's body being carried to the LZ, McCall suddenly felt a cold chill move down his back. First

Brady, now Taber. This operation had already become expensive, and they hadn't even encountered Major Thanh yet.

McCall received the totals for the NVA body count in the village. They confirmed 18 dead and had recovered 14 AK-47s, two RPG-7s, and one Chicom pistol. It hadn't been an easy night for the people of Bien Cao either. Ten had been killed in the deadly crossfire, three of them children. There were eight wounded, three seriously. Barnes and Richardson were trying to make them as comfortable as possible when Doc and his crew came walking into the ville.

Doc Hawkins looked around at the bodies that lay everywhere and at the smoldering huts and shacks. "My God. Hayes, you and Jeff help out with the wounded. There's morphine in my bag. Use it. Not too much for the kids; just enough to ease the pain. I'll give JD the bad news."

McCall didn't have to ask Hawkins if he had found Salt or Pepper; it was written on the man's face. Doc lit a cigarette and flipped the pack to McCall. "I hope the hell you're gonna tell me you got the bastards in all this mess."

McCall lit up and tossed the pack back. "Wish I could, Doc, but no such luck. We got eighteen, you got sixteen, plus the four men in the security outfit. Hell, that's thirty-eight dinks that ain't gonna be drinking tea in Saigon."

"Guess that's one way of lookin' at it, JD."

"We lost Taber. Caught seven rounds, but not before he took out five of the fuckers."

Hawkins stared down at the ground. Hell, JD. I just met Taber's ol' lady a couple of months ago when we were on R & R in Hawaii. Real nice girl. She's gonna take it hard. I'll have to write her when we're through with this shit."

Both men stood silent for a few minutes before McCall looked up and said, "You know, we shot up the wrong fuckin' bunch this morning. You know what that means?"

Doc took a deep drag of his smoke before he answered, "Hell, yes. That damn Thanh had to have heard the fireworks this morning, and right now the bastard's running for home."

McCall flipped his cigarette to the side as he said, "You got it, Doc. We're gonna have to go north to get him now."

"It's gonna be a real bitch, JD."

"I know, Doc, but we've paid too high a price to stop now. I'm getting ready to call in the situation to the ol' man. Anything you want me to ask him?"

Hawkins stared across the open area of the village at the body of Taber and at the wounded Vietnamese of Bien Cao. "Yeah, we're gonna need two medevac choppers for these people," he said, "and I'd like you to ask the ol' man if he could pull some strings and get them to set down at an American hospital unit, not one of those goddamn Vietnamese butcher shops. Shit, it wasn't their idea to get caught in the middle of all this bullshit."

McCall heard the emotion in Doc's voice. "Are you all right, Doc?"

"I'm okay, JD. Guess I'll always be askin' what the fuck it's all about. I'll get the team ready and give 'em a hand with the wounded. Just see if that hospital business is okay with the colonel. I'm really okay, boss. Don't worry."

Hawkins turned and headed for the wounded Vietnamese, stopping for a moment to look down at Taber's body. He said a silent prayer.

McCall watched his old friend and kicked the dirt in frustration as he flipped on his radio and passed his report on to Colonel Davis.

Within 30 minutes the wounded were on their way to an American MASH unit for treatment. Davis had alerted a Special Forces camp close to Bien Cao to send in a security team to police up the weapons and clean up what was left of the village. Baron would come in with the extraction choppers and remain to work with the security team to recover any documents or intelligence materials they found among the dead. He would also take care of Taber's body. Colonel Davis had wanted to say something inspiring to the team, but he couldn't seem to find the words. It came out simply, "Good job, Striker, and good luck on Plan Two."

McCall's reply had been short: "Thank you, sir. Striker out."

The conversation left Davis feeling that he had patted the team on the back with one hand and pushed them into hell with the other. . . .

VII.

Major Thanh passed the word up the line for the platoon to take a 10-minute break. They had been moving at a rapid pace for the last three hours. Thanh estimated they had covered close to 11 miles in that time, but more important, the last two miles had moved them across the DMZ into North Vietnam.

Thanh was replacing his canteen when the two Americans came over and sat by his side. Except for Thanh and a few select people in Hanoi, no one knew the actual names of the two American deserters. They were simply referred to as Salt and Pepper, names Thanh had given them.

The man known as Salt was a white NCO who had arrived in Vietnam in 1965. The first few months had been the usual army bullshit—painting, building, and just about anything else at the basecamp. It was during one of his nightly visits into Saigon that Salt had met a Vietnamese drug dealer. Drinks were bought back and forth and the conversation gradually turned to money, a subject the white NCO was more than interested in. By the end of the night, Salt had joined the drug dealer's army of pushers. Within three months he had made close to $10,000. The demand for high-grade dope in Vietnam was unending, and Salt had visions of returning to the States a millionaire. Those visions were shattered one warm night when he made the mistake of selling to an undercover CID agent. They had waited until Salt put the marked money in his pocket before they arrested him. The court-martial had taken less than two days. He was found guilty and sentenced to 10 years hard labor at Leavenworth. On the day he was moved to the airport to be returned to the States and prison, Salt waited for his chance to escape the MPs. It came during a rocket attack on the airfield. In the confusion, he got his hands on a piece of pipe and knocked out his guards. Removing his handcuffs, he took the MPs' guns and jeep and drove out of Saigon. He had no idea where he was going or what he would do. His first thoughts had been of escape. He went to the drug dealer for help but was treated like a leper —no one wanted anything to do with him. He worked his way north to Da Nang. If he could only get his hands on a fake set of orders and some phony ID, he thought, he might be able to con his way out of Vietnam. Once out, he could just disappear. The army would never find him.

Salt hung out around the local bars of Da Nang hoping to link up with an S-1 clerk willing to do anything for money, even cut him a set of orders out of Vietnam, but his luck was still going bad. The first guy he approached said that he could do the job for $2,700 and that he wanted the money in advance. Salt's supply of money was running out fast, but he agreed and paid the man. Of course, the guy had no intention of getting him a set of orders. Instead, the clerk reported the incident to the MPs, minus the fact that he'd accepted the payoff. Salt was waiting at the bar when the military police returned with the clerk. Realizing he'd been screwed over, he broke for the back door, running into two more MPs in the alley. He had drawn the .45-caliber pistol out of instinct and, before he knew it, he was firing into the MPs. He killed both of them. Racing out into the crowded streets of Da Nang, Salt lost himself among the mobs of people. That night, he lay in a stinking back room of a whorehouse and tried to figure out what to do next. The military police would be ripping Da Nang apart searching for him. Where could he go? Where could he hide? He had run out of ideas. It was the pretty young Vietnamese woman lying next to him who had given him the idea. She jokingly said, "No sweat, GI. You go Hanoi—no MP chase you there." He hadn't thought of that. Why not? The North Vietnamese might like to deal with an Army sergeant who could train their troops in the latest American tactics. It was just crazy enough to work. The next morning he stole a jeep and began driving north. He passed MPs going up and down the highway, but it was as if they didn't even see him. Salt made it to the edge of the DMZ before he was stopped by an NVA squad. He simply dropped his guns, raised his hands, and told the NVA leader that he wanted to defect to the north.

Salt was taken to Dong Hoi Province for interrogation. It was there that he met Major Thanh. The major was suspicious of the American, and the interrogation went on for a week. Salt told his story over and over, as many as 20 times in one day. Thanh had him placed in a guarded cell while his agents in the south checked Salt out. Three weeks after he defected, the white NCO was welcomed into Thanh's office and introduced to a number of high-ranking officials from Hanoi. His story had been confirmed. He was now a member of the North Vietnamese Army and would be sent to Hanoi to train NVA troops. His true identity would be kept secret, and a mask was to be worn for all propaganda photos. Thanh wanted the mask so that he could send Salt back into South Vietnam for intelligence reasons, should it become necessary.

The NVA who worked with Salt came to respect his fighting ability, his attention to detail, and his methods of instruction. More importantly, he gained the trust of Major Thanh. Salt and the major would sit for hours and talk about the United States—the government, the schools, the culture. As the months passed, a close friendship developed between the American deserter and Thanh.

Pepper was a huge black Marine who'd arrived in Vietnam with the first wave of the Johnson administration's buildup of the war. They had stormed ashore on the beach at Da Nang before the lights and whirring cameras of every major news agency in the world. The American Marines had arrived to save the day.

Pepper's problems had started long before he ever heard of Vietnam. The second oldest of a family of nine kids, he spent his youth working at any job he could find to feed his brothers and sisters and, for a black kid from Alabama, that was a daily struggle. He had grown up with the prejudice of the South and the verbal and physical abuse that came with being a black man from Alabama. This treatment ate into the youth over the years, until one day he exploded. Pepper beat three white men half to death in a fight. They had been drinking and singled him out for their insults. The first scream of "nigger" tripped the time bomb that had been ticking inside Pepper for 17 years. He used a two-by-four, his hands, and his feet to vent his rage on the three men.

It was the intervention of a Marine recruiter that saved Pepper from a prison sentence. It wasn't much of a choice for Pepper, but he had heard about the Alabama prison, and the Marines could never be that bad. He looked at the corps as a new way of life and a chance to help his family by sending money home every month. It was a dream that shattered when he found that the white man also ran the Marines. But it was not they who were bigoted now, it was Pepper. The years of struggle and suffering had festered into pure hate for anything controlled by a white man. Many of the black drill sergeants understood what the young Marine was feeling and channeled his hatred into increasingly aggressive training. Pepper nearly killed a white youth in hand-to-hand training and broke the jaw of another in bayonet practice. No charges had been filed, thanks to the black DIs. They had spoken up for the man. He may be prejudiced, they asserted, but he was going to make one hell of a fighting Marine. It was only natural for Pepper to be sent to Vietnam: If he liked to fight all the time, they would send him where he could get all he wanted.

Pepper made sure he stayed away from any white Marines at the camp and only spoke with a few of the brothers in the unit. The first sergeant and commander were both white. They were well aware of the tension the man's attitude caused at the firebase. The captain and first sergeant called him in and talked to him for over two hours. What started out as a calm discussion about the problem turned into a name-calling argument, with the captain swearing to put his black ass in jail the first time he even pissed wrong—they would be watching him. Their chance came in less than three days, when Pepper viciously beat his white squad leader. No one knew what caused the fight, but as far as the captain was concerned, it didn't make any difference. Pepper was read his rights under Article 32 by the captain; the first sergeant was in the office as a witness for the commander. Finishing the reading, the officer smiled at Pepper and told him he was going to first put him in jail, then out of the Marines. Pepper clenched his fists—the white man was taking it all away from him again. It was more than he could stand. Staring at the smirk on the captain's face, Pepper went crazy. Slamming the first sergeant into the wall, he brought his elbow straight into the man's face, breaking his nose. The captain tried to get to the pistol strapped to his side. He didn't make it.

Pepper slapped the officer with the back of his hand and grabbed the .45 from his holster. Turning to the first sergeant, he fired three times at point-blank range,

blowing the man's head apart. The captain grabbed a
fire axe off the wall and swung at Pepper, but missed.
Placing the gun on the desk, the huge black man smiled
at the officer before he attacked and took the axe away
from him. Knocking the officer to the floor, Pepper
swung the weapon with all his might, cutting the man's
head from his body. Blood splattered the walls of the
small office. Pepper ran out. There was wild confusion
at the sound of the shots that killed the first sergeant.
Some people thought the base was under attack and
opened up with machine guns and mortars. It was
during this mass confusion that Pepper worked his way
through the wire and disappeared into the jungle. He
was captured by the NVA the same night and taken to
Dong Hoi Province to undergo the same interrogation
that Salt had been subjected to. The interrogator had
again been Major Thanh, who immediately realized the
propaganda value of having two Americans defect to
the north within two months. Better still, one was white
and one was black.

Thanh found the black soldier harder to work with
than the white deserter. Pepper's insolent attitude and
hostile remarks about the Americans and the NVA
were always stated in such a way that they bordered on
insulting. The major realized this was not just a man
with prejudices, but rather a man who hated all other
men, regardless of their color. Pepper had refused to
work with Salt until he found out the man had killed
two MPs, both white. It was an uneasy alliance at best.

U.S. Intelligence tried for two years to confirm the
identification of Salt and Pepper, but the task had
proven impossible. There were over 900 MIAs in
Vietnam, and another 1,600 American soldiers AWOL
somewhere between Hawaii, Bangkok, and Vietnam.
They searched the files for the names and photos of
military personnel who had committed offenses serious
enough for a man to defect to the other side. This, too,

had proved to be fruitless: There were over 3,000 reports of murders, attempted murders, and deaths of a suspicious nature. The NVA and the VC were not the only danger in Vietnam. The other enemy the Americans faced was themselves.

After two years, no agency was certain who the two deserters, known only as Salt and Pepper, really were, or where they came from. Thanh had played the desertions to the hilt. All interviews had been conducted in Hanoi, and only proven friends of North Vietnam were permitted to speak with the two Americans. No photos could be taken unless the two were wearing their Lone-Ranger-style masks. The U.S. news media immediately picked up on the titles of Salt and Pepper, and some of the more bleeding-heart papers compared the two with Jesse and Frank James . . . seeing wrong and trying to make it right.

Thanh had seen to it that the two men had everything they wanted, from Johnny Walker scotch to long nights of sexual pleasure. They were taught the language and could carry on conversations totally in Vietnamese. In return for the lavish treatment they received, they acted as the primary instructors for the young and inexperienced recruits from Hanoi.

Only in the last year had Thanh allowed them to accompany him on operations this far south. The boredom of constantly training troops had begun to get on their nerves, especially Pepper's. They had become restless and on edge, and longed for a more active role in the war. Their continued pleas to Thanh had finally paid off. Thanh placed their request before the Central Committee in Hanoi with a letter supporting it. The Committee had been split on the issue. Those against it saw the possible loss of one of their most valuable propaganda assets. It was only after Thanh agreed to take full responsibility for the safety of the two men that permission was granted. The interrogation of

Sergeant Wathers and his team had been their first operation.

Salt leaned back and lit a cigar as he said, "Major, it's a damn good thing you let us take that break before going into Bien Cao last night."

"Yes, my friend, but not so lucky for Captain Bin's platoon, I'm afraid."

Pepper snickered. "Shit, man, we trained just 'bout every one of Bin's outfit. I'll bet they kicked ass and took names before they bugged out of there."

Thanh shifted his back against the tree as he replied, "I hope you're right, Pepper. Bin's father is an old friend, and I would hate to have to tell him of his son's death. To have gone to his aid would have been foolish. We had no idea of the number of enemy involved nor their locations. I believe whoever planned that ambush was anticipating our arrival in Bien Cao. I do not think it was a chance encounter, and when they discover they engaged the wrong group, they will come after us."

Both Americans suddenly sat up straight, disbelief on their faces. The major smiled. "Ah, I see I have managed to get your attention. Have you not wondered why I have been moving the platoon so fast?"

Salt smashed out his cigar as he said, "Hell, Major. Who'd be crazy enough to come all the way up here to chase us around in our own backyard?"

Before Thanh could answer, Pepper spoke. "Yeah, Major, ain't no fuckin' body nuts enough to come no twenty, thirty miles into North Vietnam after us. Hell, man, it'd be a damn suicide mission."

The smile was gone and Thanh's tone of voice changed. "You have spent much time with me, my black friend, but obviously your encounter with the Green Beret, Sergeant Wathers, taught you nothing. The Americans use these Green Berets for their Special Operations. They are not restricted by agreements or borders. They go where they like and do as they please, while their military leaders look the other way. True, they have never been reported as far north as Dong Hoi, but who is to say they could not find the men for such a mission. No, my brothers, do not underestimate men such as these Green Berets. And remember —their hatred for you is much greater than they could ever have for me."

Pepper rose to his feet and pulled a knife from his belt. "Let the motherfuckers come," he said. "I'll put their damn balls up their asses for 'em."

Spitting on the ground, Pepper turned and walked away, mumbling a string of cuss words under his breath.

Thanh watched as the tall black soldier moved away. Turning to Salt, he said, "Do you share your friend's words?"

Salt answered, "He is an ex-Marine. They are taught to fight well, but somewhere in the process, they lose the ability to think."

Thanh smiled once more. "And what do you think your friend should be thinking about at this moment?"

"He should consider the type of men that would risk such a mission, for they would know, as Pepper himself has said, that such a mission would have little or no chance of success. A man that doesn't fear death is more than just a dangerous man—he becomes an animal determined to succeed or die."

Thanh placed his hand on the man's shoulder. "You have learned well, my friend. You may live to see our great victory in Saigon one day. I am afraid I cannot say as much for your friend. Now come, we must keep moving. The closer we get to Dong Hoi, the more difficult it will become for those that may try to follow us."

The order was given and the NVA unit began to move once more. Thanh had only gone a short distance when he stepped to the side of the trail and, staring up into the double canopy of the trees that covered their movement, waved for the others to continue. The seconds passed as Thanh listened. The jungle silence closed in around him. The sergeant in charge of the rear-security team paused to ask if anything was wrong. Thanh shook his head. "No, Sergeant. Everything is fine."

Thanh walked up the trail to catch up with the lead element. He must be tired, he thought. For a moment back there he thought he had heard the distant sound of helicopters, but the jungle could play tricks on a tired man. . . .

Colonel Baron came in with the cleanup team and joined McCall, Hawkins, and Richardson as they went over the map of the DMZ. The older warrant officer looked up at McCall and said, "Hell, Sarge, how far north are we talkin' about?"

Pointing first to Bien Cao village, then to Dong Hoi Province, McCall said, "Well, chief, we'd like to cut this distance in half. We figure they've been runnin' three, maybe four hours by now. That'd put them just a few miles across the Z right now and heading for Dong Hoi. We plan to cut them off before they get a chance to reach the safety of their headquarters."

The younger of the two warrant officers gave a low whistle as he said, "You guys are fuckin' nuts, you know that, don't you?"

Hawkins laughed. "Hell, kid, tell us something we don't already know."

Both pilots studied the map for a few minutes before the older one said, "It'll be cuttin' it close, Sarge. We'll only have enough fuel for a one-shot setdown and maybe ten or fifteen minutes standby time outside the immediate area. After that, you get in trouble on the ground, we won't be able to hang around to get your ass out of there."

McCall stood up. Folding the map, he placed it in his pants-leg pocket. "You just get us in there, chief. We'll take care of the gettin' out part."

"You got it, Sarge. Give us a few minutes to run some checks on the birds and we'll be ready to go."

"Okay, Chief. Just holler when you're ready."

McCall, Hawkins, and Baron had spent long hours in Saigon studying the trail systems out of Bien Cao running north. They had discounted all but three as means of escape that Thanh would be likely to take in an emergency situation. McCall had selected a point 20 miles into North Vietnam where the three trails came close to intersecting. It was a shot in the dark, that was for damn sure. But it was also the only shot they had.

McCall watched the chopper crews move to their aircraft and told Doc and Richardson to get the team ready to move out.

Baron stood next to the team leader and stared around at the few homes left standing in Bien Cao. Children played around the smoldering remains of one of the huts; others had mobbed around the bodies of two dead NVA that lay in the center of the ville. They pointed to the bullet holes and blood that surrounded the lifeless forms. The families of the villagers that had been killed knelt, their hands clutched tightly to their chests, weeping uncontrollably over their loss. Others simply went about their business as if nothing had happened. For them, it was just another day they had survived.

Baron asked McCall, "JD, you think any of these people know what all this shit's about?"

McCall lit a cigarette. "Hell, sir. *I'm* not even sure what the fuck's goin' on. I'd be willing to bet ya that if you ask them what they want, they'd tell you to take all your damn Americans home and the NVA the same fuckin' thing. All they really want is to be left alone, raise their kids and their rice, and be able to walk out into the night and look up at the stars without gettin' their heads blown off. If you think about it, that's not really askin' a hell of a lot."

"Then you think they'd rather live under communist rule."

"Hell, sir, these people been here for a thousand years. These farmers' great-grandfathers harvested rice from these fields under Chinese rule, their grandfathers under the French, and now them under a combined American and Vietnamese rule. Their sons will be out there planting and harvesting the same damn field long after we're gone, and just like their fathers, they won't give a fuck who's runnin' the country. They'll just keep on pullin' up that rice crop and trying to survive."

Baron had a discouraged look on his face. Softly, he said, "Well, Jesus, McCall, what the hell is all this for, then?"

JD flipped the cigarette away. Three kids standing around him scrambled for it as he said, "Hell, Colonel, that's a question I think we'll be askin' ourselves a long time after this war's over. Guys like me and Rich, we just fight 'em. We're no good at politics. Hell, if it wasn't Vietnam, it'd be somewhere else."

Before Baron could say anything else, the chopper pilot yelled, "Okay, Sarge, we're ready to hit it."

McCall signaled Doc and said, "Get 'em loaded, Doc, it's game time."

Turning to Baron, JD stuck out his hand and said, "Well, sir, now we'll see if all that planning did any good. If ya could, sir, I'd like ya to ask the colonel to write Taber's folks back home. He was a good kid."

Gripping the tall sergeant's hand tightly in his own, Baron answered, "I'll make sure, JD. You keep your ass down out there. I want to finish that conversation about this damn war."

"I'll do my best, sir. Later, Colonel."

McCall rushed to the first chopper, climbed aboard, and waved to Baron. Then he gave the thumbs-up to the pilot. The roar of the choppers increased as their skids lifted off the ground, hovered for a few seconds, then tore out across the rice fields of Bien Cao. Looking down at an old farmer working in the field, McCall muttered to himself, "Keep workin', ol' man, you're the only son-of-a-bitch who knows what he's doin' here."

VIII.

The first chopper came in at low level and off-loaded McCall and three members of the team. The second chopper, with Hawkins and the rest of Striker, came in right behind. The men leaped from the skids and waded into the tall elephant grass.

Applying full throttle, the young warrant officer flying the second chopper banked hard to the left and began to climb. He never made it. Halfway through the roll the chopper exploded into a bright red-orange ball of fire. McCall thought he saw the body of one of the crewmen falling from the sky in flames.

The pilot of the first aircraft was on the radio. "Goddammit, where'd that hit come from? . . . Wait a minute . . . I see 'em! There, to your . . ." He never finished. The front of his helicopter exploded, fire spread its length, and it burst into 1,000 pieces. Chunks of metal and fire rained down from the sky.

Bowman was on the radio. "Jesus Christ! What the hell happened?"

Richardson answered, "Sounded like B-40 rockets. Think they came from the tree line to the right, about a hundred yards."

McCall broke in on the conversation. "Rich, take Hayes and Hotujec and find out what we got over there. Doc, you and Cowboy move in from the left. Bow, you and Murphy are on me. We'll go straight up the middle. Leader out."

Striker moved slow and easy through the 10-foot-high elephant grass. Moving too fast was an open invitation for Charlie to zero in on their position. The NVA would be watching the top of the grass for unusual movement; if they saw any, they would put all their firepower into that area. Elephant grass could hide you, but it didn't stop bullets worth a damn.

Hawkins and Barnes had covered half the distance to the trees. They paused and listened. The only sound was the slight rustle of grass caused by an occasional gust of wind. McCall whispered to Murphy, "Get Rich on that radio and find out what the hell's going on over there."

Murphy nodded and pressed the switch on the radio. "Rich, this is leader. Have you spotted anything yet? Over."

"Negative, leader. But I know those fuckin' rockets came out of this tree line. We're about twenty-five yards out at this time . . . still haven't seen any movement. Out."

McCall had monitored the conversation and said, "Shit! We're hung up out here like a bunch of blind-ass mice in a cage, and it ain't gonna take those bastards long to start rattling that cage. Come on, we only got another thirty yards."

The first Chicom grenades exploded to the left of McCall. The NVA knew the Americans were out there, but they didn't know where. The grenades didn't produce the reaction the NVA had hoped for. There was no mad scramble or panic through the grass. Striker continued its slow, patient movement through the vegetation.

Two more grenades exploded. This time they were followed by two short bursts of automatic-weapons fire. Again, the NVA got no results. McCall wiped the sweat from his eyes, smiled at Bowman, and ran two fingers through the holes in the sleeves of his jungle fatigue shirt. "The mothers cut that one a little too close."

McCall switched on his radio. "Striker, this is leader.

I think we've taken this shit long enough. I don't know how many of the bastards are in there, but it don't make a whole hell of a lot of difference anymore. The choppers started a fire in this damn grass behind us and the shit's blowin' this way—it's gonna be crawlin' right up our ass in about three minutes. We can't stay here and we can't pull back. That only leaves one way to go. Do all members roger? Over."

Striker acknowledged the message and agreed with McCall.

"Okay, then, this is the way we'll play it. First we give 'em two grenades apiece, then hit 'em head on with all we got, full auto. I know it ain't fancy, guys, but it's startin' to get pretty damn hot out here. We go in thirty seconds. Leader out."

Richardson leaned back on his rucksack and pulled the pins on two grenades. Hayes and Hotujec did the same.

McCall, Bowman, and Murphy could feel the heat on the back of their necks from the approaching fire. Doc Hawkins and Cowboy Barnes watched the second hands on their watches.

Eight grenades filled the air. The second eight were airborne before the first set hit the ground. The ear-shattering explosions came so close together it sounded like an artillery barrage. The tree line echoed with the screams of men ripped by flying metal. Striker was on its feet, breaking from the grass straight into the trees, spraying automatic death in all directions.

A few of the NVA were trying to return fire, but most of them were still dazed by the grenade attack. The frontal assault had caused mass confusion among the younger NVA soldiers.

Rich and Hotujec cut down four of the dazed troopers at the edge of the trees. Jumping over the bodies, they took down two more who were coming up on their right. Falling to the ground, both men released empty magazines and reloaded. With his breath coming hard,

Hotujec yelled over at Richardson, "You ever notice how fast the ammo goes when you're havin' fun?"

Richardson rolled to his left just as a line of AK-47 rounds tore up the ground between the two men. A short burst from Hotujec ripped the NVA's legs, stomach, and chest. Hotujec smiled. "See what I mean!"

Rich shook his head. "Man, you're gettin' about as crazy as that damn JD."

Hotujec was still laughing as the two men got to their feet and ran for the center of the tree line.

Hayes had intended to stay with Richardson and Hotujec, but a steady stream of AK fire caused him to change direction at the last second. With his back pressed hard against the base of a tree, Hayes pulled the pin on a grenade, counted to three, and flipped it to his left. At the same moment he dove to his right, rolled, and came up on his knees with his CAR-15 at the ready.

Seeing the grenade coming their way, two NVA leaped to their feet and broke from cover directly in front of Hayes, who yelled, "You lose, motherfuckers." Thirty rounds from the CAR-15 tore the two NVA apart.

McCall and Bowman had just caught five NVA in the open, cut them down, and were reloading when Murphy yelled, "JD—on your left!"

One of the five NVA they had just nailed was on his knees, his rifle pointing straight at McCall. There was a slight grin on the man's face. He had McCall cold and he knew it.

Diving forward, Murphy knocked McCall out of the way at the same instant the NVA fired. Three rounds slammed into Murphy's body before Bowman blew the top of the NVA's head off.

Crawling over to Murphy, JD held the young soldier's head in his lap. "You dumb shit, ya gotta play the hero all the goddamn time, don't ya?"

Blood trickled slowly down the side of Murphy's

mouth as he tried to talk. "Bad . . . habit, I . . . guess. It's been . . . fun . . . JD. A cough brought a gush of blood from the dying man's mouth. "Hope you . . . get the . . . fu . . . fuc . . ." Murphy was dead.

Doc Hawkins and Barnes broke through the brush. Bowman swung his rifle in their direction. "Easy, man, it's only me an' Cowboy." Seeing McCall holding Murphy in his arms, he said, "Oh shit, man, not Murphy." Bowman nodded. Doc walked over to McCall. "Anything I can do, JD?"

"No, Doc, he's gone."

Two sudden explosions in the distance claimed McCall's attention. "Doc, you and Bowman see if you can link up with Rich. Cowboy and I will cut around and see if we can get behind these assholes."

"You got it, JD. Come on, Bow, let's hit it." Both men disappeared into the thick jungle.

Standing up, McCall checked his magazine for ammo and told Barnes, "I want to get every one of these fuckers. I don't want one damn NVA to get out of here alive. We're gonna make 'em pay."

"Sounds good to me, boss."

McCall and Barnes hadn't gone 20 yards through the trees before they encountered three NVA. The men were standing less than 40 feet away when they saw McCall and Barnes. Everyone fired at the same time, with the three NVA losing the shootout.

McCall and Barnes reloaded. The trees were alive with the sharp cracks of AK-47s mixed with CAR-15s and explosions from grenades. JD yelled to Barnes, "Cowboy, split off for the center of the line and try to link up with Doc and Bowman."

Barnes waved that he understood. Just as he started to stand, he swung his rifle in McCall's direction and yelled, "JD, hit the deck!"

McCall dropped to the ground as the bullets from Barnes's rifle whistled over his head. McCall looked up in time to see the rounds ripping across the front of an

NVA soldier's shirt. The man held a B-40 rocket launcher on his shoulder—the bullets' impact drove the man backward, causing him to fire the launcher.

There were two explosions: first the backblast, then the rocket's impact in the treetops.

McCall's body wrenched as he felt sharp, burning pain rip through his left hand. Trying to focus his watering eyes on the point of the agony, he saw that a jagged piece of metal had sliced into the back of his hand. He attempted to move his arm. Shock waves of pain shot through his whole body. Gritting his teeth, he slowly rolled the damaged hand over. The metal protruded from the palm. It was shrapnel from the B-40.

Dragging himself up on his knees, McCall pulled the .44 Magnum from his shoulder holster. Cocking the hammer, he laid it by his knee. The sound of automatic-weapons fire had picked up in Doc and Bowman's area. JD knew they were catching hell.

Gently raising his left hand, he slowly turned it back and forth. The bones in the back of the hand were broken. With his good hand, JD picked up a stick and, taking a deep breath, placed it in his mouth. Biting down hard, he gripped the piece of metal and jerked it from the back of his hand. There was a loud crack as he bit through the wood in his mouth.

It wasn't until he reached for the aid pack on his pistol belt that he saw Barnes sitting on the ground with his back against a tree. He wasn't moving.

Forgetting the bandage, McCall grabbed the Magnum and moved to Cowboy's side. Barnes's eyes were open and staring—blood dripped from his nose and mouth. McCall spoke, but there was no answer. He saw a large red stain midway down Cowboy's shirt. Tearing open the front of his friend's shirt, McCall sat back on his heels and moaned, "Oh, Jesus Christ, Cowboy."

The pointed edge of a splintered tree limb was sticking out of Barnes's body, just below the rib cage. Reaching up with his good hand, McCall gently closed

Cowboy's eyes. Ed Barnes had killed the NVA, but the rocket from the launcher had exploded in the treetops above him. It had been like an air burst, blowing wood and metal downward. A three-foot piece of the tree drove like a huge knife through Cowboy's rucksack and into his back.

McCall leaned the body forward. Reaching into Barnes's rucksack, he pulled out two blocks of C-4 plastic explosive. Pushing two blasting caps into place, he positioned them under the rucksack. Pulling a pin on a grenade, JD held the handle in place and, with his wounded hand, slowly and painfully pulled the body forward just enough to place the grenade underneath the rucksack next to the C-4. He gently eased the body back so that its weight held the release handle in place. Next he positioned Barnes's hands on his CAR-15. Stepping back, McCall surveyed his gruesome work.

"Sorry, Cowboy, but I know you'd understand. This way you get to take a few more of the bastards with you."

Wrapping a bandage tightly around his damaged hand, McCall picked up his rifle and checked the magazine. He paused for a second to say a silent good-bye to an old friend and fellow Green Beret, then turned and headed for the action down the line.

Hawkins and Bowman had been pinned down from the moment they broke through the outer tree line. The bodies of nine NVA lay 10 yards in front of them. The NVA attempt to overrun the two Americans had been a costly one for Charlie. But Doc knew they were massing for another assault. Turning to Bowman, he said, "Get on that fuckin' radio and find out where the rest of Striker's at! Tell 'em we're gonna need all the help we can get, and damn quick!"

Bowman pressed the switch on the radio as bullets tore the bark off a tree only inches above his head. "Striker, this is Bow. Give me positions at this time, over."

Hotujec answered first. "We're about fifty yards to your right and working our way down the line. Just hang on, Bow. We're coming. Jeff out."

McCall came on next. "I'm on your left, Bow, 'bout thirty yards out. I'm trying, ol' buddy, but these sons of bitches just won't get with the program. Uh-oh, I got company—hang on, Bow, I'll be there."

McCall dropped the radio and swung his rifle toward the two NVA who had broken through the brush at a dead run. Spotting McCall, they came to a sudden stop. Their looks of total surprise quickly changed to desperation as they tried to swing their weapons in McCall's direction. It was too late. Two short bursts of automatic fire tore through the two soldiers. They were dead before they hit the ground. Grabbing his radio, McCall was on the move again.

Doc Hawkins and Bowman threw their last two grenades. Locking his last magazine into place, Doc looked over at Bowman. "Well, Bow, looks like we shot our wad on this one. Those shitbirds will be comin' with all they got this time."

Bowman pulled his 9mm pistol from its shoulder holster and placed it in front of him. Next came his knife. Driving the long blade into the dirt next to the pistol, he spat and said, "I got a feelin' you're right, Doc, but it's sure gonna cost their asses."

Hawkins cocked his pistol and laid it next to his knife in front of him, as he said, "Ya goddamn right. We'll make these mothers think they're in a fuckin' John Wayne movie."

Three Chicom grenades hit the ground, rolled, then exploded in front of Doc and Bowman. Behind the flying dirt and smoke came a wave of screaming NVA.

Hayes had linked up with Richardson and Hotujec. They stopped at the sound of the explosions. They could hear the increase in enemy fire and the high-pitched screams of the NVA. Hayes turned to the other two and yelled, "Damn, we gotta move it. Doc and

Bow are . . ." The first shot blew a hole through Hayes's left shoulder, spinning him around like a sand crab. The next two rounds caught the big black man in the chest, slamming him to the ground. A short burst from Richardson tore the NVA sniper's head off.

Hotujec ripped Hayes's shirt open. Blood squirted from the two holes in the man's chest. Tearing the wrapper from his aid pack, Jeff pressed the thick pad over the holes. With his other hand he pulled a tube of morphine from his shirt pocket.

Rich knelt down and held the pad in place while Jeff broke the seal on the tube and jammed it into Hayes's arm. "How bad is it, Jeff?" Rich asked.

Hotujec looked up. He didn't have to say anything. Rich could tell by the look in Jeff's eyes.

Hayes coughed. Blood trickled out of his mouth as he tried to speak. His breathing became short and hurried. "It's bad enough . . . asshole, goddamn . . . shame." He coughed again, and more blood ran from his mouth. Richardson wiped the sweat from his friend's face. "Don't try to talk, Don. JD and Doc will get us out of this shit somehow."

Hayes forced a grin. "Hell . . . man. I'm already . . . out of . . . the shit . . . god, I'm . . . so . . . tired. Hayes's eyes slowly closed. He was dead.

Hotujec lowered his head and looked at the ground. Richardson reached across Don's body and gently folded the man's hands on his bleeding chest. After removing Hayes's magazines and grenades, he stood up. Hotujec wiped his eyes and stood next to him. There was nothing left to say. The gunfire from Doc's position erupted once more. Jeff glanced at Rich and nodded in the direction of the firefight before he said, "Let's go kick some ass!" Both men checked their weapons, took one last look at Hayes, and disappeared into the jungle.

McCall figured Doc and Bowman had to be close by. Only minutes ago he had heard the unmistakable sounds of a Magnum and 9mm pistol mixed with the sharp cracking of AK-47s. Now there was nothing. The jungle was silent. Crawling into the thick cover of some palm leaves, McCall listened for any sound of movement. The bandage around his hand had turned bright red. He thought of using morphine to ease the pain, then changed his mind. This was no place to be stumbling around half-high.

Rolling onto his side, JD started to key his radio when he heard someone moving through the brush. Whoever it was, they were moving carefully. McCall laid the rifle aside—it would be useless in the thick leaves—and pulled out his Magnum. He quietly cocked the hammer. For all he knew, he could be the only member of the team still alive. The movement stopped only a few feet to his front.

The voice on the radio startled McCall. It was only a whisper, but it sounded unnaturally loud. "JD, this is Rich. What's your location?"

It took McCall a few seconds to realize why the voice had been so loud. Moving his hand quietly into the folds of the palm leaves, he gently eased them apart. He saw the back of Richardson's head. Again the radio crackled. "JD, come in. Where the hell are ya, man?"

"Right behind you, sweetheart."

Richardson and Hotujec jumped as McCall pushed the leaves apart.

Rich's voice was still a little shaky as he said, "Jesus, JD. Ya scared the shit out of us!"

"Sorry, man. I didn't know who the fuck was out here till you keyed that radio."

Both men saw the bloody bandage around McCall's hand. Jeff said, "Looks like you caught one, boss."

"Yeah, shrapnel from a damn B-40. Probably the same one that took out the choppers."

Jeff looked past McCall and asked, "Where's Cowboy?"

"The Cowboy didn't make it this time, Jeff."

Hotujec couldn't hide the loss he felt on hearing McCall's simple statement. It had been Ed Barnes who taught him all he knew. They had been together for a year. Now, he was simply gone. Turning away from the other two men, Jeff wrapped his arms around his knees and, lowering his head, began to rock slowly back and forth.

Richardson started to put his hand on the kid's shoulder, but McCall shook his head no. It was something Hotujec would have to work out on his own.

Rich moved his fingers lightly through the dirt and said, "Hayes didn't make it either, JD."

"Damn," said McCall as he leaned back. "Have you heard anything from Doc or Bowman?"

"Nothing since Bow called to ask our position. Jeff and I thought we heard a couple of pistols cut loose 'bout five minutes ago."

"I heard the same thing. Doc was carryin' a .357 Mag and Bow had a 9mm."

Hotujec had regained his composure. He said, "What the hell's going on, JD? One minute the fuckin' NVA are thicker than whores on Hay Street. The next minute the place is quiet as a damn churchyard. Where the hell did they all go?"

"I wish I could tell ya, Jeff. Right now, your guess is as good as mine." McCall paused for a moment, then asked, "You guys didn't happen to see anything of our boys Salt and Pepper, did ya?"

Rich answered, "Hell, JD, you can bet your ass we'd have been screamin' on the radio if we had."

The frustration was clear in McCall's voice as he said, "Boy, we're doin' just great on this motherfucker. In less than twelve hours we've tangled with two NVA units, and neither one of the mothers was the one we're lookin' for. An' we still ain't got any fuckin' idea where Thanh and his boys are right now. Shit."

The three men sat in silence, each with his own

thoughts. It was McCall who finally said what they were all thinking: "Well, fellows, I think we've put it off as long as we can. Let's go have a look-see."

They moved in the direction of Doc's last known position. There hadn't been a shot fired for the last 15 minutes, and neither Doc nor Bowman had come up on the radio. They didn't have to go far. Scattered among the trees at the edge of a clearing lay the bodies of 10 NVA. Stepping over bodies every 15 to 20 feet, Richardson made his way into the clearing and waved the other two men forward.

NVA bodies covered the area. Doc and Bowman had been pinned down in a shallow bomb crater beyond the edge of the tree line. Charlie had tried to flank the two Americans; that accounted for the bodies at the edge of the trees. Judging from the number of dead NVA, it had been a costly maneuver.

With his rifle at the ready, McCall began to move out slowly into the clearing. Richardson broke off and headed left along the trees. Hotujec went right. JD glanced at each of the bodies as he passed them. One had shrapnel wounds, another bullet holes; over there were three in a group, all shrapnel hits—must have been a grenade. The closer McCall got to the crater, the more bodies there were. At the very edge of the shallow hole, the bodies were stacked two and three high. McCall was taking short steps as if to prolong having to look in the hole. But he knew what he was going to find, and that slowing down his forward movement was not going to change anything.

The final charge had been a simple matter of numbers. One massive, human wave against two men who would not have had a chance to reload before the wave swept over them.

McCall stood at the edge of the crater, his rifle hung loosely at his side. Richardson and Hotujec joined him. Doc Hawkins lay on his back—half his face had been shot away, his right arm hacked off at the shoulder. There were no less than 15 holes in his body. A dead NVA lay across Doc's legs, the tip of a knife sticking out of his back. Bowman lay a few feet away, face-down. There was a gaping hole in the back of his head. It was hard to tell how many bullets had been fired into the body, but it had been enough to tear it apart. Bowman's left hand held the broken handle of his knife.

Richardson did a slow turn, looking around the crater. "Christ, JD, there must be close to forty dead NVA around this hole."

McCall stood silent for a moment, then in a quiet voice replied, "Yeah, Doc would have figured that made it just about even."

It was starting to get to Hotujec. First Cowboy, then Hayes, and now Doc and Bowman. Turning away from the sight in the crater, he asked, "What d'we do now, JD?"

Richardson didn't wait for the answer. Jumping into the hole, he released the straps on the two American rucksacks that lay off to the side.

"Oh shit, JD." Richardson held up what was left of their PRC-25—it was the primary radio. "This mother's had it. All we got left now are the URC-10s, and they ain't worth a fuck for long range."

McCall was still staring at Doc's body. "They'll have to do, Rich."

Throwing the worthless piece of equipment out of the hole, he went back to the rucks and removed what was left of the C-4 plastic explosives.

McCall spoke in a haunting, solemn tone. "Doc and Bow must have really fucked over that final wave or they wouldn't have left that shit behind." Turning to Hotujec, he said, "You look white, kid. Ya gonna be okay?"

Hotujec had felt nauseous from the moment he saw

the bodies in the hole. He had to look away for fear that the vile-tasting contents of his stomach, which had rushed into his throat, would spew forth at any minute. In all his missions with Barnes, he could not remember seeing anything that had upset him as much as this. Taking a deep breath, he said, "I'll be okay. My God, JD, how do you two guys do it? I mean, doesn't this bother you people?"

"After you've been here as long as me and Rich, there ain't nothin' you haven't seen. You never get used to it, kid, but ya gotta learn to accept things for what they are and go on with the job."

The feeling of nausea passed. Jeff said, "JD, do you think the ol' man would say anything if I asked to quit this recon shit when we get back?"

McCall placed his hand on Jeff's shoulder, "Not at all, kid. If you weren't gonna ask him, I was. You feel well enough to help Rich down there?"

"Sure, boss. And thanks. I mean that."

"No thanks needed, Jeff. Rich, I'm gonna check some things out. You know what to do. Don't place any booby traps this time. I got a feeling we're gonna need all the shit we can carry before this show's over. Jeff, you check out Doc and Bow's URC-10s. If they're operational, turn one of 'em on and place it somewhere out of sight over in those trees. Bring the other one with you."

Hotujec started to answer, but McCall was already walking away. He watched as the tall Green Beret disappeared into the trees.

"McCall and Doc were pretty close, weren't they, Rich?"

"Yep. They went back a lotta years together. JD might not show it, but this shit got to him, too. He's hurtin' inside, but ain't about to show it. That's why a lotta people call him a hard-core son of a bitch. But I know him. He's hurtin' real bad."

Rich and Hotujec finished the task of removing the explosives and ammo from the crater. Climbing out of the hole, they took one last look at the bodies of the two men they had laughed with only yesterday. There was a moment of silent good-byes before the two turned and walked away, neither man looking back.

SOLDIER OF FORTUNE

INTRODUCTORY OFFER

9 issues for only $18.95

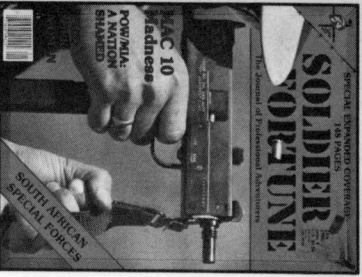

Save over 29% off the 1 year single copy price.*

☐ Payment enclosed (must accompany order)

☐ MasterCard   ☐ VISA

Card # _____   Exp. Date _____

Signature _____

Name: _____

Address: _____

City: _____   State: _____   Zipcode: _____

BTBKF7

BUSINESS REPLY MAIL

FIRST CLASS   **PERMIT NO. 8**   **MT. MORRIS, IL.**

POSTAGE WILL BE PAID BY ADDRESSEE

SOLDIER OF FORTUNE

P.O. Box 348

Mt. Morris, IL 61054-9984

IX.

Major Thanh raised one arm and motioned for Salt to move his squad around to the right. With the other he waved Pepper to the far left. Turning to his sergeant, he whispered, "Move your fire team forward at staggered intervals. If you come under fire, try to keep the enemy centralized while the flank squads close off any chance of escape."

The sergeant acknowledged and began moving his people forward.

Pepper moved up behind his point man and asked why he had stopped. Without answering, the man pointed to an open area through the trees. Pepper counted eight dead NVA soldiers on the ground. The point man lightly tapped Pepper's arm and pointed to the right of the open area. The black soldier slowly shifted his cold eyes left to right, suddenly spotting the American leaning against a tree with a rifle across his legs. Reflex action caused Pepper to drop to the ground, his weapon aimed at the motionless figure against the tree.

The point man knelt down and, grinning at his black squad leader, slowly drew his finger across his throat, indicating that the American was dead. Realizing he had made a fool of himself, Pepper jumped to his feet. There was fire in his eyes as he stared hard at the point man. The NVA soldier's grin disappeared. He spoke in a nervous tone. "I did not mean any disrespect, sir, but the man has been dead for some time."

Pepper's large open hand caught the man flat across the face, the blow spinning the smaller man halfway around. "Ya don't laugh at your superiors no time. Now, ya just be glad that's all I'm gonna do to ya."

A thin line of blood had appeared at the corner of the man's split lip. He bowed his head slightly as he said, "Thank you, sir. It shall not happen again."

"Ya goddamn right it won't. Now bring me that radio."

Pressing the switch on the handset, Pepper made the call. "Snow White, this is Blackjack, over."

"Blackjack, Snow White, go."

"I've got eight very dead NVA and one dead American on my side. What d'ya got over there?"

Salt replied, "We've got six NVA down and one U.S. dead. By the way, Blackjack, this GI is a black dude."

"Big fuckin' deal. Motherfucker should'a kept his black ass in the States. Has the dude got his weapon with him?"

"That's a negative, Blackjack."

Major Thanh's voice was loud and clear over the radio. "Snow White, Blackjack, this is Tiger One. Use extreme caution in all areas. Watch for booby traps of personnel and weapons. Do you roger?"

Both men acknowledged the message. Tiger One said, "I have found two Americans dead in my area also. When you are sure your positions are secure, I want you to join me at my location. I am at the forward edge of the tree line. Tiger out."

Salt and Pepper passed the instructions on to their team leaders and headed for Thanh's position. They stood at the edge of the crater. Pepper was the first to speak. "Holy shit, man. Look at all them dead NVA scattered around here. What the hell these here boys tangle with? The whole fuckin' U.S. Marine Corps?"

Salt was still surveying the sight as he answered,

"No, buddy, I'd bet my money on a Special Forces team."

"Oh, come on, man! You tryin' to tell me a handful of them Green Berets killed all them guys we found in the woods and this whole fuckin' bunch too? Hell, you been listenin' to all that bullshit about them guys, you're startin' to believe the shit yourself. Just how the fuck y'know it was Green Berets?"

The white American never got a chance to answer. Thanh had stepped up behind the two men and had been listening to their discussion. Thanh said, "And you, my black friend, have not listened to enough of those stories. The two dead Americans in that hole are Green Berets, as well as the two you both found in the woods."

There was sarcasm in Pepper's voice as he said, "Aw hell, another fuckin' Beret expert. You wanna tell me how the hell you two know them guys are SF?"

Thanh smiled. Slowly bringing his hand from behind his back, he brought the rigid object directly up, only inches from Pepper's face. The move caused Pepper to step back. He couldn't hide the startled look that appeared on his face as he stared at the bloody arm that had been crudely hacked from Doc Hawkins's body. Halfway between the wrist and the elbow was a tattoo: a pair of jump wings with a green beret sitting on top. Above the beret were the words *Special Forces*.

Pepper had hate in his eyes. He started to say something, then thought better of it. Instead, he spit at the major's feet and walked away.

Salt gave a short laugh and said, "It would appear that you have made our black brother feel like the proverbial ass."

Discarding the arm and wiping his hands, Thanh replied, "Our black brother is starting to get on my nerves. I am a patient man, as you know, but this man begins to wear that patience very thin. Come, we must try to determine how many of these madmen they have sent into this area."

The two had only moved a few feet when the jungle silence was shattered by two rapid explosions. Grabbing Thanh, Salt threw his commander to the ground, then fell beside him with his rifle searching for any possible target.

An NVA soldier broke through the jungle and into the clearing, his arms waving frantically. He was screaming for a medic. Salt moved from Thanh's side and ran up to the man. The two spoke for a moment before Salt waved for the medic to go with the soldier.

Salt walked over and pointed to Pepper. "You're gonna need a new point man and maybe two replacements. They didn't bother to check out that American body against the tree. The point man got his shit scattered for a city block and two others were wounded, one of 'em pretty bad. You knew that fuckin' body was rigged—that's why you asked me if that American I found had a rifle."

Pepper showed little concern as he said, "Fuck 'em. I told the dumb bastards to check everything out before they touched anything—it's their own damn fault."

Thanh stepped between the two men before an argument started.

"It is truly unfortunate, but there is little we can do about it now. We have more pressing matters to discuss than one man's stupidity. I am convinced that the ambush at Bien Cao and the sudden appearance of these Green Berets are more than just coincidence. While we were moving this morning, I thought I heard the sound of choppers in the distance. It would appear I was correct."

Pepper asked, "How many do you figure were in this firefight?"

"That is hard to say. There is wreckage from two UH1H helicopters in the field out there."

Salt said, "If I remember correctly, these Special

Forces recon teams like to work in small teams of eight to ten people. Two choppers is all they would need. We know for a fact that four of the Americans are dead as hell, so that could only leave four to six members of the team runnin' around out here."

Pepper still found all this hard to believe. "You guys got any idea how many dead NVA there are scattered through this area? Ya telling me a few of these green beanies did all this damage? It ain't possible."

Thanh looked at the black soldier and said, "If it were any other unit but Special Forces, I would agree, but these are not ordinary troops. I would think they were handpicked and, as such, you can be assured that they have spent countless hours planning for this operation. I find it hard to believe they are the type of people to quit before their mission has been accomplished."

Speaking in a loud and critical voice, Pepper said, "Major, you keep sayin' 'their mission.' Since you seem to think you're a fuckin' expert on these guys, just what was their mission?"

Thanh looked the black soldier in the eyes as he quietly said, "To kill the three of us!"

The look in Thanh's eyes and the calmness with which he had made the statement sent cold chills down the black soldier's back. For the first time since this operation started, Pepper felt fear run through him. It didn't last long. "Shit, Major, you're talkin' out your ass. Next thing ya gonna try to tell me these dead guys out there are the same bunch that set up that ambush in Bien Cao."

"That is a very good possibility, my friend."

"Hell, Major, ya know the odds of those clowns picking the route we took back to the north?"

"Granted, the odds would seem impossible, but a detailed study of the area by a determined group such as this would cut those odds down considerably. You have only to look around you to see my point. They missed picking our route by only one hour and a distance of one mile—that was hardly a lucky guess, gentlemen."

For the moment Pepper was willing to accept the major's theory. "Okay," he said. "Let's say you're right and these are the same people from Bien Cao and they came in here on them choppers that are smokin' out there. It's like Salt said a while ago, they done lost four folks, an' whoever got out of this shootout alive is more than likely bustin' ass for the DMZ and home, so what's the fuckin' problem?"

Thanh hated to admit it, but Pepper had a good point. Between the action in the village the night before and the obvious life-and-death struggle that had occurred here, it would seem logical for the few survivors there may have been to return to the south. . . . Logical, that was the word that bothered him. Thanh had battled these Special Forces many times over the years and had learned the hard way to expect the unexpected from these Green Berets. His thoughts were interrupted as Pepper snapped his fingers in his face. "Hey, Major, ya still with us? I said, what's the problem?"

"I was thinking of what you just said, my friend. I cannot convince myself that this team of Americans would work so long and hard and come so far, lose four of their friends, then turn and run. They were picked for this mission because of their ability to accomplish their operation at all costs, and with the loss of these four, I feel they will be more determined than ever."

There was a slight snicker in Pepper's voice. Placing his hands on his hips, he said, "Well, big fuckin' deal. We've handled these hotshots before, and we can do it again. If you're that damn worried about the assholes, let's hunt the bastards down an' wipe 'em out."

Thanh was amazed that the huge black soldier could stand in the middle of this slaughter and still not appreciate the capabilities of the men they were about to pursue. Thanh said, "That is exactly what we are going to do. We will not return to our headquarters until we have eliminated every member of this team. Is that understood?"

There was excitement in Pepper's voice. "Now you're talkin', Major."

Salt didn't find Thanh's choice of action all that exciting. Unlike Pepper, he had more than a little respect for these Green Berets. Even now, as he looked around at the total destruction the small group had reaped on its enemy, he felt a spark of admiration. These men with the green hats had pride and the guts to back it up. He couldn't help but wonder where he would be today if he had become a member of that elite group instead of a damn grunt, but that thought only lingered for a moment. He could never go back. Thanh took notice of the reluctance in Salt's voice as he answered, "Yes, sir, I understand."

Hanoi didn't know it yet, but they had lost an entire NVA platoon, and Thanh had no intention of letting his people meet the same fate. They would track down and eliminate the survivors, and hopefully this would discourage Saigon from sending any more people this far north again. Thanh would also sleep better at night, knowing there were no Green Berets creeping through his window to cut his throat.

It had taken Thanh's unit an hour to recover the weapons and ammunition from their fallen comrades. Thanh ordered the equipment buried and the coordinates radioed back to headquarters. The bodies were to be left where they lay. There would not be time to bury the dead—Thanh hoped to close in on the Americans before dark. Trackers were sent out and the platoon briefed on its mission.

Waving his troops forward, Thanh began the hunt. . . .

*   *   *

Colonel Baron nodded as he passed Davis's aide. Tapping on Davis's door, he entered the office. "Sir, we just received a confirmation from Cooper's people. Major Thanh was definitely outside of Bien Cao last night."

Davis didn't bother to look up. Baron moved to the front of the desk and said, "Something's gone wrong, hasn't it?"

Davis looked like a tired old man as he picked up the photographs and passed them to Baron. "Those were taken about two hours ago by one of the Air Force high-altitude reconnaissance planes. They picked up a beeper on the emergency frequency."

As Baron sat down in a chair to go through the photos, Davis continued. "As soon as the flyboys saw what they had, they blew up the pictures and rushed them right over to my office. The coordinates are on the back. We can stop the search for those two choppers that left Bien Cao this morning—they never made it out of there."

Baron continued to study the pictures as Davis walked to the bar and fixed a couple of drinks. Setting one in front of Baron, he said, "What do you think, Jess? Did Striker find our boys or not?"

"I don't think so, sir."

"Care to explain your reasons?"

Shuffling through the photos, Baron selected five and laid them out on the coffee table. Pointing to the first one, he began, "Well, sir, in this one you can see the remains of the insertion choppers. Judging from the wide area of the wreckage, I'd say they were hit in the air after the insertion. The second picture has a better angle. You see, sir, there are only five bodies in the wreckage area. If Striker had been on board when they went down, we'd have a helluva lot more bodies in that area."

Taking a sip of his drink, the intelligence officer

continued. "This one confirms that at least part of the team was on the ground. The body against the tree is wearing tiger stripes. Striker was wearing tigers when they went in this morning."

Davis tapped the photo and said, "Of course, you noticed that the man against the tree still has his rifle across his legs."

"Yes, sir. Knowing McCall, I'd be willing to bet you that the body is booby-trapped."

Davis nodded in agreement. Baron pulled out a fourth picture and pointed to the center area. "Now, here we have two more members of the team in that crater. Notice how the number of dead NVA increase the closer they get to the hole?"

Davis leaned over the photo and studied it for a moment, then said, "They got pinned down, and Charlie used a mass assault to overrun their position."

"Exactly, sir. And from the looks of it, our people gave them one hell of a fight before they went down. See the AK-47s that are lying all over the place? Charlie got his ass kicked so bad he didn't have enough people left to recover those weapons."

Davis turned his attention to the fifth picture. "And what about this one, Jess? It looks like the same shot to me."

"It's pretty close to the same one, sir, but taken from a slightly different angle. I didn't catch it the first time either."

Shuffling through the pictures again, Baron picked three more from the pile and placed them above the fifth. There was the jungle, the edge of the open field, then the tree line and, finally, the crater. "Sir, as you know, the U-2 takes six photos per second."

"Right, Jess, I understand that. But what do you see in that picture that I don't?"

Pulling a pen from his shirt pocket, Baron drew a circle around a group of NVA bodies at the far right of the fifth picture. "Look at this area and tell me what you see, sir."

Davis set his drink on the table and stared at the photo for a few seconds before he said, "I'll be damned, Jess. I wouldn't have seen that if you hadn't drawn that circle."

"I know, sir, I almost missed it myself. Somebody on Striker figured a good intel man somewhere along the line would spot it."

In the circled area of the photo, the bodies had been arranged in such a manner that a person on the ground wouldn't notice anything unusual. But from the air, the bodies formed an almost perfect arrow pointing north. Granted it wasn't a big arrow, but it was there. Davis moved back to his desk and said, "So, we know now that someone from Striker survived that shootout. But how many, and who?"

Baron leaned back as he said, "We can confirm at least three members of the team KIA from the photos, but there could be more in that thick jungle cover around the crater. We'll try to blow these up a little more and concentrate on the areas around the hole."

Colonel Davis sat silently at his desk for a moment and slowly turned a pencil between his fingers before saying, "Jess, why are you so sure that the dead NVA in these pictures are not Thanh's?"

"Two reasons, sir. First, McCall, Hawkins, and I agree that Striker picking the exact route that Thanh would take back north would be a hundred-to-one shot. They'd have to be awfully damn lucky. And, if you'll excuse me for being less than optimistic, Striker hasn't had a hell of a lot of luck since they started this operation. Second, whoever is left alive out there placed those bodies that way to let us know they were continuing the mission. Therefore, no Thanh."

"My God, Jess, we planned this mission for ten people, sent in eight, and now we can confirm at least three of them dead, maybe more. That only leaves four or five to take on Thanh and his outfit."

"Yes, sir, I agree. You asked me for the best we had for this operation. I gave you ten of the very best in the business. They won't quit until either Thanh's dead or they are."

Davis turned his chair toward the double French doors of his office. He stared out the windows, his eyes fixed on the bright yellow-and-red-striped flag of South Vietnam that hung over the Presidential Palace. "What are Striker's odds, Jess?"

"I'm afraid I'd have to say slim to none, sir."

Without turning to face Baron, Davis said, "Thank you for being honest, Jess. I want you to get hold of Colonel Taylor at Air Wing Command and also Colonel Hyatt at 5th Group Headquarters. Inform them of the situation and tell them we will keep them posted on further developments."

Baron stood to leave, and Davis added, "Also, let CCN and CCS know that we have KIAs, but have not been able to confirm ID at this time."

Davis's voice dropped off to a low whisper at the end of the statement.

"Yes, sir." Baron quietly closed the door on his way out and informed the aide that Davis was not to be bothered for the next half-hour.

The rains began at last light. The storm front moving into the area would remain for at least the next 72 hours. The three survivors of Striker One waited until dark, then found shelter under a large outcropping of cliffs at the base of a mountain. They leaned back against the rocks, totally exhausted.

McCall had ignored the pain in his hand while they were moving. But now, sitting in relative safety with darkness closing in around him, the pain reminded him of the damage. Each throb shot pain all the way up his arm. The rain had turned the bandage into a faded mess. Placing the hand in his lap, McCall unwrapped the bandage. Each movement brought new pain.

Hotujec and Richardson moved to each side of JD as he removed the last layer. The hand had swollen to almost twice its normal size. The swelling in the back of the hand had caused the open wound to protrude. Gently turning the hand over, he saw that the raw, red gash in the palm looked even worse than the back.

Richardson shook his head as he said, "Damn, JD, that thing's gotta be givin' ya hell."

Before McCall could answer, Richardson pulled a tube of morphine from his pocket. "Here, boss, you're gonna need somethin' to get through the night."

McCall's voice had lost its authoritarian tone. "No, Rich. Every damn NVA from here to Hanoi must have heard that fuckin' firefight this morning. They'll be out lookin' for us tonight, rain or no rain. We're gonna have to be ready for 'em."

"Shit, JD. This is Rich, your ol' partner, man. Ya ain't gotta play this damn John Wayne shit with me. I know you're a hurtin' motherfucker. Hell, me and Jeff can rotate the security for tonight. Now get that fuckin' sleeve up, asshole."

McCall started to protest, but saw it would be useless. He slowly nodded in agreement. Hotujec gently pulled the sleeve up and whispered, "See how you are? Here me and Rich are gonna be up all night, and you're bitchin' about a free ride on some of Uncle Sugar's best shit. Hell, JD, ya know what those protesting dopeheads would pay for a shot of this shit? An' you're gettin' it for free. This fuckin' army's all right, man."

Passing the tube to Hotujec, Rich winked at his tired team leader. "'Night, 'night, boss."

The needle went into the vein. McCall leaned back and closed his eyes. The throbbing pain began to disappear, replaced by the coolness of the rain and fading bright colors. McCall entered a world beyond pain, beyond war, beyond worry. Within minutes he was sound asleep.

Checking to make sure JD was totally out of it, Rich reached gently for the wounded hand. Lifting it slowly, he looked at both holes.

"Jeff, we're gonna have to clean this damn thing up or he's gonna have one hell of a case of infection by tomorrow night."

Hotujec jerked the straps on his rucksack and pulled out a poncho, a penlight, a sulfa pack with bandages, and, finally, a clear-plastic package of saline.

"Rich, once I get under the liner, I'll flip the penlignt on for a few seconds . . . you check me out. . . . If there's no light showing, an' we're good to go, you tap me and I'll get to work on this thing. Granted, I ain't no medic, but you're right, we gotta do something or JD's gonna lose this hand."

Sitting with his legs crossed, Hotujec brought the liner over his head. Bringing McCall's hand under the liner, he tucked one edge of the poncho around the arm and flipped on the penlight momentarily while Rich moved around the huddled shape to make certain no light was visible.

Rich tapped the liner and whispered, "You're good to go, Jeff."

Hotujec flipped the light back on. Within the limited confines of the poncho, the small light provided a good view of the wound. With the light between his teeth, Jeff removed his knife and punched a small hole in the top of the saline bag. Moving his head to focus the light on the gaping hole in the back of JD's hand, he tipped the bag and flushed the dirt and debris from the red, torn flesh. Turning the hand over, he repeated the treatment. Jeff knew Rich was right. It wouldn't take long for infection to set in. They could try to keep it cleaned out, but that wasn't going to be enough for a wound this bad. It was only a matter of time. Using the gauze from the packet, Jeff dried the hand, tore open the pack of sulfa powder, and poured it into both wounds.

Richardson tapped the liner again. "How's it goin', Jeff?"

"Almost got it, Rich. Just a couple more minutes." Folding two pieces of the fine mesh gauze into small pads, he placed one over each hole and wrapped the heavier gauze around the hand, leaving the fingers exposed. Tearing a piece of tape from the roll, he fastened the ends of the bandage in place. Leaning back slightly, he looked at the job he had just finished. "Not bad for a weapons man, if I say so myself." Flipping the light off, he pulled the liner from his head and, folding it once, placed it over McCall.

Richardson looked down at his sleeping team leader. "Whatcha think, Jeff?"

Hotujec was busy repacking his rucksack. "It's a nasty hole, Rich. Now, I ain't any doctor, but I'd say we got maybe forty-eight hours before infection locks onto that hand. Once it does, it'll spread damn fast. Any longer than that and he's gonna lose that hand and maybe the whole fuckin' arm."

Richardson knelt down next to Hotujec. "What if we get him out of here in the next twenty-four hours?"

"I just don't know, Rich. Hell, man, I'm a friggin' weapons man, but it makes sense that the odds would be a hell of a lot better. Why, you think we can get him to give up an' head for home?"

Richardson sat back against the rocks, the futility clear in his voice. "I must be out of my mind. There ain't no fuckin' way we're gonna get JD to leave here until he has ol' Thanh's head on a stick. He'll cut that hand off himself before he'll go home without getting that asshole."

Hotujec nodded in agreement. "I got a feeling Thanh's gonna have something to say about that."

Rich chuckled quietly. "Hell, Jeff, I can't count the number of dead NVA I've seen since I been runnin' with JD, an' they all thought they had somethin' to say about dyin', too!"

Hotujec slid up next to Rich and said, "You know, it's kind of funny I don't know JD any better than I do. I mean, hell, we been workin' in the outfit for a year now, and I've heard him say more in the last two weeks than in twelve months."

Rich just smiled and said, "Hell, don't feel bad, kid. JD just don't like to get too close to a lot of people in this business. The first two months I worked with him, he called me Sergeant Richardson . . . not Rich or my first name . . . just Sergeant Richardson. That crap went on for about three or four operations, until he finally loosened up a little. I asked him one day, "'Why all the Sergeant shit?' He told me he was just waitin' to see if I could stay alive for more'n sixty days."

"But, hell, Rich, you been with the guy almost three years now. Just how long's he been here?"

"The year I got here, JD was supposed to be headin' home. But they extended him another six months so he could help break in some of the new guys from Bragg. Y'know, McCall showed up in Vietnam with thirty-three other guys from Bragg in the early days of this gangbang. They didn't know a fuckin' thing except what they were told in school. By the time I got here, JD and Doc Hawkins were the only two left out of that thirty-three. The rest were either killed, missing, or so fucked up that they were sent home in pieces. The brass all said McCall just had a natural talent for this kinda work. And his Chinese mercs thought the guy was the best damn thing since Genghis Khan—they'd follow him anywhere he wanted to go."

"Jesus Christ, Rich, that's gotta be almost five

straight years of this shit. That's enough time to screw up a guy's head permanently. Why the hell has he stayed here so damn long?"

Rich shifted his position and checked on JD. The team leader was sleeping soundly. "I'm not really sure, Jeff. JD never says anything about leavin', an' I don't ask. But I got a good idea it has somethin' to do with the Major Nichols incident."

Hotujec could tell by the expression on Richardson's face that the man had let something slip that he had not intended to say. Jeff sat up straight and said, "What incident, Rich?"

Richardson didn't answer the question. Instead he said, "Guess I'll take the first watch. You get some sleep."

Jeff put his hand on Rich's shoulder. "Like hell you are. We're in this fuckin' deal together, all three of us. I figure I've held up my end and I got every damn right in the world to know everything about the people I'm gonna be dying with. Now, you want to tell me what the hell the Nichols deal's all about, or do I keep you awake all fuckin' night?"

Richardson stared at Hotujec for a second before saying, "I guess you're right, kid. But I'm gonna tell ya somethin'. This deal happened a couple years back, and JD don't exactly care for people that talk about it, so ya better keep it to yourself."

"You got it, Rich."

"Well, it was 'bout the fifth month I was with JD. We came off this real bad operation, lost half the damn team. Now, JD'd been with them Chinese for goin' on two years, an' man it really got to him losin', half of 'em. We got off the chopper at the pad that night and this Major Nichols, our fucked-up S-2 officer, gave out with the sorry-'bout-this and sorry-'bout-that shit, and how he wanted a detailed briefing right away, especially a solid number on the body count. Well, JD wasn't in no mood to talk to anybody right then, especially this Major Nichols. Ya see, the operation had been the major's brainstorm from the beginning. The guy had big visions of a high-level staff job in Saigon, but he had to pull off somethin' really big that'd draw the attention of the big boys. So the asshole comes up with this idea of a HALO infiltration onto the Ho Chi Minh trail, with the idea of blockin' the damn thing for a few hours while the Air boys did a number on the backed-up convoys.

"Now, me an' JD never turned down a mission goin' anywhere, so it was no big surprise that we were picked for the job. JD was more worried about the little guys on the team. Like I said, he was real close to those Chinese. He asked a lot of questions at the briefin', and Nichols had all the right answers. Hell, that briefin' made it sound half-ass easy and impressed the shit out of the boys in Saigon. The only thing wrong with the whole dog-and-pony show was that our boy Nichols hadn't coordinated half the shit he had put out at the briefing, and his estimates of expected enemy contact weren't even close."

Hotujec listened intently to Rich's every word.

"Well, we go screamin' in there from twelve thousand feet with twelve of our best Chinese mercs and hit the ground shootin' and blowin' the shit out of everything movin' on the ol' Ho Chi Minh trail. In less than thirty minutes we got Charlie's traffic backed up for five miles. Of course, the NVA ain't sittin' on their ass holdin' their dicks in their hands. They started flankin' us on both sides. But we ain't worried, see, 'cause our boy Nichols told us we got two reinforced Mike Force Companies standin' by to rush in like the cavalry and save our butts at the last minute."

Hotujec interrupted. "Let me guess, Rich. . . . No Mike Force, right?"

Rich leaned over and spat before he continued.

"Hell, no, there wasn't any fuckin' Mike Force! What we got were two more recon teams from CC Central. So now we had thirty-six mothers trying to hold the Ho Chi Minh trail against two damn battalions of hard-core NVA. Let me tell ya, boy, it can't be done.

"Anyway, the shit really starts hittin' the fan and we're takin' casualties faster than we can count. The Air boys' big attack on the convoys consisted of three fuckin' Phantom Fours makin' two passes each, then leavin'. Hell, Charlie had that shit cleared off the road before the jets crossed back into South Vietnam."

Jeff whispered, "Jesus Christ."

"I don't think he could've helped that damn situation. Hell, JD saw how hopeless it was and called for an immediate extraction. By then, we had lost one complete team from CCC and the other one was so damn shot-up that it was all they could do to throw a grenade every once in a while. We had five of our Chinese killed and two wounded. JD calls for an out, and Nichols comes back on the radio and tells us to hold till the Air Force can get another shot at the convoy. Well, ol' JD tells the man politely to fuck off an' gave the man our status on KIA and WIA. It didn't make any difference to Nichols. The son of a bitch wouldn't release the choppers for the extraction, so we did the only thing we could—we broke off contact and tried to drag our wounded back to the Z and South Vietnam. Man, we took an ass-kickin' every step of the way. The guys that were left from CCC got caught in an ambush, an' there wasn't a motherfuckin' thing we could do to help 'em. That really hung heavy on JD's shoulders. We lost a total of nine Chinese before that fuckin' Nichols finally gave in and released the extraction choppers to come in and get us out of there."

Hotujec shook his head. "God, I'll bet JD was mad as hell."

"Let me tell ya, kid, the guy was way past the mad

stage. He kept sayin' he was gonna kill that major the minute we got off the choppers. An' if you could've seen the look in his eyes, brother you would have known he wasn't bullshittin'. No, sir, not at all."

"Well, go on, Rich. What happened next?"

"Well, we land at the CCN chopper pad and, sure enough, Nichols comes runnin' up to us with his hand stuck out, but JD ain't shakin' hands with this asshole. He tells JD he wants an after-action report and detailed debriefing right away. I kept tryin' to get the major off to the side and tell him to let that shit go for now, that JD ain't in a mood to be fuckin' around with damn reports, but the asshole just kept goin' on about how sorry he was things hadn't worked out and all that bullshit. Now, all this time, JD ain't sayin' a word. He just stands there . . . staring at Nichols. I suppose JD finally figured the guy wasn't worth killin', 'cause he told Nichols to fuck off, that he was goin' to his room and have a drink. If the major wanted a damn body count, he should put his ass on that damn chopper and go out there and count 'em himself. Then he just walked away."

Hotujec whispered, "Jesus, I can just see JD doing that, too."

"Well, Nichols went fuckin' crazy. He started screamin' all kinds of shit about bringing JD up on charges for disrespect, insubordination, and just about everything else they got in that damn rule book of theirs. JD didn't even bother to turn around. He just kept walkin' off the pad. Then Nichols really stepped on it, man. He screamed some shit about JD losin' all them folks out there because he hadn't followed orders and had run when the fightin' got too hot."

"Damn, Rich. This guy Nichols must've been a real wacko."

"You got it, kid. As soon as that major said that shit, I knew he had fucked up royal, 'cause JD stopped walkin', dropped his rucksack on that damn pad, and just stood there for a minute . . . like he was thinkin' it over in his mind. Then I saw JD's right arm go to his shoulder holster, and when he turned around, he was holdin' that big-ass .44 Magnum an' it was pointin' right at the major's chest. Colonel Turner was the commander back then. Him an' the sergeant-major were just drivin' up to the pad when JD pulled the gun. Now, like I said, them Chinese had been with JD a long time. When he pulled that Magnum, them boys dropped all their rucks and locked and loaded their weapons and formed a semicircle around ol' JD. You better believe them boys were gonna shoot the shit out of anybody that tried to bother JD.

"The colonel and the sergeant-major were screamin' at McCall, but he wasn't hearin' anybody. As far as he was concerned, there wasn't nobody on that pad but him and Major Nichols. That major didn't know what the hell to do when JD started walkin' at him. He just kept lookin' around for somebody to help him, but there wasn't nobody movin'. . . . So he starts pleadin' with McCall to put that big-ass gun away. But, man, it was already too late by then. I think everybody there knew JD was gonna kill the guy, and the major saw real quick that there wasn't one guy gonna go up against those Chinese to save his ass—so he did the only thing there was left to do. He went for the .45 strapped on his hip. Hell, JD let the guy draw it and fire twice before he brought that Magnum up an' put a slug dead-center in Nichols's chest. The guy was dead 'fore he hit the ground. Everybody just stood there starin' at the body."

"Goddamn, Rich. You mean nobody did anything?"

"You got it, kid. I think everyone was kinda in a state of shock. Everybody but JD, that is. He walked over, picked up his ruck and, just as cool as ya please, walked up to Colonel Turner, handed him the Magnum without sayin' a word, and headed for the team house with the Chinese right behind him."

Jeff Hotujec sat quietly for a few minutes before he said, "My God, I can't believe it!"

"Well, ya better believe it. 'Cause I was there when the major went down hard on that pad. That was a little over two years ago, I reckon."

Leaning forward, Jeff whispered, "Well, tell me something, Rich. Since JD did blow a hole through a U.S. major, what's he doing here instead of breaking rocks in Leavenworth?"

There was a slight grin on Richardson's face as he said, "That's why a lot of damn people think that it's just another one of those wild-ass stories comin' out of this fucked-up war. They figure iffin it was true then McCall would be locked up someplace for 'bout a hundred years, but he ain't."

"Well, just how the hell'd he get away with a thing like that?"

"Jeff, that's one I can't answer. It was kinda strange how things worked out after the shootin'. The sergeant-major came down to the hootch about an hour after it happened. JD was sittin' on his bed with his back against the wall and a tall glass of bourbon in his hand. He hadn't said a damn word in all that time, and me and the Chinese weren't about to say nothin'. He would just sit there, sip his Jack Daniels, and stare at the wall. The sergeant-major came in and told me to go for a walk or get drunk, just as long as I left them alone. Hell, who was I to argue with a sergeant-major? I took his advice and went to the club an' got totally wasted. When I woke up the next mornin', JD, the colonel, and the sergeant-major had left for Saigon. I didn't see JD for almost a week. I found out he'd paid what was left of the team a bonus an' put them on three-weeks leave back to Taiwan. If any of 'em said anything about what happened they would be fired and dealt with accordingly. What that meant I'm not sure. So, anyhow, I ask around the whole camp what the hell was goin' on, an' for once nobody really knew. Six days later JD's back with the sergeant-major, the colonel was stayin' in Saigon with a new assignment, and JD's carryin' around his Magnum again."

"Well, Rich, you're JD's best buddy. You mean he never told you what went down in Saigon?"

"Not a word to this very day, kid. All I know is, nothin' ever came out of that shootin'. The colonel got blown away in a bomb attack on a restaurant or some damn thing an' the sergeant-major was killed in a mortar attack a few months after that. So ya see, there ain't a whole hell of a lot of people left alive that know what kinda deal was made in Saigon. JD went right back to runnin' recon and gettin the shit missions as usual."

Hotujec looked over at the sleeping form of McCall, then back to Richardson. "I guess they figured he wouldn't serve any worthwhile purpose in a damn cell at Leavenworth. . . . I wonder how many years they sentenced him to in this fucked-up country?"

A look of sadness came over Richardson's face as he stared down at the ground and muttered, "Life . . . an' he'll keep runnin' till they kill him."

"Well, from what I've seen, Rich, that'll take some doing."

"Yeah, he's one tough mother, that's for damn sure. Look here, man, you get some sleep. I'll wake ya in about four hours."

Hotujec didn't argue. They hadn't slept in the last 48 hours. Lying back on his rucksack, Jeff was asleep within minutes.

Richardson moved a few yards forward of the rocks and into the thick jungle cover before settling into position. He activated the silent beeper on his radio and placed it on the ground next to him. He would remain in this position for the next four hours listening for any sound of trouble. For now, there were only the sounds of the tree frogs, the distant cry of a lizard, and the slow, steady patter of the raindrops in the trees. All was as it should be in the darkness of the Vietnamese jungle.

X.

Major Thanh halted his platoon. Taking the radio from his RTO, he ordered Salt and Pepper to find shelter for their men and get some sleep—the search would resume at first light. Thanh moved his troops out of the rain and under the trees to where the wide, broad leaves interlocked to form a near-perfect, water-repellent roof. Ordering that security be posted, Thanh slowly lowered himself to the ground and leaned back against the trees.

Exhaustion had begun to set in. His 42-year-old body reminded him that he was no longer the strong, virile youth who once ran these very mountains and jungles against the Japanese and, later, the French. Now here he was again, only this time he was fighting Americans.

Staring into the darkness that slowly closed in around him, Thanh listened to the gentle sound of the rain on the leaves above his head. It was a relaxing sound to a man who had known nothing but war for most of his life. He had been born in the city of Haiphong in 1925. His early memories traveled through his mind as the tapping of raindrops increased its symphony overhead.

The only calm, the only feelings of joy, had been in those early years: the carefree playing of a child with other children, the deep-felt love of his mother and father, the continuous but loving pestering of his two older sisters. As a child, Thanh had seen nothing wrong or even unusual about the presence of so many French people in his country. There was only time for fun. But as with all children, growth brought knowledge and the realization of what was truly going on around him. By the age of 13, he began to understand his father's resentment of their French masters. The time for play was over, replaced by long hours of hard work rewarded by meager amounts of food and little hope for a better life.

World War II and the invasion and occupation by Japanese forces brought promises from the French of a free Vietnam, governed by Vietnamese, if the Vietnamese would help defeat the invaders. Thanh saw this as an opportunity not only to fight for his country, but also as a new way of life for his family. At the age of 15, he joined a Vietnamese guerrilla unit and conducted hit-and-run operations against Japanese forces all over the countryside. By his sixteenth birthday, Thanh had become a squad leader and had over 40 kills to his credit. It had been Thanh's bravery and command abilities through the last two years of the war that had brought his name to the attention of the Vietnamese commanding general, Vo Nguyen Giap.

Giap had invited Thanh to his headquarters; after the meeting Thanh, at the age of 18, was commissioned a lieutenant. Even though the commission came in the closing days of the war, it was Thanh's proudest moment.

The war over, Thanh returned to his home in Haiphong, confident that things would now improve for him and his family. He took his parents and two sisters to Hanoi that September of 1945 to hear the words of a man whom he'd heard much about but had never met. They stood among the crowd of thousands under an overcast sky as the man read a paper called the American Declaration of Independence. It had been chosen because it contained the dreams and hopes of all the people of Vietnam. Having finished reading, Ho Chi Minh proclaimed Vietnam's newfound freedom.

It was a freedom that was short-lived. Twenty-one

days later, French soldiers stormed the city hall of the new government and arrested the Vietnamese representatives. Ho Chi Minh barely escaped. By midnight the French were once more the rulers of Indochina.

The takeover outraged the Vietminh soldiers who had fought so long and hard against the Japanese. They were ready once more to take up arms and fight for the freedom they knew they had earned. Ho Chi Minh urged patience as he struggled to find a peaceful solution to the situation. General Giap and the Vietminh agreed. They would do as Ho asked. Meetings in Paris, Hanoi, and Geneva went on for over a year, yet Ho Chi Minh still asked for patience.

For Thanh, as well as all Vietnamese, that patience ended on the twenty-fifth of November 1946, a date Thanh would never forget. An argument over import duties erupted between Vietnamese and French officers at Haiphong harbor. This incident gave the French the excuse they had been waiting for: an opportunity to show the Vietnamese their power, establishing once and for all who was the master and who the slave.

They gave the people of Haiphong two hours to evacuate the city. At the end of that time, the French navy would begin shelling the harbor. The time limit was, of course, impossible to comply with; the French had known that from the start. The guns opened up right on time. Over 6,000 men, women, and children were killed in the barrage, among them Thanh's mother, father, and sisters.

The Haiphong incident was more than even Ho Chi Minh could tolerate. If the French wanted a war, they could have it. The time for patience had drifted away with the fading smoke of the navy guns. Thanh was given command of his own platoon of Vietminh soldiers. He had hardly known a year of peace. Now he was alone, his family gone. There was nothing left but war.

The fighting raged for seven and a half years. In that

time, Thanh was wounded no less than six times. The fatal blow was struck against the French at a place called Dien Bien Phu. The battle for that valley had lasted eight long months and, in the end, the French not only lost a battle but a country.

Thanh was 29 when the war was over. He had hoped for a unified country, but it was not to be. An east-west parallel had been established across the center of Vietnam. Those who wished to stay in the north under the now communist rule of Ho Chi Minh were more than welcome. Those who did not want the new government were free to go to the south. This had not been what Ho had originally wanted, but was a concession to the war with France. General Giap and Ho Chi Minh had agreed that the years of battle—first with the Japanese and then with the French—had taken their toll on the Vietnamese people. There would have to be a time to rebuild. There would be another day to turn their eyes to the south.

Thanh spent the next five years receiving political and military indoctrination in Moscow and Peking. It was at the Military Institute in Moscow that he first learned of the United States's elite group of "advisors" known as Special Forces. The Russian instructor classified them as America's "Dogs of War." They were not to be feared, the instructor said, but extreme caution should be used when engaging these men in combat. Thanh read between the lines of his instructor's comment. These were soldiers that had earned the respect of even the Russians.

His training complete, Thanh returned to Hanoi and was immediately promoted to the rank of captain. Having specialized in interrogation and terrorist tactics. Thanh was ordered to go to the south and assist his Vietcong brothers in their struggle. The council gave him a free hand in his handling of the situation. Thanh became Hanoi's chief avenger. Not only individuals, but entire villages, suffered his wrath. His methods, called ruthless by some, proved most effective throughout the south. As his reputation grew, so did the approval of his superiors in Hanoi. Within three years of his return from Moscow, Thanh was promoted to major.

In the summer of '63 Thanh reported increased numbers of Green Beret "advisors" from the United States in the south. The advisors' expert training of South Vietnamese units had improved their effectiveness. The numbers of Vietcong killed and wounded had grown steadily since the advisors' arrival in Vietnam. They were going to be a force to be dealt with. Thanh asked for the assistance of hard-core regulars from the NVA army. Ho Chi Minh declined the request. Should the situation become worse, he said, he would reconsider Thanh's request.

Thanh's military career reached its peak with the conversion of the two American deserters to the NVA cause. He personally presented Salt and Pepper to the high council in Hanoi for questioning. They had been well prepared by Thanh to answer any and all possible questions.

The questioning lasted one hour. At the conclusion of the session, the council was so impressed with the two Americans and the confidence that Thanh had shown in them that they gave them both the rank of lieutenant in the NVA and placed them under the command of Major Thanh.

The two Americans soon became as effective at interrogation as their leader. Their loyalty to Thanh and the NVA cause had been tested and proved many times in combat. Pepper had been especially valuable in providing intelligence about U.S. Marine bases and recon tactics after the huge troop buildup of 1965 and 1966. In the years they'd been with him, both men had accounted directly or indirectly for over 500 American and an unknown number of Vietnamese dead.

Yes, Salt and Pepper had both done much to further

Thanh's career and to assure him a place on the high council when the war was over.

A young NVA soldier appeared suddenly in front of Thanh, interrupting the major's reverie. He held out a poncho and said, "Comrade Major, I would be most honored if you would accept my cover to protect you from the cool dampness of the night."

Thanh smiled as he looked at this young soldier, a mirror of himself so many years ago. Thanh asked, "How old are you, comrade?"

The boy straightened. "I am fourteen, sir."

Thanh reached out and took the poncho from the young hands as he said, "It is I who shall be honored to wrap myself in the cover of such a brave freedom fighter as yourself. Thank you."

Pride shone on the boy's face as he saluted smartly and departed. Thanh leaned back. Wrapping the poncho around his shoulders, he wondered if the boy would ever see his fifteenth birthday.

In such moments, Thanh felt deep hatred for all Americans. He had been robbed of his youth by war, and now this boy, like so many others under his command, was spending his youth on a battlefield when he should be in school learning the intricacies of mathematics, the wonder of literature, the beauty of poetry. But this could not be, not so long as Americans continued to interfere in the politics of Vietnam. This was their war. What right did these Americans have to be here? Had they not seen what had happened to the Japanese, the French? No difference; they would meet the same fate as the others. What saddened Thanh was the thought of all the young soldiers who would have to die to achieve that goal.

For that very reason, Thanh had begun to consider this his last operation. He had lost the callous hardness that war required. He could no longer remain insensitive to the destruction of youth required to rebuild his beloved Vietnam. Such feelings had no place in these jungles—they were an open invitation to a quick and sudden death.

He would seek a staff job in Hanoi. No one would voice an objection—he had done more than his share for the cause. Now the years and the old wounds he had suffered over them were slowly but surely taking their toll on him.

Pulling the poncho tighter around him, he rolled onto his side on the cold damp ground. Yes, that was what he would do. He would find a good staff job in Hanoi. Salt could take over the operations out of Dong Hoi. He was well liked and trusted by the NVA command. Pepper, on the other hand, was becoming a problem. His attitude over the past few months had gone from bad to worse. It was a situation that would have to be dealt with sooner or later. For now Thanh needed the services of the ex-Marine, but afterwards . . . Better yet, the Americans might get lucky and take care of the problem for Thanh.

Closing his eyes, Thanh thought of how pleasant it would be to dine at a fine restaurant, sip fine wine, and, most of all, enjoy the company of a beautiful woman. Even now, with the rain slowly falling and the coolness of the night blowing gently against his weathered face, the thought of a woman warmed his soul.

Wrapped in the boy's poncho, Thanh drifted off into a sound sleep. In his dream, she had the shiniest long black hair he had ever seen. She whispered his name. . . .

The rain had stopped when dawn broke upon the horizon, but low clouds still blocked out the sky, promising more rain. Hotujec slowly rubbed the cramped muscles of his right leg before trying to stand. Richardson had awakened him at two in the morning for guard duty. Nothing unusual had happened during the night, and Jeff had made periodic checks on JD to make sure he was all right. Hooking his radio back onto his web gear, Hotujec moved out of the jungle brush and back to the camp. McCall was just waking up when Jeff walked up to him and said, "How's the hand feeling, boss?"

"Like someone used it for a fuckin' dart board."

"Yeah, I'll bet. I did the best I could on it last night."

Rubbing the sleep from his eyes, McCall replied, "Looks a hell of a lot better than it did last night, kid. Thanks. Damn, I sure could use a hefty shot of Jack Daniels right about now."

"You sure you're old enough to drink?" The remark came from Richardson, who had just sat up and was rubbing the sleep from his eyes.

"Fuck you, Rich."

Hotujec moved to the edge of the rocks and returned with three dehydrated LRRP meals he had prepared earlier. "You guys want to keep cussin' each other or eat?"

"Well, would ya look at this, brother Richardson? We're gettin' breakfast in bed this morning. Jeff, you're all right."

Setting the plastic bag on his lap and stirring the contents with a plastic spoon, McCall asked, "Anything movin' out there last night?"

Hotujec answered, "Naw, just the usual stuff. I figure anybody that might have been out there last night did the same thing we did—just holed up somewhere to wait out the rain. An' man, it really started comin' down about four this morning."

McCall nodded. "Yeah, and it don't look like it's gonna move out of here any time soon, either. You guys remember to turn on those radios last night?"

Spitting out a rock-hard bean that had refused the water treatment, Rich said, "Hell yes. You think you're travelin' through this exotic countryside with a couple of rookies?"

McCall grinned. "I can see already this is gonna be a long day."

The meal finished, JD flipped open his map and pointed to two heavy red lines on the map. "Well, boys, it's like this. Colonel Baron, Doc, and I went over every possible route that we thought Thanh might take to get back home, and we came up with these two as our best bet."

Placing the point of his pen an inch to the right of the red line marked "number one," McCall continued. "Right about here is where I figure our choppers put us in." Moving the pen upward, he stopped next to the red line. "We should be right about here and, if I'm right, that trail is just on the other side of these cliffs about eight hundred to a thousand yards away. Now, ya know we're not sure if our boy Thanh will be comin' this way, but this is all we got to go on. Myself, I just got a feelin' the bastard's out there somewhere an' he ain't far off, either."

Richardson studied the map for a moment. "I don't know, JD. I'd sure as hell feel a lot better if we had some solid intel on that guy."

"I know, Rich, so would I. But losin' those radios on the infil limited us to the URC-10s. They don't have enough range to reach our firebases below the Z, and Moonbeam's flyin' too fuckin' high to monitor voice contact. But at least they can pick up the beeper signals for a fix on our position, so they know where we're at."

Rich moved his finger up the map. "Yeah, an' ya can bet your ass they've noticed which direction we're headin'."

"Hell, Rich, you didn't have anything else to do today, did ya?" said JD, as he grinned and winked.

Hotujec glanced at McCall but didn't say anything. He was beginning to realize why Richardson spoke so highly of his friend and team leader. The guy never thought negative and never gave up on anything. Here they were—the three of them, all that remained of an original 10-man team, standing 15 miles inside North Vietnam with no artillery, no air support, no commo, and nothing but bad guys all around them. Yet McCall made it sound like no more than a stroll through the woods to the corner bar.

Returning the glance, McCall asked, "Is there anything wrong, Jeff?"

Jeff shook his head. "It's nothing, JD. Go ahead, I'm listening."

"Well, like I said, that trail should be pretty close. We'll move up to the outer edge and establish an observation point. We'll give it six hours and see what we come up with. Now, we all know what Thanh looks like, and it sure as hell won't be hard to spot Salt or Pepper. So, if it's all the same to you two guys, I'd rather not shoot up just anything or anybody runnin' up an' down this trail. I feel that's all we've been doin' since we started this damn gangbang. If we get a lot of traffic, I'll snap a few pictures for the G-2 boys back in Saigon and we'll let them move on through. If our targets show up, we go balls to the wall with all we got. Hell of a plan, don't ya think?"

Rich and Jeff both nodded in agreement. Once the men had all their gear packed, McCall and Richardson moved out. Jeff made one last check of the area. Using a tree branch, he brushed out the boot prints that had been left at the edge of the clearing near the rocks. Then, throwing the limb into thicker jungle cover, he ran to catch up with the others. Striker One was on the move again.

XI.

Colonel Baron had received two messages this morning. The first was from Colonel Taylor, commander of Air Command. Moonbeam had received another beeper signal during the night. The coordinates were included in the message. However, the second message had been totally unexpected: Colonel Howard, the CCN commander, and Colonel Whitington from CC Central wanted to see him as soon as possible. They had arrived in Saigon a little past three in the morning and were staying at the Americana Hotel. They would be waiting for his call.

Shaving and getting dressed, Baron decided to skip breakfast to arrive at his office by 0700 hours. He ordered his aide to call the two colonels at the Americana and set up an immediate meeting. He also asked if Colonel Davis had arrived yet. The aide gave him a negative. Baron was to be informed the moment Davis came in.

Entering his office, Baron went right to the map board and plotted the coordinates he had received from Air Command. Stepping back, he stared at the bright-red square he had drawn on the board. Striker One was still alive, and whoever was running the show was still heading north for Dong Hoi Province.

Baron moved to the safe in the corner of his office, pulled out yesterday's photos, and spread them out on the coffee table. Next, he removed the records of the 10 members of Striker One and placed them next to the pictures. At least five of the men whose names appeared on these records no longer existed. Brady had been killed during the training phase. Taber had bought it at the gunfight in Bien Cao. How many were left, and who? Who was running this team? Baron had an idea—but that was all it was, an idea.

He was certain Striker had lost both of its main radios on the infil or during the battle action shown in the photos; otherwise, contact would have been established with one of the bases along the DMZ. There had been no reports of normal communications. Only the steady beep of the emergency radios had been heard each night. Jess Baron lit a cigarette and stared aimlessly at the pattern of the smoke; he had never felt quite so helpless.

Baron was so deep in thought that the distant sound of tapping on his door didn't register until his aide entered with a hot cup of coffee. Placing the cup on the colonel's desk, he said, "Sir, Colonel Howard and Colonel Whitington are on their way over, and Colonel Davis just arrived a few minutes ago."

"Thank you. I'll be in the ol' man's office. When our visitors arrive, bring them down to Colonel Davis's office."

"Yes, sir." The aide turned and left the room.

Gathering the files and photos, Baron picked up his coffee and headed for Davis's office.

Davis was pouring coffee when Baron walked in.

"Morning, Jess. Do you need a refill for that cup you're carrying?"

Placing the stack of photos and files on the table, Baron said, "No, thank you, sir. I thought you'd want to see these messages right away."

Davis set his coffee down and moved to his desk for one of his favorite cigars. "What'd we get, Jess?"

"We received another message from Air Command

at 0530 this morning. I was right. Whoever is still alive in Striker consider themselves still operational. They're heading north for Dong Hoi Province."

The flame from Davis's lighter never reached the tip of the cigar; he pulled it from his mouth. "Jesus, Jess, there can't be more than four or five men, at the most, left from that team."

"I know, sir. That's what I've been working on this morning. I've been trying to figure out just who in the hell could be left alive out there. I'm almost positive about one."

Davis walked to the window. Looking out over the city, he quietly said, "It's suicide, Jess. You know that, don't you?"

Baron paused a moment before he answered. "Yes, sir. You and I know that. But those men out there haven't even considered that idea."

Davis slowly twirled the unlit cigar in his hand for a few minutes before he turned away from the window. "Jess, I want those men out of there. I don't care how you work it. You'll get anything you need for the operation, but goddammit, I want those men out of there and back home. God knows they gave it a good run, but it's hopeless to go on under these odds." Davis was emphatic.

Baron noted the emotion in the older man's voice. It was more like that of a worried father than a military commander.

Baron said, "Sir, I wish that were possible, but I'm afraid we've got three things working against us. For one, the weather up north has the entire area socked in. We couldn't get anything in for at least the next seventy-two hours. Second, Striker's last location has been fixed at about fifteen miles north of the DMZ. Even if we could get choppers in the air, there's little chance we could sit them down that far north. Charlie has the whole area covered with ground-to-air missiles and thirty-seven-millimeter anti-aircraft guns. We'd be

lucky to get one out of ten choppers even close to
Striker."

Baron watched the look of hopelessness on Davis's
face as he slumped down in his chair and put his face in
his hands. "You said there were three reasons,
Jess. . . ."

"Yes, sir." Baron shuffled through the files. Finding
the one he wanted, he handed it to Davis. "That's your
third reason, sir. JD McCall."

Staring at the name on the thick file, the colonel said,
"McCall? I don't understand, Jess."

"Sir, you wanted ten of the best people we had for
this operation. JD McCall was one of the first ones I
got. I believe you know he's the guy that saved my ass
from that fuckin' Thanh and his boys on my last
operation. That file you have in your hand contains
enough information to award McCall the Medal of
Honor at least seven times over. He has never refused a
mission. He has a 98-percent success rate on those
missions. His reputation as a hard drinker is well-
founded, but it has never interfered with his ability to
prepare and execute his missions. Hell, he's proven that
by staying alive this damn long. But one thing stands
out above all else, sir. Once he starts something, he
finishes it. He'll finish this or die trying."

Davis flipped through the file. "Okay, Jess. The guy's
a solid professional. But the fact remains, he's in a
hopeless situation here. He must realize that."

Davis became silent, in deep thought. He studied the
file once more before saying, "I still want some type of
plan put together to pull this team out of there. I have a
feeling that this is one operation McCall might reconsider his position on and welcome a chance out of this
fuckin' mess."

Baron stared at the ceiling for a fleeting second as he
considered what he was about to say. The old man
wasn't going to like it, but he was going to hear it
anyway.

"I don't think you understand, sir. You see, one of the other things I found out about McCall was that once he gets on the ground in a target area, he considers himself the *total overall commander*."

Davis was on his feet in remarkable time for a man his age. His voice thundered. "What the hell do you mean, mister? Are you telling me that this man will not follow *my direct order* to remove his team from the field?"

"Respectfully, sir, JD McCall won't come out of there until he's finished what he started. If you take choppers in there before he has completed this operation—or at least had a chance to—he'll tell you to go fuck yourself . . . *sir*."

The veins in Davis's neck stood out and a flush of red came over his face. "I'd have that bastard's balls, too. I saw a notation in reference to an 'Eyes Only' Report in that file. You have any idea what that's about?"

"No, sir. I tried to check it out and was told to forget it."

"Obviously, our boy McCall has let his cocky attitude be known before."

Trying to relieve the tension he felt, Baron said, "Yes, sir, but you have to admit the mother's got class."

Davis walked over to the map. Staring at the large red square that was Striker's last known location, he tapped it with his finger and laughed. "You're right, Jess. The bastard's as crazy as hell, but you've got to admire his style." Davis thought a few minutes longer and then as an afterthought added, "You really think he'd tell me to shove it if I ordered him out of there?"

Baron was grinning over the top of his coffee cup. "Without a doubt, sir."

Davis's voice had returned to normal. "My God, George Patton would roll over in his grave."

Both men were laughing now as the aide knocked and entered.

"Colonel Howard and Colonel Whitington are here, sir."

"Thank you, Captain," said Baron. "Tell them it will only be a few minutes."

"Yes, sir." The captain closed the door as he left.

"Jess, you have any idea why they're here?"

"Well, sir, you did tell me to notify their commands that we had KIAs on this operation. I would imagine they're here to find out what happened to some of their best recon people."

"Of course—you're right. They'll want to know what we're doing to recover bodies and the status of any survivors. What do you suggest we tell them?"

Baron looked over to the map on the wall; his eyes seemed to penetrate the bright red square representing the last known location of any survivors. Then, looking Davis straight in the eye, he said, "Colonel, I'd tell them the truth—give them the whole operation from the beginning to our present situation. The security of the operation is no longer needed and, for all practical purposes, Striker One has been neutralized. You say you want those people out, sir. I'm not going to bullshit you: right now I don't see any possible way it could be done. Maybe what we need is a couple more experienced people to take a look at it and see what they come up with. It could be I've looked at it so long I'm missing something. But that decision is up to you, sir."

Davis sat quietly considering the advice of his intel officer. He knew Jess was right, of course. The great plan to capture or kill Thanh, Salt, and Pepper was now a total shambles. Striker had made a good run at it, but the cost had been high. At least five members of the team were confirmed dead, not to mention two complete chopper crews, and there was no way at this moment of knowing the condition of the survivors. To make matters worse, Thanh and his two renegades were still running around out there. Each hour that passed increased the odds against Striker. All North Vietnam would soon be searching for them, if they weren't already. The hunters had become the hunted. Baron's profile on McCall left little doubt that it was McCall leading the survivors. . . . They were still heading north.

Davis made his decision. "Tell them to come in, Jess. I'll get us all some coffee before I start the briefing."

Baron nodded and went to the door. "Colonel Howard, Colonel Whitington, would you come in, please."

During the hour-long briefing that followed, the two visiting officers occasionally glanced over at each other but never interrupted. Davis concluded the briefing by handing the Air Force photos to the officers and saying, "There you have it, gentlemen. We have three positive dead in those pictures, and whoever's left is heading for Thanh's headquarters in the north. We are certain the three men we've spotted in the photos are part of Striker. Colonel Baron was with them the morning they left Bien Cao—they were all wearing tigerstripe uniforms."

Colonel Howard looked slowly through the pictures, a million thoughts running through his head. Without looking up, he muttered, "I'd be willing to bet you money JD McCall is the guy leading whoever's left of Striker."

The room was silent, and all eyes were on Howard. A slight smile had appeared on Baron's face. He realized he had an ally who agreed with his theory on McCall.

Davis asked, "You want to explain how you came up with that from just the photos, Bob?"

Howard selected three pictures and lined them up on the table.

"Well, Colonel, McCall stands over six-foot-four. Look at the bodies in the crater. Now, unless I've forgotten a lot since my early days at the O&I school,

this picture was taken at twenty thousand feet, repro-
duced, and blown up at least twice. Now, using photo
altitude-conversion measurements, that would make
the bodies in that hole under six feet tall." He pointed
to the second photo. "The same principle applies to the
body against the tree. With the adjustment for body
position, I'd say that man was at least four to five inches
under six feet." Tapping the third and final one, he said,
"And this one, Colonel Baron, I think slipped by you.
Quite understandable, I might add. I missed it the first
three times I looked at it, too."

Everyone crowded around Howard as he continued.
"Notice the heavy foliage to the right of my finger.
Now look real close at the small opening between the
two layers of leaves. Slowly move your eyes from the
tips of the leaves to about midway down the branch."

Baron was the first to spot it. "Jesus, that's a pants
leg! And tigerstripe pants at that. There! Just beyond
the base of the trees, you can barely see it. Isn't that a
jungle boot?"

"Very good, Colonel Baron," said Howard.

Davis was still trying to find the cause of Baron's
excitement when Howard shocked the group once
more.

"Now, gentlemen, can anybody show me the second
body in that picture?"

The whole room was stunned. Especially Baron. He
had spent hours going over these photos. Granted, he
had not spotted the pants leg, but missing two bodies in
the same picture was too much. There was self-doubt in
his voice as Jess Baron said, "Really, sir. I've been over
these things a hundred times; I may have missed one,
but two?"

Davis and Whitington sat silently, watching Howard
and Baron. Howard asked, "Do you have a magnifying
glass?"

Baron was on his feet. "Yes, one moment, I'll get it."

He left the room and returned moments later, passing the glass to Howard.

Howard's voice was calm. "Now, Colonel Baron, I want you to know I am not doing this to embarrass you, nor is it any reflection on your competence as an intelligence officer."

"I understand, sir."

"Good. Now take the glass and look at the edge of that small burnt-off area just short of the foliage."

Baron did as he was told. Slowly moving the magnifying glass over the picture, he searched the area Howard had pointed out. One pass, two, then a third. On the third sweep he found it.

Baron sat calmly for a second. Then, looking up at Howard, he said, "How in the world did you spot that without this glass?"

Howard sat back in his chair, lit a cigar, and replied, "The irregular pattern of the black, burnt grass in contrast to the green foliage. But don't feel bad, Colonel. I was the OIC of the Operations and Intelligence School at Fort Bragg for three years. But that was a long time ago."

Davis and Whitington were waiting for someone to tell them what the hell was going on. Davis was the first to ask. "Would you two care to let us in on this great discovery of yours?"

Baron turned the photo so that it faced both officers and gave Davis the glass. Moving Davis's hand to the point in question, he said, "Notice the black stripes and irregular lines mixed in with the green of the palms, sir."

Davis stared hard at the image through the glass. He saw it, but he didn't really want to. Dropping the magnifying glass, he slumped back into his chair and quietly said, "My God, that means there are only a maximum of three people alive out there, and they're still heading north."

Colonel Whitington didn't bother to look at the photo. He too sat back in his chair. "Well, that convinces me. The only guy out there with enough balls to take on Thanh and the whole fuckin' Vietnamese army with only three people has to be JD McCall."

The room had fallen silent, but at the mention of McCall's name every eye in the place focused on the map that hung on Davis's wall. Unknown to any of them, all four were thinking the same thing: McCall was either crazy as hell or the bravest bastard they had ever had the chance to serve with.

That thought moved Baron to his feet. "We've lost a hell of a lot of good people on this operation, gentlemen, and I'd just as soon we didn't lose what's left of Striker One."

Howard agreed. "Well, we're sure as hell not going to get them out of there by just sitting here."

Whitington asked, "What'd you have in mind, Bob?"

Howard moved to the map and studied it for a moment. Then he turned to the others and said, "Colonel Baron pretty well summed it up. The weather up north is worse than lousy and it's going to stay that way for a while. I also agree that choppers wouldn't last fifteen minutes that far north, even if the weather were to clear. Finally, I agree with the colonel's evaluation of McCall. You tell the guy he's got to come out now and he'll tell you to get bent. It's obvious that JD figures this mission already has a heavy price tag attached. He's still movin' north."

The frustration was clear in Davis's words. "But goddammit, Colonel, it's the act of an insane man. There are only three men left. Even if he reaches Thanh's headquarters, they couldn't possibly last five minutes in that situation. What you're telling me, Colonel Howard, is that McCall is leading a suicide mission."

"Not at all, Colonel Davis. What I'm saying is that

McCall knows the weather's against him and that TAC air or chopper support is out of the question. He's already lost five people, that's true. But if you'll notice, his last position places him fifteen miles north of the DMZ, and that was at 0630 hours this morning. If he's moving right now, and you can believe me, he is, he's closer to Dong Hoi Province than he is to the DMZ. No, Colonel, McCall hasn't gone off the deep end just yet. He figures he's closer to the target than he is to getting help from us, and to be honest, sir, given our present situation, I'd have to agree with him. To McCall, there's no reason to turn around now. The price has already been paid."

Once again there was silence in the room, each man alone with his own thoughts. Colonel Whitington was the first to speak. Moving from his chair to the map, he said, "I think you're right, Bob. McCall would have only two options. Either turn back or drive on for Dong Hoi. I would imagine that were any of us in the same situation, we'd see the choices the same way."

Jess Baron and Davis both nodded in agreement. Whitington continued, "Now, we know McCall is determined to reach Dong Hoi and attempt to complete his mission. But I must also agree that three men have little, if any, chance of staying alive in there to complete such an operation. I'm not saying we can change McCall's mind about this, but what if we could get him some replacements for the people he's lost? I believe that's a deal McCall would go for."

Howard was on his feet. "Hell, yes. You're talking about a HALO infiltration to reinforce Striker."

Whitington answered, "You got it, Bob. I know for a fact I've got at least ten people at CCC, and I'm willing to bet you've got a few at CCN. Hell, between the two of us we got the best damn skydivers in the fucking world."

Davis glanced at Baron, then turned to the other two colonels. "Can we pull it off with that weather going on up there?"

Howard traced the distance from the red pin in the map to the suspected location of Thanh's headquarters in Dong Hoi. "Colonel, I believe—and I think Colonel Whitington will concur—that if we start scrambling everything right now, there is more than a seventy-five percent chance we can get Striker some help. I can get my people from CCN over to the Da Nang air base in no time. Colonel Whitington can send a message to his S-2 and have his people in Da Nang within a couple of hours. If you get us a hangar and some security people around it, I think we can pull it off."

Davis was up and moving to his phone. "You've got it, Colonel. Anything else?"

"Yes, sir, we'll need a C-130 rigged for high-altitude low-opening."

Davis turned to Baron. "Jess, get Colonel Taylor at Air Command on the line. He can handle the hangar and aircraft problems for us."

The atmosphere in the room had changed suddenly from one of hopelessness to one of excitement and enthusiasm. There remained one last desperate chance to save the mission as well as the heroic survivors of Striker One.

Howard and Whitington left for the communications room to transmit their messages to their respective units. As usual, the mission would be all volunteers, and HALO personnel were preferred. No one would know what he was volunteering for, nor what would be required of him, until the volunteers were secured in the hangar at Da Nang.

Baron left to contact Air Command and set up transportation for Davis, himself, and the two colonels. After placing the files and the photos in his safe,

Davis stopped at the map and stared at the bright red pin that represented the lives of three men. Quietly, he said, "Don't move too fast, McCall. . . . We're coming."

XII.

━━━✕━━━✕━━━✕━━━✕━━━✕━━━✕━━━✕

Thanh halted his platoon near the Phu Wai River which ran between the two major trails coming out of the north. It was here that he would join forces with the young and ambitious Captain Quan and his platoon. Thanh had hoped to capture the few remaining Americans without any assistance, but after hours of criss-cross searching through the area, no trace of them had been found. He was certain they were still nearby, but the size of the area was more than one platoon could handle alone. He radioed Dong Hoi, informed them of the situation, and requested immediate assistance. He also instructed headquarters to alert all NVA units moving south to be on the alert for possible contact with an unknown number of Green Berets. Should such contact occur, he was to be notified at once. For now, there was nothing to do but wait for Captain Quan.

Thanh knew the captain well. Quan's rise through the ranks was due to his use of his father's name. Nui Di Quan had been a hero of the French war and was highly respected by all North Vietnamese military leaders. Thanh himself had pulled strings in Hanoi to have the high-spirited officer assigned to command in Dong Hoi. This had been done as a favor at the request of the elder Quan, who was an old friend of Thanh's. It was a favor he later regretted. The young Quan was forever bringing up his famous father's favor with the high committee and, on more than one occasion, he hinted to Thanh that he would hold a powerful position in the new government once the war was over. It was a thought that sent cold chills down Thanh's spine. The captain might be the son of a famous freedom fighter, but the father's qualities are not always transferred to the son. Thanh had found it necessary to reprimand the young man more than once on his careless disregard for the lives of the troops in his command. If it had not been for the friendship and respect he had for Quan's father, Thanh would have sent the captain back to Hanoi long ago. But to do so would dishonor the elder Quan, and Thanh could not find it in his heart to do that.

If there had been any other commander available at Dong Hoi headquarters, Thanh would have ordered Quan to stay in the rear and placed another officer in charge of his platoon. But that had not been the case: Captain Quan was already en route to the link-up point along the Phu Wai River—and to his fate.

The dull, throbbing pain had begun again in McCall's hand. Ignoring it, he kept his eyes on the open end of the trail and listened for the slightest sound to indicate anything or anyone coming his way. Hotujec was concealed 20 yards up the trail from McCall. Richardson had taken up position 15 yards to McCall's left and down the trail.

In the past three hours they had watched two NVA companies and one platoon moving south. They had passed within 10 yards of the three Green Berets.

McCall shifted his position to relieve the pressure on his badly swollen hand. It didn't help. The movement shot pain all the way up his arm. Silently cursing, he heard two quick hissing sounds over his radio, then silence. Richardson had broken squelch twice on his radio to signal McCall and Hotujec that more traffic was coming down the trail.

McCall lay perfectly still and peered through a small opening in the jungle cover at the end of the trail. He saw the NVA point man come around the bend with his rifle at the ready. This was something McCall had noticed about the groups that passed earlier: they too had been moving with rifles ready and showing more caution than usual. The NVA normally moved through their own areas at a casual, relaxed pace, coming up on full alert only when they were within a few miles of the DMZ. But that sure as hell wasn't the case today.

The point was obviously nervous. Every few yards, he would stop, squat down, and stare into the jungle on both sides of the trail. Watching his cautious advance, McCall knew the alarm was already out—there were Green Berets in the area.

Three more NVA moved up beside the lead man. Two of them knelt down by his side. The third stood with his hands on his hips. McCall couldn't hear what was being said, but it was a sure bet that the one standing was angry at the point man. He began to wave wildly in all directions. The point man stood and pointed to both sides of the trail. McCall's heart skipped a couple of beats as the man pointed to his side of the trail. Had he spotted them?

Another NVA came around the bend and approached the group. Immediately all argument stopped. The new arrival and the point man exchanged words. McCall knew he was either a high-ranking noncom or an officer, but there was little doubt the man was in charge. McCall watched him grab the point man by his shirtfront and shake him like a rag doll.

No longer concerned with maintaining silence, the officer screamed at the man. "You cowardly son of a pig! You would hold up my entire platoon because of your cowardice! Do you fear a few Green Berets that much? The Americans that Major Thanh reported have more than likely put their cowardly tails between their legs and run away to the south. And you hold up my unit because you see ghosts in the shadows among the jungle vines! You are a fool as well as a coward, old

man! We are due to link up with Thanh within hours!
Are you trying to embarrass me by making the major
wait for me?" Raising his hand, he held it high as if he
were going to strike the man. The point man flinched as
he awaited the expected blow. It never came. Bringing
his hand down, the officer screamed, "Go to the rear of
the platoon. You are of as much use to me as a
frightened child. I will deal with you later."

Another soldier was assigned to the point, and the
column moved past Striker and disappeared down the
trail. McCall pressed the switch on his radio and
whispered, "Jeff, Rich, close in on me ASAP." Within
minutes the three had regrouped and moved back away
from the trail. McCall spread the map on the ground.

Jeff asked, "What was all that yelling about, boss?"

In a whisper McCall answered, "It was one hell of an
interesting ass-chewing being given to that point man.
Any doubts we had about Thanh's location have been
cleared up for us. He's a couple of hours down that
trail. Those guys that just passed us are on their way to
link up with him. All we gotta do now is stay on that
platoon's ass until that link-up. Then we've got 'em."

Richardson slowly shook his head. "Damn, would ya
listen to this crazy fucker? There's only three of us and
he says we got 'em! Hell, JD, you know Thanh don't go
no place without at least a platoon, and with this bunch
hookin' up with him, you're talkin' about close to a
hundred fuckin' NVA in the whole mess."

McCall grinned for the first time that day. "Hell,
Rich, where's your sense of adventure, that ol' spirit of
excitement? Hell, son, you're a fuckin' Green Beret—
people *expect* you to do these thrill-a-minute heroics."

"Screw you, JD. That old 'We're Green Berets' shit
ain't cuttin' it this time. You know we gotta get the hell
out of here. It was gonna be bad enough takin' on
Thanh and his bunch, but with another platoon hookin'
up with him, there ain't no fuckin' way three of us can
take on them mothers."

McCall stood up and folded the map. "Well, Rich, to quote a famous man of our time, 'A man's gotta do what a man's gotta do.'"

Richardson stared in amazement at McCall for a moment. "Just who the fuck said that?"

JD's voice was calm and quiet. "Gary Cooper. I think it was in *High Noon*."

"Hell, don't worry, Rich, we'll give them a chance to surrender first," Hotujec said after he quit laughing.

"Now, see what ya went and did, JD. You made this damn kid about as nuts as you are. I knew you was gonna be a bad influence on him."

All three men were quietly laughing. Striker's spirits ran high as they moved off in the direction of the trail. The days and hours of uncertainty about Thanh's location were over. They were no longer looking for a needle in a haystack. They only had to follow the unsuspecting NVA and they would be led to their prize. All three men knew they might have only one chance at Thanh or the two renegade Americans, but that was all they wanted. One shot. A lot of good men had already paid for that chance, and JD McCall wasn't going to let them down.

Air Force security guards with rifles and dogs patrolled the blocked-off sector of the Da Nang airfield as three vans with blacked-out windows drove up to the hangar. Colonel Howard directed all but two of the men inside, then introduced the two men to Colonel Baron. "Sir, I'd like you to meet SFC Mel Smith from Command and Control Central and Lieutenant Ed Esswain from Command and Control North."

Handshakes were exchanged all around before the colonel asked, "Sergeant Smith, how many men did you bring with you?"

"Ten, counting myself, sir."

"Lieutenant, how about you?"

The tall lanky officer replied, "Ten, sir, including me.

But we must have had at least fifty who wanted to go along."

Concern appeared on Colonel Baron's face. "What do you mean, Lieutenant?"

Esswain read the look and quickly answered, "Oh, don't worry, sir, there hasn't been any security leak or anything. Nobody really knows what this is all about. Just a lot of folks guessing. Shithouse rumors, you know."

Baron kept pressing. "Just what are they guessing at, Lieutenant?"

"Well, sir, the boys back at CCN are bettin' this has got something to do with JD McCall and Richardson. Barnes and Hotujec, too. You see, McCall and those guys have got a lot of friends back there."

Colonel Howard motioned in the direction of the hangar. "Well, gentlemen, a team with that many friends ought to have their asses saved, so why don't we go in and figure out just how we're going to do that. Colonel Whitington is inside with the rest of the team."

The five men moved past the large double doors and into the relative coolness of the hangar. Baron looked around the briefing room that had been quickly thrown together. The volunteers sat along benches that consisted of no more than two-by-eight boards propped on top of ammo boxes. To the front stood a podium and, beyond that, a huge map board covered with parachute silk.

Colonel Whitington called for attention as Colonel Davis entered the hangar. The volunteers rose as one.

Davis moved to the podium. "Take your seats, gentlemen. First, I'd like to thank each and every one of you for being here. It demonstrates your courage and belief in the Special Forces motto: 'Anytime, Anyplace, Anywhere.' Again, thank you. Now, since you are all from either CCC or CCN, my next statement is doubly hard for me." Davis paused a moment to clear his throat before continuing. "Gentlemen, approximately forty-eight hours ago a hand-picked team of eight SF personnel engaged a platoon of NVA while on a classified operation. That engagement resulted in the death of five members of that team. Those who were killed have not been identified. We have not had voice communication with the survivors, so we have no way of knowing for sure who's still alive out there." Davis paused again and then read the list of 10 names of the Striker One force. "Sergeant Brady was killed during the training phase of the operation and Sergeant Taber was killed in an encounter with an NVA unit in the village of Bien Cao. So you see, men, that means there are only three survivors out there. I would like to add that our aerial photos have confirmed over sixty dead NVA in the battle that occurred on the insertion LZ."

This news brought a wild cheer from the men in the hangar. Someone yelled from the back, "Hell, sir, those guys would have called that about even." This brought more yells from the group, and lifted the depression that had fallen over the men when Davis first began.

"The team is code-named Striker One." Davis continued, "I say 'is' because there are one to three members still alive. As I said, the lack of voice communication makes it virtually impossible for us to positively ID the survivors, but my staff and I, as well as Colonel Howard and Colonel Whitington, are convinced that one of them is JD McCall."

The announcement brought another burst from the group.

"Hell, Colonel, from what I hear, JD McCall could kick ass back to the DMZ all by himself."

"You have a point there. But you see, gentlemen, McCall has no intention of coming back to the south. He is driving on with his mission."

The statement brought absolute silence to the room. Turning to the map, Davis pulled the silk cover from the board, revealing a brightly colored map of the DMZ and North Vietnam. A large red circle marked off an area some 15 miles past the black border indicating the DMZ. The hangar came alive with soft mutters and low whistles. Picking up a pointer beside the podium, Davis placed the tip in the red circle.

"Here is the last reported position of Striker One. We know this position to be accurate. Whoever is still alive out there has been sending out signals on the URC-10 emergency beeper. The Air Force can track that signal to within twenty-five yards of the radio. Now, Colonel Howard has assured me that McCall is neither insane nor suicidal, but tells me that if I ordered him out of there, McCall would have no qualms about telling me to go fuck myself."

This brought a roar of laughter and nods of agreement from many in the room.

"Therefore, gentlemen, since Striker One has elected to continue this operation, we have decided to give them some help. That is why you are here. You will conduct a HALO infiltration into this area, link up with Sergeant McCall or whoever is still running the show out there, and assist them in completion of the mission."

Davis paused to let his words sink in, then said, "I realize that you are all volunteers. I also realize that this is the first time since you volunteered that anyone has informed you of the scope of the operation. Therefore, if any members of this group wish to reconsider, I want you to know that no one will think any less of any man who wants out. I'll give you all a ten-minute break outside. Those personnel that return will be the rescue team for Striker One." Davis put the pointer down and walked away.

Not one of the volunteers moved or spoke.

Lieutenant Esswain stood up and looked at the men before him. "I take it you all feel the same way I do—there is no need for a break. Am I right?"

The entire group answered as one, "Yes, sir!"

The lieutenant nodded, then turned to the colonel. "Sir, if it's all right with you, we'd like to continue with this briefing. We're on Striker One's time now."

In his haste to link up with Major Thanh, young Captain Quan neglected his rear security; it was easy for Striker to follow close behind. The NVA platoon had been moving for almost an hour and were making good time. That was fine with McCall. The sooner they reached their destination, the better. McCall would follow this group to hell for one shot at Thanh—he owed that much and more to Doc Hawkins and the others—but he knew what that shot would cost. The plan was simple: once the link-up between the two NVA units had been made, Striker would move into the best possible position for a shot at the targets. If Thanh were alone, all three Green Berets would zero in on him. If Salt and Pepper were with him, McCall would take out Thanh, Richardson would go for Pepper, and Salt would be Hotujec's target. After firing, they would drop back a hundred yards, regroup, and prepare for a last stand. It would be pointless to run. After the first shot, NVA would be as thick as flies on a dead cow. The best the three men could hope for was a clean shot to end their lives quickly, but it was better to go down fighting than running. By sundown today, Striker One would cease to exist, but then, hopefully, so would Major Thanh. McCall watched the last man of the NVA platoon round a bend in the trail. Out of habit, he flipped on his URC-10 before following.

Smith and Esswain moved through the aircraft checking each man's equipment. They had been airborne for half an hour. The steady roar of the C-130's engines filled the plane. They were still 30 minutes out from Striker's last reported position.

Completing their checks, the two team leaders returned to their seats. Esswain looked over at Smith and said, "You know, I kind of like the code name Colonel Baron gave the rescue team. It sounds like a good name for a movie: *Deliverance One*."

Smith nodded, "Yes, sir, and you can bet your ass it's gonna be one hell of a shindig."

"You got it, Smitty. Especially going in there in daylight. It shouldn't take Charlie long to get on us once we hit the ground."

"I'm not so sure, sir. We've got heavy cloud cover and the rain on our side, and we're going in high enough that nobody can hear the plane. Our real problem is going to be getting everyone together once we're in there."

Smith pulled a pack of cigarettes from his pocket and offered one to Esswain. The lieutenant declined. Smith lit up and replaced the pack before he said, "Hell, sir, we've got some of the best skydivers in the world on this airplane right now."

Esswain leaned back into the webbing behind his seat. "I know, Sergeant. I'll just feel a hell of a lot better when we're on the ground and moving."

No sooner had Esswain made that statement than the crew chief appeared from the front of the aircraft and headed for the two team leaders. Putting his cigarette out, Smith tapped the lieutenant's shoulder and said, "I think you're about to get your wish, sir."

Both men were on their feet as the chief leaned forward and yelled above the engine noise, "Sir, we've got a new fix on Striker One. We're only ten minutes out. You've got heavy clouds leveling out at eight hundred feet with a light drizzle."

"Thanks, Chief." Esswain turned to the rescue team and, holding both hands up, yelled, "Ten minutes!"

The men began making last-minute checks on their equipment. For some, the 10 minutes would seem like a lifetime. Adrenaline flowed, hearts beat faster, cold sweat appeared on foreheads. Sergeant Smith would be the jumpmaster. Holding up six fingers, he began giving the jump commands: "Six minutes." Pointing to one side of the aircraft, he yelled, "Outboard personnel, stand up!" Half of the team rose to their feet, grabbing the anchor cable to steady themselves as the heavy C-130 bumped and rocked its way through the stormy sky.

"Inboard personnel, stand up."

"Check equipment!"

"Sound off for equipment check!"

The count echoed its way to the rear of the aircraft as each man yelled his number and slapped the buttock of the man in front of him. "Twenty, okay, nineteen, okay, eighteen, okay. . . ." The count ended with Lieutenant Esswain raising his thumb and yelling, "All okay!" Smith acknowledged the signal with "Stand by!"

The crew chief reached above his head and pressed a red button. The whine of hydraulics joined the roar of the engines as the tailgate of the big bird slowly began to open wide. A loud click signified it had locked in place.

Deliverance One stared at the open space before them. Below lay a carpet of white clouds. Smith turned and pointed to the first man in line, then to the edge of the tailgate. Lieutenant Esswain moved forward, followed closely by the rest of the team. Palms wet and cold with sweat were made colder by the force of the cool air blowing through the plane.

The crew chief raised a finger. "One minute!"

Smith acknowledged and passed the word down the line. Stomachs tightened, silent prayers were uttered. Then it came. The green light flashed and Smith was yelling, "Go, go, go!" Esswain threw his body from the rear of the aircraft out into the swirling wind and thick clouds below. The rest of the team was right behind him. In a matter of seconds the plane was empty. The crew chief reached for the switch once more. As the tailgate closed, his eyes swept the length of the long C-130 and he felt a slight chill inch up his back. Had it been the cold wind? Or had it been the momentary realization that he had just opened the door to hell and cast 20 men to their fate? The tailgate locked in place.

Captain Quan brought his platoon to a halt as he double-checked his position on the map. He estimated that Thanh should be only a short distance ahead. He would let his men catch their breath now that they were back on schedule. If he gave them a rest, they would appear in good shape when he linked up with the major. There would be no signs of the obvious haste made to make up for the tentativeness of his point man.

McCall watched the last two men of the NVA platoon stop, then drop to the ground, exhausted. The NVA officer had given his people a well-deserved break. It would be welcome for the members of Striker as well.

Richardson had just leaned back against the trunk of a dead tree when he heard a noise about 15 yards down the trail. It sounded like wood breaking, but he wasn't sure. McCall and Hotujec were across the trail from him, but they apparently hadn't noticed the sound. Picking up a small rock, Rich tossed it across the trail to get their attention, then motioned McCall across the trail. As McCall started to cross, he heard the same sounds behind him. Motioning Richardson to take cover, he moved back into the jungle and stared up at the trees.

Hotujec moved quietly to McCall and whispered, "What the hell is going on, JD?"

"I wish the fuck I knew, Jeff. There's something or somebody up in those trees."

The sounds were coming from all around the three Green Berets. One after another tree limbs sharply cracked, some landing at McCall's feet. Richardson scrambled across the small trail. "What the hell, JD?"

McCall shook his head. "I can't tell you, Rich, but if I didn't know any better, I'd swear those were fuckin' paratroopers bustin' through those trees."

"Shit, man, I didn't know ol' Charlie had paratroopers!"

Any reply was cut short by an NVA soldier's scream of "American, American!" Automatic-weapons fire rattled the jungle, followed by more yelling and gunfire.

One member of the Deliverance team broke through the trees and rappelled into the center of the trail, landing less than 10 yards from the last man in Thanh's platoon. Shocked by the sudden appearance of an American paratrooper, the NVA had screamed and fired at the same time, completely missing the American. Unhooking his snap link from the rappelling rope, the American dove into the brush.

McCall turned in astonishment to the other two members of the team. "Did you two guys see what I saw?"

Hotujec said, "Goddamn, JD, you must know somebody—that was a damn American paratrooper."

A smile started across McCall's face. His first thought was of Jess Baron and Colonel Davis. They hadn't let him down. There was still a chance to pull off this mission and go home. Enthusiasm and confidence were back in his voice. "Well, hell, let's help get 'em out of the trees. Then we're gonna kick some ass." Breaking cover, McCall made for the trees across the trail.

Hotujec caught Richardson shaking his head. "What's the matter, Rich?"

"That mother's got more lives than a fuckin' cat."

"I can't disagree with that, brother, an' you can bet your sweet black ass I'm gonna stay as close to that cat as possible."

Rich winked as he said, "I hear that, man! See you

later, Jeff. Keep your ass down, ya hear?"

"You got it." Both men melted into the jungle growth.

Captain Quan dove under cover at the first sound of gunfire. The NVA sergeant had moved to the rear of the column to determine the reason for the weapons fire. It seemed to be coming from the last two men in the column, but was spreading fast among the others. Yelling for the troops to cease fire, the old NCO closed in on the last two men, who were still firing sporadic short bursts in all directions.

Grabbing the barrel of one of the men's rifles, the sergeant punched him in the face, screamed for the other to quit firing, and demanded explanations from the two men. Then he reported back to Captain Quan.

Quan listened intently to the report, his face showing anger and contempt. "I am surrounded by idiots and cowards. The fools must have seen one of the Americans Major Thanh is searching for. Their story of a man coming down from the trees on a rope is only their cowardly fear running wild. Major Thanh is waiting for us less than a mile from here, Sergeant. Do you realize the opportunity we have before us? I, Captain Quan, shall present these Americans to Major Thanh as a gift." There was smugness in his voice as he addressed the NCO.

The sergeant was more than twice Quan's age. Without looking at his commander, he asked, "What are your orders, Captain?"

Quan became a wild man. Throwing his arms in the air, he screamed, "What the hell do you think I want you to do, you old fool? Capture the sons of bitches, of course. Must I do everything in this command?"

The sergeant hesitated for a moment, then asked, "I understand, my captain. But, what if the two men did see what they say? That could mean that the Green Beret devils have parachuted reinforcements in to help those whom Major Thanh seeks. They could be all around us at this very moment."

Quan's face turned crimson. "I shall report this insolence when we return to headquarters, Sergeant. Tell me, did you hear a plane before these supposed paratroopers were seen? Of course you didn't. Do you think the Americans are crazy enough to risk their paratroopers to rescue a few men who were obviously expendable to begin with? Now, quit acting like such an old fool. You are my senior NCO and have many years of service to our country. Now, do as I say. Bring these Americans to me and I shall forget this conversation ever happened."

Shrugging his shoulders, the old veteran replied, "Yes, sir," and left to gather his squad leaders together. Within a matter of minutes, NVA squads were moving through the jungle in search of their quarry.

McCall stood at the base of the tree and watched intently as the paratrooper rappelled down the rope and landed next to him. The man was so involved undoing the snap link from his rope that, at McCall's unexpected appearance, he jumped backward, tripped over a tree root, and fell to the ground. As he fell, the paratrooper reached for the 9mm pistol in his shoulder holster—a useless gesture since McCall's rifle was already pointed at his chest. Leaning forward, JD said, "Easy, Claude, I'm on your side."

The paratrooper slowly released the hammer of the automatic and leaned back on his elbows, his eyes taking in the height of the man before him.

"Sergeant JD McCall, I presume?"

McCall grinned. "Nice touch, kid. I don't think we've met."

Unhooking the snap link and getting to his feet, the man responded, "Mel Smith, C an' C Central. Heard you might need a hand."

McCall held up the bloody, bandaged hand for Smith

to see. "Not funny, Brother Smith. How many guys did you bring with you?"

Smith was still staring at the bandage. "Sorry about that, man, uh .. . . I brought twenty fightin' mothers with me."

Retrieving the sergeant's rifle, McCall threw it to him as he said, "Well, Smith, I don't know about their mothers, but their sons are about to have one hell of a hard day at the office. Let's see how many of your crew we can find before the shit hits the fan."

"You're the boss." The men headed in the direction of another tree-shattering landing in progress.

Richardson watched the black paratrooper inch his way down the tree. As the man's toes touched the ground, Rich leaned around the tree and said, "Hey, bro, glad to see ya could drop in."

At the word "Hey" the man's eyes had closed, expecting a bullet that never came. Slowly, the eyes opened to see a set of pearly teeth grinning at him. His voice was still shaky as he said, "Jesus, man, you coulda' given me a fuckin' heart attack!"

Rich slapped the man on the back. "Hell, brother, before you get out of this damn deal, you may wish that you *had* had a fuckin' heart attack! Now, get your stuff together and let's get the hell out of here. By the way, what's your name?"

Grabbing his rucksack and rifle, the man said, "Brown, Phil Brown. You Hayes or Richardson?"

"They must have briefed you guys pretty good. I'm Richardson."

"Glad to meet ya. Is McCall still alive?"

"He was the last time I saw him. If we're through with the Sunday-tea chat, Brown, I'd like to go and see if that's still true."

"Let's go." Brown followed Richardson as they headed back for the trail.

*   *   *

McCall told his group to find cover. Someone was coming their way.

Smith knelt at McCall's side. "Are they good guys or bad guys?"

Without turning around, JD answered, "Could be either one. We were tracking an NVA platoon before you guys dropped in. Their rear security fired up one of your people. They didn't hit him, but they sure as hell know we're here."

The sound of the movement came closer. McCall's finger tightened on the trigger, his eyes locked on the broad leaves of a palm tree 15 yards to his front. As the leaves moved, he whispered to Smith, "Get your people ready."

The seconds passed. Then McCall said, "Hold your fire, they're ours."

Hotujec pushed through the leaves and spotted McCall. Moving up next to him with eight of the Deliverance team, Hotujec smiled. "Hi, boss. I found these guys wandering around out there."

McCall was not smiling back. His voice was firm as he said, "You almost got your fuckin' ass shot off, Jeff. Have you seen Rich?"

Jeff's smile disappeared. "No, JD, he's on the other side of the trail."

McCall reached for his radio but didn't have a chance to use it before automatic-weapons fire broke out across the trail 30 or 40 yards away. There were three grenade explosions and increased weapons fire. Forgetting the radio, McCall began yelling orders: "Smith, take five people and go around the left. Jeff, take another five and break right—that's Rich over there. Watch yourselves, they know we're in here but they don't know how many of us. Now, go."

As the two groups departed, McCall turned to four more members of the relief team. "Now listen, I got a real good friend over there gettin' his ass kicked, and I intend to go in there balls to the wall, so if any of ya don't feel up to it, then stay here!"

The four men slowly looked at one another. One young member of the group answered for the rest. "Sergeant McCall, that wasn't necessary. We had enough balls to come in here to save your ass."

McCall realized he fucked up. He knew it was a combination of the pain in the hand, the frustration with the whole mission, and now his concern for Richardson. "Sorry about that, you guys. This just ain't been my week."

The young kid answered, "No sweat, Sarge."

"Okay, then get ready. We go in fifteen seconds."

Magazines were checked and grenades unhooked from web gear. McCall's yell resounded through the trees as he leaped to his feet and broke across the trail, followed closely by his new team.

Richardson had been trying to help another paratrooper out of the trees while Sergeant Brown stood guard when a squad of NVA stumbled into them. In the firefight that followed, Brown killed three; but before he could reload, one of the NVA broke through and emptied a 30-round magazine in the direction of Richardson and the hung-up paratrooper. The first rounds caught Richardson in the legs, knocking him to the ground. The paratrooper was hit by the main burst and died instantly. Brown would have been dead too but for the timely arrival of three members of Deliverance One. They finished off the remaining NVA with a solid wall of automatic-weapons fire.

Brown started to help Richardson, but another NVA squad had been attracted by the gunfire and had Richardson's whole group surrounded and pinned down. Gripping his legs tightly in a vain attempt to cut off the pain, Richardson heard that wild rebel yell that he had heard so many times over the years. That sound did more for him than morphine ever would: JD was coming.

The rifle fire increased to Richardson's right. That

would be the direction JD would come from. Screaming above the sounds of weapons fire and grenade
explosions, Rich yelled, "Hold your fire! Hold your
fire, goddammit!"

Hearing the command, Brown ran to the others and
repeated the order. It was then that they realized they
were no longer taking fire. The NVA had shifted all
their fire to the crazy Americans coming straight at
them from the right.

McCall broke through the jungle growth at a dead
run, colliding with an NVA coming from the other
direction. The impact knocked both men to the ground.
As the NVA made a grab for the weapon he had
dropped, JD pulled his Magnum and fired twice. The
first round lifted the NVA several inches off the ground,
the second blew out his right lung. The four men with
McCall were laying down a steady volume of fire into
the trees to their front. JD signaled for grenades and,
within seconds, five explosions erupted along the edge
of the trees. Through the dust and smoke, one NVA
soldier staggered out into the open, his uniform torn
and dotted with small red spots. He was literally cut in
half by the Deliverance team.

As desperate men fought to survive, rifle fire and
ear-shattering explosions mingled with screams and the
cries of wounded and dying men. All this destruction in
an area of less than three square blocks.

Captain Quan had kept one squad with him at his
command position. He could hear the heavy exchange
of gunfire and the continuous explosions. He didn't
have to be a West Point graduate to know that his
platoon was engaged with more than a handful of
shot-up, struggling Americans. If only he could contact
his sergeant to learn what was going on around him.
What if the man *had* seen an American sliding down a
rope from the trees! Paratroopers would have to use
rappelling ropes to get down from the thick overhead
canopy. There could be hundreds of them around him

right now. A sick feeling spread through Quan's stomach as he whispered for three of his men to move in closer around him. He wondered where Major Thanh was. Surely he could hear the fighting—he was supposed to be less than a mile from this very position. Where was he?

The old NVA sergeant of Quan's platoon held his squad silently in place, waiting. . . . He had fought the Japanese, the French, and the Americans. His young captain was no more than a gleam in his mother's eye when the sergeant was killing Japanese, being tortured in French prisons, and suffering the loss of a wife and children at Haiphong harbor. The NCO had taken the captain's youth into consideration in all dealings with him. After all, age becomes accustomed to youth. The young officers were always seeking new ways to gain popularity with the staff in Hanoi. What better way than to cloak oneself in glory in combat? But Quan did not seem the glory type. True, his father's deeds were well known, but the young Quan did not have the courage of his father. Of this there was no doubt in the old sergeant's mind. He would not let a young fool be responsible for his death or his squad's, all of whose members were as young or younger than their commander.

As the sound of battle intensified, one of the younger members of the sergeant's squad asked quietly, "Sergeant, why do we wait? We must join our brothers in the fight now."

The old man fixed blazing eyes on the soldier. "Be silent, you young fool! I have lived these many years by using my wits, not by acting foolhardy. If you wish to live as long, you will keep quiet and do as I say."

Lowering his head like a reprimanded child, the soldier nodded and moved back to his position.

The sounds of raging battle had shifted in front of the sergeant's position to his left. The old man listened intently to the automatic-weapons fire. The young members of his squad did not realize that he was trying to count the number of Americans around them by the distinctive, high-pitched crack of their weapons. By separating and pinpointing the positions of those sounds, the old man guessed that there were 10 to 13 Americans to his front and left. He also knew that guessing in this game could be fatal. He would hold his squad in position, waiting and watching as the situation developed. When he was certain of what he was facing, he would act. Not before.

Keeping his bodyguards around him, Captain Quan withdrew farther into the jungle cover. Wiping the sweat from his face, he gripped his rifle with a tightness that turned his knuckles white. Where was Major Thanh? Where was his platoon sergeant? What was happening? These questions jammed Quan's frightened mind. Sweat dripped from the young officer's forehead, a combination of jungle heat and human fear. His dreams of impressing his superiors with the capture of the Americans had disintegrated into a desperate desire to survive. If only Major Thanh and his platoon were here. If only he could talk to him. That last thought brought the young officer to his feet. He had the radio frequency Major Thanh was operating on. Headquarters gave it to him before he left Dong Hoi. All he had to do was radio Thanh and all would be fine.

Calling the communications man to his side, Quan set the frequency. He was still upset with himself—he had let fear override logic—but now his confidence returned. Once he linked up with the major, they would destroy these worthless Americans.

Pressing the mike, Quan tried to calm his shaky voice. "Major Thanh, Major Thanh, this is Captain Quan, come in." There was no reply.

"Major Thanh, this is Captain Quan. Come in, please."

The seconds passed; still there was no answer, only steady hissing from the handset.

Quan's regained confidence began to disappear. A third time he tried, his voice less sure this time. "Major Thanh, this is Captain Quan! We are completely surrounded, we need your help. Major Thanh, please come in!"

Before he could key the handset for a fourth try, a voice came back, "Captain Quan, this is Major Thanh. Remain calm, we are coming to your aid. I will contact you when we are in position. This is Major Thanh, out."

Breathing a sigh of relief, the young captain smiled. A second later, a bullet tore through his back and out the front of his chest, the impact driving his face into the ground. That shot was followed by a burst of automatic fire. Captain Quan and his squad were dead.

Stepping over the officer's body, Hotujec moved over to the commo man and pulled the radio from the body. Striker had finally had some luck—the radio didn't have a scratch on it. Checking the frequency dials, Jeff glanced down at Quan's body. "Thanks, Captain. Now we'll have Thanh come to us."

Jeff Hotujec hadn't lost a single man in his encounter with Quan. But Sergeant Smith and his team had not been so lucky. They had moved wide right, crossed the trail, then cut back left. Hearing the increased rifle fire from McCall's assault, Smith had gathered his people around him for final instructions before they made their assault. They never got the chance to discuss it. The ambush had come from all sides at the same time. Within ten seconds it was all over. Smith and his entire team lay either dead or dying.

Lying on his back with three gaping holes in his chest, Smith stared up through the trees at the low-hanging clouds while his life leaked slowly from his body into the soil of Vietnam. Each breath forced blood from his nose and mouth. It was a strange

feeling. There was no pain, yet he couldn't move. What
the hell was it all about? Who'd make the payments on
his car? Shouldn't have dropped that pass against Ohio
State. . . . The last thing Sergeant Mel Smith saw
before he died was an NVA standing over him. The
man seemed so old.

XIII.

Major Thanh tossed the handset of the radio to Salt. "That cowardly dog Quan has gotten himself pinned down! I swear that after this is over, I will see him thrown out of the army, famous father or not. The fool didn't even think to use call signs over the radio! He has now identified not only himself, but also me, by name."

Pepper shook his head in disgust. "Major, that fuckin' kid's scared shitless, that's all."

Thanh's stare was less than friendly as he said, "And what about you, my black friend? Are you scared of these Green Berets?"

The veins in Pepper's neck began to swell as a look of pure hatred crossed his face. "You ain't never seen the fuckin' day you're gonna see me scared of you *or* a bunch of overrated. . . ."

Thanh cut him off before he could finish. "Enough! We have work to do. I want this business with the cursed Green Berets finished before the day is over. Salt, you will work with me. Now, let's move. We must at least try to save that fool Quan."

Thanh turned and walked up the trail in the direction of the distant gunfire. Salt prepared to follow, stopping in front of his angry partner and whispering, "Cool it, man. I'm going to need you thinking straight when this shit hits the fan. The major's just upset. This is gonna be his last operation, he told me so himself this morning."

Pepper checked the magazine in his rifle as he

watched Thanh walk away. The hate was still in his eyes as he looked at Salt, "You got *that* shit right, man! This is gonna be that asshole's last mission. That's a promise."

Before Salt could reply, the big black soldier had moved out. Salt hurried to catch up with Thanh, but his thoughts were on Pepper's last words. Thanh had pushed the man too far this time. He hoped he was wrong and that Pepper would forget about it once the battle was underway, but he had a gut feeling that that wasn't going to happen. Pepper had every intention of blowing Thanh away the first chance he got. Salt realized he couldn't let that happen—for two reasons. One, he really did like Major Thanh. They had talked many times—he of his family in the United States, and Thanh of his love for Vietnam. The second reason was simple. If Thanh was killed by Pepper, the remainder of the NVA would blow them both apart. They wouldn't care who had done the shooting. It was a thought that was still on his mind as he walked up to Thanh's side.

Thanh looked thoughtfully at the deep concentration on his friend's face and said, "You have a worried look, my friend. I know you have respect for these men we will soon battle, but that is not fear I see in your eyes."

"No, sir, it's not that. I was just wondering what would happen to us once you return to Hanoi?"

Placing his hand on Salt's arm, Thanh answered, "There is no need for you to worry about such things. You have not only been a loyal comrade but also a true friend with whom I could talk. For these reasons I plan to take you out of these jungles and back to Hanoi with me as part of my staff."

Thanh's piercing eyes watched for Salt's reaction as he continued. "Unfortunately, I cannot say the same for your black brother."

Salt stopped in the trail and placed his hand over Thanh's. A burden had been lifted and there was sincerity in his voice as he said, "Thank you, Major. I find it a great honor to be called your friend, and I pledge that as long as I can draw a breath, no harm will come to you."

Thanh knew Salt spoke from the heart. Squeezing his shoulder in acknowledgment, Thanh motioned for Salt to move on up to the front of the platoon. Thanh fell in behind him. He could feel the cold eyes of Pepper on the back of his neck as he slowly moved forward. Thanh knew that before this day was over either he would kill the black man or Salt would do it for him.

The weapons fire had become sporadic in all directions. McCall pressed his radio switch. "Rich, this is JD. Come in."

"JD, this is Rich. Where the hell are you, man?"

"Sorry, ol' buddy, but we've been kinda busy. Give me three quick rounds for orientation."

Three shots echoed 30 yards to McCall's front. "Got ya, Rich. What's your situation?"

"I had five of these rescue guys with me for a while, but now I'm down to one. A guy named Brown. He's been doin' a helluva job keepin' them assholes off us, but we sure as hell could use help pretty damn fast."

"You got it, partner."

"JD, watch yourself coming in. There's at least five or six of the bastards between us. We haven't seen 'em, but they're out there somewhere."

"Roger, Rich. You hang in there. I'll get hold of Jeff and we'll come in together. JD, out."

McCall had barely said "Out" when Jeff came on. "JD, I monitored. I'm about twenty-five yards to Rich's right. Over."

"Roger, Jeff. We go in two minutes."

"Roger, JD, we'll . . ."

Two explosions rocked the trees to McCall's front, followed by a heavy volume of AK-47 automatic fire.

McCall yelled into his radio, "Forget the two minutes, Jeff. We're going now! Hit it! JD, out."

McCall and his team were on their feet and moving at a dead run. Hotujec's people were doing the same. Both teams hit Richardson's location at the same time. Richardson was going hand-to-hand with one NVA while Brown had just blown an NVA off his chest with a 9mm round through the guy's head. From behind a tree came another NVA swinging a machete. McCall and Hotujec both fired at the same time, catching the man in a crossfire and tearing him to pieces. The remainder of the team made quick work of four other NVA. It was quiet now except for the grunts and groans coming from the life-and-death struggle between Rich and the NVA soldier.

Jeff pulled his pistol to kill the NVA. McCall grabbed his hand. "Rich can handle it. Let him."

Jeff started to say something to McCall about the blood on both of Richardson's pants legs, but then realized it wasn't needed. McCall knew Rich was wounded. Jeff knew the two men had been together for years. If McCall said let it go, he had a reason.

Richardson flipped the NVA over onto his back. Holding the man's knife hand, he brought his knee up hard between the NVA's legs. The man's face crumpled in pain. Rich squeezed and shook the wrist holding the knife until it dropped free, then released the empty hand. Rich placed one hand on the crown of the NVA's head and the other on his chin; with a quick twist, he broke the man's neck. With his breath coming in short gasps, Rich pulled himself off the lifeless form and leaned back against the trees. Looking up, he saw McCall grinning at him.

McCall said, "Boy, you niggers sure fight dirty!"

"Fuck you, McCall!"

"Not today, sweetheart. I got a splittin' headache. How's the legs?"

"It hurts like hell!"

McCall pulled his knife and began cutting away

Richardson's pants legs as he said, "Jeff, check out the other Americans. See if any of 'em are still alive."

"Roger, boss."

Brown came over and knelt beside Richardson, his face covered with blood and sweat—the blood was from the head wound he had inflicted on the NVA. Pushing Rich's sleeve up, he started to give him a shot of morphine.

Rich grabbed his hand. "Hey, man, I don't need none of that shit."

Continuing his work without looking up, JD said, "You're gonna take the shit, anyway, an' that's a fuckin' order." Before he could object further, Brown jabbed the needle into Richardson's arm.

"Ouch! God almighty, man. You ain't in no fuckin' dart-throwin' contest!"

"Sorry, man. I can't stand needles. I like to get it over with quick."

McCall finished cutting away the pants leg and gently raised and lowered the right leg. Pain shot across Rich's face but he didn't say anything. JD moved to the left leg. The minute he started to raise it, Rich cried out.

"Oh, Jesus, JD."

Trying not to show concern in his voice, JD said, "The two rounds in the right leg went straight through, but the two that caught you in the left must have splintered a bone. You lay on back and me and . . . What'd you say your name was?"

"Brown. Phil Brown."

"Well, Brown, let's fix this old cripple up before he starts cryin' all over us."

Richardson was amused in spite of his pain, but he could tell by the look on Brown's face that the man thought JD McCall was a total wacko.

Lieutenant Esswain appeared. Brown introduced McCall.

McCall shook hands as he said, "Sure was glad to see

you drop in, sir. We figured command had wrote us off."

"Glad we could make it, McCall. But to tell you the truth, if you hadn't left that beeper of yours on, there's no telling where we would have come down. It was a thousand-to-one shot coming down where we did."

"Well, Lieutenant, it's about time we started having a little luck on this gangbang. Up till now, the damn thing's been an uphill battle all the way."

"From what I hear about you, Sergeant McCall, you make your own breaks. Colonel Baron told me I could learn a lot working with you and, from what I've seen so far, he didn't exaggerate."

McCall lit up a cigarette and took a long drag off it. "Colonel Baron said that, did he? I'm surprised he isn't with you."

"Oh, he wanted to come, believe me. Colonel Davis said no way!"

"How many folks did you bring in with you, Lieutenant?"

"Twenty, counting Sergeant Brown and myself. We've got nine still alive here. I'm not sure about Sergeant Smith."

McCall said, "He was with me for a while. I sent him and five others around on the flank, but haven't heard from him since."

Hotujec walked up just as JD finished. "JD, we heard one hell of a heavy volley go down behind us before you gave me the order to move out."

More as a statement than a question, McCall said, "Ambush."

Jeff nodded. "Sounded like it."

McCall dropped his cigarette to the ground. "Lieutenant, Jeff and I will go out and check around for Smith. I'd like you to set up a perimeter around Sergeant Richardson and hang tight until we get back."

"No problem, Sergeant McCall. Colonel Davis said

you'd be in charge and that if I had any doubts about it, just to ask you."

"Thank you, sir. Jeff, you ready?"

"Yeah, JD, but I want to show you something first."

Hotujec swung the NVA radio up in front of McCall. "Took it off the commander of this NVA outfit. Guess who he was talking to before I blew his shit away?"

A knowing grin crossed McCall's face. "Our boy Thanh!"

"You got it."

"Any chance he knows we've got this thing?"

"No way, boss. I waited until the captain was through transmitting. I heard Thanh tell him he was heading this way and that he'd give him a call when they were in position."

McCall turned to Brown and asked, "Sergeant Brown, I know you people had to have brought some radios in with you. Am I correct?"

Brown nodded. "We brought in three, but one was destroyed in the trees and Sergeant Smith had the other two with his people."

McCall looked at Hotujec. "Now we really got to try and find Smith, and damn fast. Those radios are worth more than gold right now." He turned to Brown. "Jeff and I are going out and make a sweep for Smith. The lieutenant said something earlier about you knowing three different languages. Is that right?"

"Yes. Thai, French, and Vietnamese."

"Out-fucking-standing. I want you to monitor this NVA radio while we're gone. When the lieutenant gets back here, I want you to tell him to round up all the AK-47s and ammo that he can find and bring them into the perimeter."

"You got it, JD."

A light rain had begun to fall as McCall and Hotujec moved slowly and silently through the jungle. McCall tried to analyze how many NVA were possibly still roaming around. Captain Quan had been leading a platoon. Subtracting the number of known dead NVA, McCall figured there were at least ten unaccounted for. Either one squad had broken and run, or they were sitting in position waiting to ambush the hell out of anything that moved their way. To make matters worse, JD knew that Thanh was moving into position and that he would be coming up on that radio again, and soon. Time was important, but so was finding Smith.

McCall knelt down on one knee to listen for any sound of movement. There was nothing but the sound of raindrops against the leaves of the jungle canopy above his head. Hotujec faced to the rear and did the same. Both men studied the dense jungle for any sign of movement or irregular patterns.

Jeff whispered, "JD, maybe that squad did split when the shit hit the fan."

McCall didn't answer. He had been fighting this war for over four years now, and one thing he had learned in that time was that there was a hell of a difference between a Vietcong and a damn NVA regular. A VC would fire a few shots at you and then run like hell, but if an NVA opened up on you, brother, you better make sure you brought your lunch because you were going to be there all day. That guy wasn't runnin' nowhere. It was experience that gave McCall a deep gut feeling that these boys hadn't run—they were waiting. . . .

Having watched Sergeant Smith die, the old NVA sergeant moved his squad back into the thick jungle cover. The young soldier who had been scolded by him earlier stared in awe at his gray-haired leader, as did the entire squad. What stories they would have to tell once they returned home!

Slowly wiping the rain from his tired eyes, the old man watched intently for any sign of movement. It had been 15 minutes since he had heard the last sound of gunfire. He wondered who the victors had been. Were there ever any victors in this game? If he had been winning this war all these years, then why was he hiding now? No, it wasn't the victory or the victors, it was the survivors that mattered. Scanning the jungle once more, the old man decided he would wait another 30 minutes before moving.

The minutes seemed like hours. One of the younger NVA soldier's legs cramped, and the urge to relieve himself increased the pain. The sergeant had reminded them that they must remain perfectly still and in position, but the pressure was becoming unbearable. If he wet his pants, his comrades would surely tease him forever.

Slowly removing his hand from his rifle, the young trooper began a slow roll onto his side; even this slight movement brought new life to his half-paralyzed legs. He found that he could not undo the buttons of his pants in this position, yet the thought of relief being only moments away intensified his urgency to get them undone. He pushed himself up on one elbow, his fingers working frantically at the fly. He could feel the wetness rushing forward. In final desperation he jerked at the buttons with such force that he pulled himself off balance and fell over on his back. The dead tree branches that he landed on cracked with a force that startled the whole squad. All eyes turned toward the soldier with the wet spot spreading on the front of his pants. His humiliation deepened with his effort to roll back over on his stomach: more noise from the crackling branches. He could feel the sergeant's eyes burning through him. Regaining his position, he dared not look the old man in the face. Instead, he buried his face in his hands, hoping the others could not see him cry.

McCall quietly released the white-phosphorus grenade from his web gear and signaled Jeff to do the same. The sound of the cracking limbs had come from a heavy clump of palms less than 15 yards away. Choosing each step carefully, McCall and Hotujec moved closer to their target. Both men gripped the grenades tightly, and slowly pulled the pins. McCall felt the instant pressure on the long, thin, spoon-like release, awaiting only the release of his hand to begin its deadly five-second countdown. McCall held up three fingers; Jeff nodded. On the count of three, both men heaved the heavy grenades into the palms, then dropped to the ground. There was a slight popping sound as the releases flew off the grenades. Somewhere in the clump of palms someone screamed, "Grenades!" With their rifles on full automatic, McCall and Hotujec waited.

The wait wasn't a long one. There were two shattering explosions. Then huge clouds of white smoke billowed upward into the jungle canopy, the flying steel stripping the trees of leaves, limbs, and bark. The fortunate ones died instantly, the others screamed in untold pain as the phosphorus burned through their bodies.

One NVA with his shirt and hair on fire broke through the palms. JD and Jeff opened fire simultaneously, spinning the man 360 degrees and into the ground. Smoke rose up from the lifeless form as the white-hot phosphorus continued to burn.

Two more NVA soldiers broke from the smoldering cover, their uniforms smoking. Jeff fired a short burst, cutting one of them in half. McCall brought the other one down with two shots to the head. As the body slumped to the ground, JD noticed the huge wet spot on the front of the man's pants.

The smell of burnt wood and scorched flesh hung heavy in the air. McCall waited until the thick smoke had all but disappeared before he moved forward. JD signaled Jeff to cover him. Stepping over the smoldering body of one of the NVA, he could see the ripped and torn bodies of the rest of the squad among the palms. The sizzling sound the phosphorus made as it burned through flesh reminded McCall of bacon cooking.

As McCall turned to wave Hotujec forward, he caught a sudden movement out of the corner of his eye and dropped to his left. A bayonet ripped through his shirt sleeve. Grabbing the barrel of the rifle behind the bayonet, JD jerked the NVA soldier down. Pain shot through McCall's body as the NVA fell on his injured hand. Hotujec brought his rifle up to fire, but the two men were too close together. He couldn't fire—he might hit McCall.

Throwing his leg up and over the NVA, McCall rolled on top of his chest. He pinned one of his arms down long enough to reach up and pull his K-Bar from its sheath in his web gear. As JD raised the long, razor-sharp knife, his eyes met those in the half-burnt face of the old gray-haired man. The eyes showed no fear. Instead, the old NVA sergeant stopped struggling, lowered his arms to the ground, and muttered painfully, "End this burning hell for me. . . . Do it quickly, please." McCall hesitated for only a moment, then brought the knife down through the dying man's heart, killing him instantly.

Jeff handed McCall his rifle. Both men stared down at the old man. "He asked me to make it quick," McCall said in a strange tone. JD had seen something beyond the pain in the man's eyes. It was like a glimmer of relief.

"Jesus, JD, how old do you think he was?"

"I don't know, Jeff, but you can bet he's seen a lot more combat than either one of us ever will. I've got a feeling we'll find Smith and his people around here someplace close. I'll give the lieutenant a call on the URC-10 and let him know we're all right. You check around, an' be careful."

Hotujec didn't have to go far. Less than 30 yards away, he found Smith and the other members of his team—they had been cut to pieces. There would be no burial, only a location noted on a map for a small group of men that had played the game and lost.

Major Thanh brought his platoon to a halt. The two explosions and the weapons fire had come from the west. He estimated the distance at 800 yards. The firing had not lasted long and now it was quiet once more. Salt and Pepper moved up alongside the major and awaited their orders.

Pepper leaned forward and said with a slur, "What's the matter, Major-baby, you gettin' cold feet?"

Thanh didn't bother to turn around. "Impatience has cost more than one man his life. If you desire to test that theory, then by all means feel free to do so."

"All right, by God, I will!" Pepper responded hotly. "I'm not afraid of these motherfuckers."

Salt started to say something but the major stopped him. "No. Let the fool go."

Raising his voice so that the other members of the NVA unit could hear him, Pepper said, "I'm a fool, am I? Well, we'll see who looks like the fool when I tell headquarters how the legendary Major Thanh stood by and let a fellow officer and his whole command go into battle on their own without even making an effort to help them. When they find out it was me who went to the fuckin' rescue, we'll see who comes out lookin' like a fool."

Thanh now stood face to face with the black soldier, his hand resting on the grip of his PPK pistol. Salt moved back a few feet and slowly shifted his rifle in Pepper's direction. The final confrontation was about to go down. . . . The tension of the moment was shattered by four thunderous explosions that rocked the jungle. Massive rifle fire erupted to the west. All three men dropped to the ground, the confrontation forgotten.

Salt inched up next to Thanh. "Jesus Christ, Major, that firefight's close by. You better check with Captain

Quan. That's a hell of a lot of firepower for just a few Americans.''

Thanh agreed and grabbed the handset of his radio. "Captain Quan, this is Major Thanh. Come in.''

Waiting a full minute, he tried again, "Captain Quan, this is Major Thanh. What is your situation?'' It was only after he had unkeyed the handset that Thanh realized he had made the same mistake he had earlier accused Quan of making. In the excitement, Thanh had forgotten to use the radio call signs.

A muffled voice came over the radio. "Major, this is Quan. We have the Americans surrounded, but I do not have enough men to close the circle. What is your position?''

Thanh hesitated for a moment as he studied the mike. "Something is not right. That does not sound like Captain Quan's voice.''

Three more rapid explosions echoed through the trees as the sound of automatic-weapons fire picked up. Pepper screamed, "Goddammit, Major. The man's in a fuckin' firefight! You said yourself he was a shaky officer at best—naturally he don't sound the same! The mother's scared shitless!''

Thanh still hesitated. Pepper could be right, he thought, but still there was something about the whole situation. . . . Quan's voice came over the radio again pleading for help.

Pepper was not about to let this opportunity go by. "What's the matter, hero? You don't even trust your own damn officers now?''

Thanh's reply was interrupted by the voice of Quan speaking rapidly, the excitement apparent in his words. "Major, where are you? I am losing too many men. We cannot close them in without your help. Major Thanh, are you still there?''

Pepper never took his eyes off the major; he was enjoying every minute of this. Thanh still did not answer. Pepper stood up and sneered at Thanh. "Hero, my black ass!"

The black soldier moved to his squad, and Thanh could not hear what he was saying. However, it was obvious from the looks Thanh was getting from the squad that the conversation was about the major's refusal to engage in the firefight to help Captain Quan. Thanh fought back the urge to kill Pepper. He hated to admit it, but for now he needed the big man to lead the squad in the upcoming battle. But afterward . . . that would be a different story. Thanh pressed the mike switch and spoke calmly into the radio. "Captain Quan, this is Thanh. We are located some 800 yards east of your location. How many enemy are you engaged with at this time?"

"Major Thanh," the voice replied, "so very good to hear your voice. We estimate there are no more than six to eight Americans still alive, but they are putting up an honorable fight, sir."

"Very well. Where do you need my platoon the most, Captain?"

"The opening of the circle is to our east. Since you are already there it would accomplish my plan if you could move your people up to the base of the hill that should be directly in front of you. There is a small ravine at the base. I believe the Americans will attempt to break out in that direction. Your unit shall provide the blocking force."

"I understand, Captain. We shall start moving immediately. You keep our friends occupied until we are in position. It should not take us more than 20 minutes. Once that time limit has passed, you will let up on your weapons fire. We shall then see which way the rabbit runs. This is Thanh, out."

The major gathered his troops around him. "Gentlemen, we have a situation that should not take more than an hour of our time. Captain Quan and his platoon have pinned down the Americans we are seeking. He has left them only one direction in which to escape. We shall move in that direction and serve as a blocking force for Captain Quan. As far as we know, the Americans do not know we are here. I wish to keep it that way. Strict discipline and absolute silence must be maintained once we move into position. Are there any questions?"

No one spoke.

"How about you, my impatient friend?" Thanh's words were aimed at Pepper. "Do you think you can contain your urge to die, at least until the Americans are in sight?"

Pepper only smiled. "We shall see who dies, Major."

"So we shall. Now, let's move out."

Thanh glanced at Salt as he walked past. The American nodded and smiled. After today they would both get out of these stinking jungles and spend the rest of the war in Hanoi. . . .

Sergeant Brown replaced the handset on the NVA radio and turned to McCall. "Well, what d'you think? Did he buy it?"

McCall winked. "Hell, Brown, you even had me convinced! I'm glad to see all those months of language school in California weren't wasted on beach bunnies and booze. Ya done good, Brown."

JD turned to Rich. "Okay, buddy, I'm leavin' four guys with you. I want them scattered out and firing those AKs, mixed with a little M16 crap every now and then. Lieutenant, you and I will split the rest of the people and head for that ravine. You got your C-4 and claymore mines?"

"Roger, JD, we're good to go."

McCall paused and offered his good hand to Esswain. "Lieutenant, just in case things don't turn out right, I want you to know it's been a pleasure workin' with you."

The lieutenant shook the tall, blond sergeant's hand and said, "Been an experience for damn sure, JD. But don't worry, we can pull it off."

"Hope you're right, sir. Ya better get movin' now. We'll be along in a few minutes."

"Right. Okay, guys, let's hit it." As Esswain and half the team pulled out, JD and Hotujec knelt down by Richardson. McCall unhooked a grenade from his web gear and handed it to him. "Rich, you keep these guys firing for about five minutes after we move out, then pull 'em in real close and find yourselves a place to hide. If we don't make it back here, you wait until dark, then start headin' south to the DMZ. You shouldn't have anyone trackin' you—they'll figure they got us all."

Richardson tossed the grenade back to McCall, "Hell, man, you're gonna need that damn thing more than me! And I don't need no four fuckin' bodyguards neither!"

McCall stood up and said, "Man, you're really a pain in the ass sometimes, do you know that? Remind me to fire your black ass when we get back. But till then, mother, you're gonna do this shit my way. Come on, Jeff, we gotta get movin'."

Hotujec placed his hand on Richardson's shoulder. "You be cool, man."

"You too, Jeff—an' try to keep an eye on that long, lanky piece of shit for me."

"You know it, buddy."

McCall had already walked away without looking back. Rich watched as the last man of the team vanished into the jungle. He knew McCall was right —there was no way he would have been able to help out in the battle with his fucked-up legs. He also knew why JD had left four men with him. If it went down wrong in the ravine, Rich would have two men for security and two to carry a stretcher. Rich knew all this, but it didn't make him feel any better.

Esswain and his team had finished placing the C-4 explosives along the slope of the ravine. The claymore mines were wired and positioned at the south end. McCall and Hotujec had done the same thing on the north end. There was nothing to do now but wait. Thanh was no fool. JD knew the only chance Striker had would be to catch Thanh's people by surprise. The NVA outnumbered them three to one. The first 30 seconds would determine the winners from the losers.

A light rain began to fall as the sounds of the fake firefight to the east slacked off, then stopped altogether.

XIV.

Thanh checked his watch. It had been exactly five minutes since Captain Quan had begun the sporadic weapons fire. The platoon was still not in position and he knew that his verbal exchange with Pepper had cost them valuable time. From the edge of the trees, Thanh could see the gently sloping ravine Quan had spoken of. He knew he should send out scouts, but there was no time. The rifle fire from Quan's position had stopped now. The Americans would be trying to break out at any moment, and Thanh had to have his people ready.

Waving to Pepper's squad, Thanh motioned them to the right slope, then pointed to Salt and the left slope. Both men acknowledged the signal and split off to their assigned areas. Thanh would swing wide right and block off the end of the ravine with his squad.

McCall and Hotujec watched from the crest of the north slope as Thanh gave his orders.

"We got 'em, Jeff," whispered JD, as a grin of satisfaction spread across his face.

"Yeah, man. All three of the bastards in one barrel," replied Hotujec.

The two Green Berets kept their vigil as the two traitors split up, one left, one right. The one called Salt was approaching with knowledgeable caution. But the black guy was moving his people with total disregard for even the basic tactics of movement. No flankers, no point, just a mob of people rushing along the side of the hill.

Jeff whispered, "I count fifteen to the right side and fourteen on the left. But I don't see that fuckin' major."

"I got the same count, Jeff. That asshole Thanh is moving his people around to cover the end of the ravine. You wanna take a bet on that, kid?"

"Hell no, JD. My question is, will the son of a bitch come out in front of us or behind us?"

"Little late to change the battin' order now, Jeff. We'll just have to play it the way it falls. One thing for damn sure. At the rate that black guy's movin' he'll be on top of the lieutenant in a few minutes." Grabbing his radio, McCall said, "Lieutenant, give that black cat another twenty yards, then blow hell out of 'em. Be ready to cover your ass when you do. That major's still movin' around somewhere in those trees across from you. Out."

Pressing his selector switch to full automatic, McCall waited and watched as the faces of the NVA soldiers became clearer with each step they took. He thought of all the death and destruction that brought these two forces to this place and time. Within the narrow slopes of this valley would come the final confrontation.

The sound of distant thunder rolled up through the valley. The light rain that had begun earlier became a steady downpour. . . .

Esswain held the detonator for the claymores in his hand. For each step Pepper took, Esswain increased the pressure on the handle.

Every part of the valley seemed to explode instantaneously. Esswain, Brown, and Hotujec had fired their claymores within seconds of each other. In those few seconds, 3,000 ball bearings tore a destructive path through the rain-soaked ravine. The echoes of the explosions mixed with the screaming of men ripped apart by the lethal steel balls. Pepper's whole squad had been caught in the main blast and were gone. Pepper himself lay writhing on the ground, screaming, both of his hands gripping his mangled legs in a vain attempt to keep them attached to his body.

Salt's caution had paid off. His squad had not moved completely into the killing zone. He had lost two men and two were seriously wounded. Looking across the ravine to the other side, he saw Pepper holding his legs and rolling on the ground.

Salt waved his squad in the direction of the trees at the crest of the slope. As he struggled to gain a foothold in the wet grass, bullets came from everywhere at once, tearing up the ground around him. He still had nine members of his squad left alive. They were trying to lay down some type of cover fire for their team leader.

Reloading, one of the NVA jumped to his feet and began running up the slope, screaming and firing on full auto. Ten feet from the top, a bullet blew his head off. Salt knew if they could reach the top of the crest and the cover of the trees, they would have a chance. He watched as another squad member made a wild dash for the crest. This one reached the top only to be torn to pieces by rifle fire. Another prepared to make the charge, but Salt waved him back. If they were ever going to get over that crest, it was going to take a synchronized assault. Pulling two grenades from his web gear, he signaled the rest of the team to do the same. On the count of three they all tossed the grenades over the crest. The explosions vibrated through the valley and men cried out in agony as hot chunks of metal shredded their way through flesh and bone.

McCall could tell from the screams that he had lost more of his force. But the payback was going to be a bitch. Laying his rifle down, he picked up the detonator and waited.

Salt heard the screams from above. The sound gave him a surge of hope that he might still escape this hell. Yelling the order to advance, he moved with what was left of his squad for the crest of the slope.

Fifteen yards from the top, Salt slipped in the wet grass and fell hard to the ground. Bringing himself up on his hands and knees, he started to rise again, but his eyes immediately focused on an object that lay only yards from him. It had been covered with grass and mud, but the heavy downpour and his fall had dislodged one of the blocks from its concealed position. The rain gave the white block of plastic explosive a strange shimmering beauty.

Salt's eyes followed the wire coming from the C-4 up to and along the rim of the ravine. As his eyes followed the twisting, turning wire, he felt an indescribable terror come over his body. His eyes didn't have to follow the wire far.

McCall stood on the crest of the ridge, his rifle cradled in his arm with the bloody bandaged hand, and the detonator held high in his other hand.

The remaining members of the squad stopped suddenly, momentarily stunned by the unexpected appearance of the American on top of the hill. That moment cost them their lives, as McCall's team rushed over the crest and cut the NVA troopers down. They then shifted their rifles to Salt. The white deserter reluctantly threw his rifle to his side and raised his hands.

"Don't fire!" yelled McCall. "Fall back, we still have a squad of NVA runnin' around loose out here somewhere."

The team quickly moved back under cover, leaving McCall and Salt face to face.

The two stared at each other. Salt knew it was over. He would not get the chance to sit out the war in Hanoi. He would reap no benefits from his defection. He would become no more than another number broadcast on the ABC news, a fatality of the war in Vietnam. He wondered on which side of the board they would place his number: good guy or bad guy. It didn't seem to matter. There was still one chance left, a slim one, but at least it was worth a try. Sitting back on his heels with his hands clasped behind his head, Salt disguised his terror with a forced voice of professionalism. He spoke to McCall.

"Well, Green Beret, it would seem you have accomplished your mission. Your commanders will give you anything you want when you bring in me and that nigger over there." Salt nodded toward the hillside where Pepper lay motionless. "I commend you on a job very professionally done. Might I ask your name?"

McCall didn't move even a facial muscle as he prolonged his searing stare into Salt's eyes. Slowly lowering the detonator, he replied, "Sergeant JD McCall."

A look of recognition came over Salt's face, quickly replaced by an overwhelming look of despair. "Oh, yes. I've heard of you, Sergeant McCall. Do you realize you are highly respected in the north?" Seeking to regain his composure, Salt continued, "You are known for your outstanding professionalism. After this, your name will be known in all parts of Vietnam as the man who captured Salt and Pepper. You should be very proud."

McCall's voice had no feeling as he said, "Since you seem to know so much about me, would you care to tell me your name?"

Salt relaxed visibly. At least he had McCall talking. The detonator hung loosely in his hand at his side. Salt was still alive. Hell, going back for a court-martial was better than being dead. At a court-martial he could claim they had tortured him to the point that he had become a mental slave to the NVA, and how they had repeatedly broken his spirit and taken away his will-power to resist. Yes, a good lawyer and a convincing story might just get him out of this mess. Hell, the way the kids in the States were protesting the war right now, he could even become a hero to some. After these mental calculations, Salt answered McCall's question with a confident voice.

"Does it really matter what my name is, Sergeant McCall? The important thing is that I am your prisoner."

McCall's expression didn't change as he listened to this man who had tortured and killed his American brothers. The man had a point. McCall could take him back. It would even the score for the Nichols incident. He could go home again.

A slow, menacing smile spread across McCall's face as he said, "Fuck it!"

With one quick jerk of his hand, McCall fired the detonator. Half of the slope disappeared in a ground-shaking explosion. Along with it went an American who had chosen the wrong side in the game. Dropping the detonator to the ground, McCall calmly said, "Your name's shit now, asshole."

Lieutenant Esswain and Sergeant Brown moved their team down the slope to where Pepper lay wounded. Esswain waved the rest of the team across to link up with McCall. He and Brown would catch up with them in a few minutes.

Pepper's huge hands still gripped his torn legs. Brown knelt down by the black soldier's side and said, "Take it easy, man. I'm gonna do what I can for you, so just try and relax. Lieutenant, let me have some of that morphine you're packing."

Esswain hesitated before he said, "I don't think JD really gives a shit about keeping this bastard alive. If anything, you'll just be saving the poor bastard to face that big-ass Magnum of McCall's."

Brown stood up and glared at the officer. "Now look, Lieutenant, just because this black guy got a little screwed up in the head don't give McCall the right to blow him away. Besides, our orders from General Davis were capture, if possible. Well, I'm capturing this man and he's my prisoner. Now, give me that fuckin' morphine."

Esswain shook his head in disagreement but pulled the box from his shirt pocket and handed it to Brown. "Okay, man, okay. But if I were you, I wouldn't promise this dude that he has a hell of a lot of time left on earth."

Brown didn't answer. He knelt back down, pulled Pepper's sleeve up, and injected the painkiller. Tossing the box back to Esswain, Brown said, "Why don't you go on, Lieutenant, and remind McCall this man is my prisoner. You can send a couple of guys back to help me carry him."

"Are you sure, Brown? We still don't have a fix on that major and his people."

"Hell, yes, I'm sure, sir. Now, go on. McCall will need your help up there if he does find Thanh. Hell, don't worry. This guy's not going anywhere."

Brown had a good point. Both Pepper's legs were ripped beyond saving. That much damage, Esswain noted, would have killed an average man. But Pepper was a hell of a lot bigger than the average man.

Esswain glanced across the ravine. His team had just moved over the top on McCall's side. "OK, Brown. If you're sure you want to do this . . ."

"I'm positive! Now, get the hell out of here." Pausing a moment, Brown added, "I mean, get the hell out of here, *sir*."

Esswain grinned. "Okay, just watch yourself. I'll send some folks over to help you move him." With that, Esswain moved down the slope.

The morphine brought Pepper instant relief from the

burning pain and, for the first time since he had been hit, he removed his hands from his legs. Looking at Brown, he said, "Thanks, brother. Them white boys are all motherfuckers."

Brown had dropped down in a prone position next to Pepper and was watching the lieutenant move down the slope. "Don't 'brother' *me*, you asshole. You deserve everything you got. That lieutenant is right, you know. When JD McCall finds out you're still alive, he's liable to come down here and blow your balls off for you."

Pepper's voice sounded unconcerned as he said, "Is that the same guy that almost nailed us at Bien Cao?"

"You got it, man. And he was willing to chase your black ass all the way to Hanoi if he had to."

"Well, tell me somethin', man. You're with this guy McCall, so why the hell you helpin' me?"

Keeping his eyes on the lieutenant, Brown answered, "I ain't been here as long as McCall. I guess I just haven't gone kill-crazy yet. I figure these NVA must have screwed with your head pretty good while they had you locked up and I don't buy all the fucked-up stories I've heard about you and that guy they call Salt. I'd like to see you have a chance to explain what the hell happened, that's all. Jesus, we got enough black guys dyin' in this fuckin' war without killing 'em ourselves."

Pepper pushed himself up on his elbows and looked at the tangled mess that had once been his strong, powerful legs. "What a fuckin' mess! Claymore mine, right?"

Brown glanced at the man's legs, then at Pepper. "Yeah, McCall's idea."

Pepper moaned, then said, "Guess your lieutenant was right. This guy McCall didn't plan on taking any prisoners—"

"You got it, man," Brown interrupted. "Now, why don't you let me worry about McCall and you just lay back and ride out that drug trip I just gave you."

Esswain had stopped halfway down the slope and looked back up the hill. Brown waved him on as Pepper continued to talk. "Just one more question, Sergeant Brown. . . ."

Still waving at the lieutenant, Brown said, "If it'll shut you up, man, what's the question?"

"Well, I just wondered if you knew some other Special Forces guys named Wathers, Moore, and Todd . . . I think that was their names—they were screamin' so fuckin' much, it's hard to be sure if that's right."

Brown's hand stopped, suspended in his final wave to the lieutenant. He brought it down slowly and turned to look at Pepper.

Pepper had a wide grin on his face as he prodded in an unusually soft tone, "Well, did you know them, Brown?"

There was no longer a look of compassion on Brown's face. "You're goddamn right, I knew them."

The grin vanished from Pepper's face. "Good. Give 'em this when you see 'em!"

Brown saw it coming, but it was too late. Pepper's left arm swung wide and down with a powerful thrust. The 12-inch K-Bar knife split the spinal cord between the shoulder blades and came out the front of Brown's chest, pinning him to the ground. As Brown tried to scream, nothing but blood came from his mouth.

Pepper leaned close to Brown's ear and whispered, "Ya want some morphine, you fuckin' white man's nigger?"

It was wasted bitterness. Brown was dead. Prying the rifle from the dead man's hand, Pepper checked the chamber, then struggled to roll over into a prone position. The pain in his legs almost made him lose consciousness but, with one final push, he got into position. Slowly raising the rifle, he sighted in on

Lieutenant Esswain, who was now almost at the bottom of the hill. Slowly squeezing the trigger, Pepper gathered all his strength, forced it to his lungs, and screamed, "Lieutenant!"

Esswain stopped, turned, and looked back up the slope. The bullet shattered the young officer's skull before the sound of the shot echoed through the valley.

Pepper released the rifle and rolled over on his back. Staring up at the colorless sky, rain falling lightly on his dying body, Pepper whispered, "Told you them damn Green Berets weren't shit. . . ."

The rain continued to fall, but on uncaring eyes. Pepper was dead.

From the crest of the north slope, McCall lowered the binoculars and gazed at an invisible spot on the ground. Hotujec walked up to him. "Who fired that shot, JD?"

Without looking up, McCall answered, "A dying man who took his hatred with him . . . but it doesn't matter now. How many people have we got left?"

Jeff peered down at the ground to see what his leader was staring at, but seeing nothing but the brown earth of the Vietnam jungle, he answered, "That grenade assault by Salt cut us pretty thin. Counting you and me, we have seven—that's not counting the lieutenant and Sergeant Brown. They haven't come in yet."

McCall didn't say anything. The spot on the ground had become a buffer against the inner pain that McCall was feeling.

"Did you hear me, JD? As soon as we get the lieutenant and Brown linked up, we can move out for Rich's position."

McCall looked up slowly. Handing Jeff the glasses, he said softly, "The lieutenant and Brown won't be joining us. They're staying down there. Come on, we've got to get out of here. That damn major's still running around here somewhere, and I want that bastard's ass."

Hotujec held the glasses to his eyes and surveyed the mass of bodies that littered the green grass below. Slowly lowering the glasses, he drew in a sharp breath before he said, "It's over, JD. It's time to go home."

McCall angrily turned to the young sergeant. "Like hell it is, kid! I came out here to kill all three of those motherfuckers. I say when this operation's over."

Hotujec had expected the outburst, but was determined not to back down. "That's bullshit, JD. Look at your hand; the damn thing's twice its normal size. If we start back right now, you might be able to save the damn thing."

McCall's voice was tense and unemotional as he drew each word out slowly and clearly. "It's *my* fuckin' hand. If I have to cut the damn thing off myself, I will. But that major's going to pay."

"Oh, sure. And what are you gonna do about Rich's legs? You gonna cut *them* off too? You gonna drag his ass all around this pisshole just because you have to prove something? It's over, man. Jesus, JD, you already done more than they expected anyway. Now, let's take Rich and go home."

McCall looked out across the valley. He knew what Jeff said was true. The hand had become so painful that the slightest movement sent jolts of pain to every nerve in his body. Rich was lying back there with holes in both legs, and within the next 24 hours his pain would become unbearable. McCall had lost count of how many people were already dead from this operation, but it had cost too much. Salt and Pepper were dead—that was some consolation. Hotujec was right. It was time to go home.

"OK, Jeff, round 'em up. We'll go back, pick up Rich, an' head for the DMZ. This weather's supposed to start breaking sometime tomorrow. The closer we are to the Z the sooner we get picked up. You hang on to that

NVA radio. Since Smith's were destroyed, that's our only sure FM link with the firebases."

Hotujec had been watching McCall warily as he pondered silently. Now he smiled. "Hope there's no hard feelings about me soundin' off like that, JD."

"Hell no, kid. You done everybody a favor. Thanks."

Jeff nodded. "Anytime. I'll bet Rich is having a cat right about now."

"Yeah, you better give him a call on the emergency radio. Tell him we're headed back to his location. We should be coming in about thirty minutes from now."

"Okay, JD," a relieved Hotujec said, as he pulled his radio and walked away.

McCall took one last look into the valley below at the lifeless form of Lieutenant Esswain and said softly, "Sorry things worked out like they did, Lieutenant; you done good, sir, you done real good."

Picking up his rifle, JD McCall walked off into the jungle. They were going home. . . .

Major Thanh and his squad had made it halfway to the end of the ravine when the claymore mines went off. He placed his people under cover, took the squad leader, and moved to the edge of the ridge. From there he watched the life-and-death struggle as it unfolded below.

Thanh watched as Pepper rolled in pain on the side of the slope. He felt a moment of pity for the loud-mouthed black soldier. If only they had trusted his instincts. Now it was too late; Thanh was only able to watch as his people were destroyed before his eyes. And he watched Pepper shoot the American at the base of the slope, and realized that he had witnessed one man's ultimate act of defiance.

He had felt a sudden flow of hope for Salt as the white soldier rushed up the incline. He listened in vain as the squad leader who lay next to him whispered, "Hurry, hurry, only a little farther." That hope was shattered when Thanh grabbed the squad leader's arm and whispered, "There, on the crest of the ridge."

Staring across the valley of death, Thanh saw the tall American holding a rifle in one hand. He did not have to guess what the man held in the other. Thanh knew that the man who had planned this ambush was a professional, and would have explosives planted along all routes of escape, especially the slopes.

Thanh watched the exchange of words between Salt and the American. He saw Salt relax for a moment, then in the next moment saw his friend vanish in a cloud of smoke and flying earth.

Thanh lost control of his feelings in the seconds that followed, and would have given away his position if it hadn't been for his squad leader. Thanh's only thought was to open up on the American who stood so brazenly on the rim of the ravine, and to bring him down in the same cold, callous, professional way the Green Beret had ended Salt's life. The squad leader grabbed the barrel of the major's rifle and reminded him that they were still unsure of the strength and location of the rest of the Americans. To fire now would surely get them all killed.

Those few seconds of intervention allowed Thanh to regain his composure. He removed his finger from the trigger of the rifle and placed his hand flat on the ground. The hand was trembling, but the squad leader pretended not to notice and looked away. Thanh lowered his head to the weapon and closed his eyes. It never seemed to end. The constant killing, the fear of having friends, of loving someone. He silently asked himself if it would ever end. Now he would have to track down this American who had killed his friend. It was the code of the game.

The two NVA watched McCall and his team leave.

The squad leader asked if they would go home now, or follow the Americans.

"We must go after them, comrade. It is the way of these things. We cannot return home until all of them are dead or we are."

The squad leader didn't say any more as the two men departed to round up what was left of one of North Vietnam's crack units.

The battle with Salt and Pepper had been a costly one. Of the 20 people Esswain and Smith had brought in, only eight were still alive. Of those eight, three had frag wounds, but were able to fight. Rich was completely out of action with his bad legs; McCall's hand was getting worse. He could feel fever setting in—a sure sign of infection. Jeff had been the only member of the original Striker team who'd been lucky. He didn't have a scratch.

McCall gathered his ragtag team around him and spread the map on the ground so that all could see it. "Gentlemen, I figure we are less than eighteen miles from the DMZ. It's almost noon, so if we move in the next thirty minutes we should be able to make the Z by first light tomorrow. Colonel Davis should have a Mike Force in the area sometime late this evening. Once we link up with them we're home free. Are there any questions?"

One of the Deliverance team that had been with Richardson during the battle asked, "Did we get all three of the targets, Sergeant McCall?"

"No, I'm afraid not," McCall replied. "We did nail the Salt and Pepper team, but Major Thanh got away. The honorable major chose to sit this one out. He never got into the shootout. But he's still out there somewhere. Keep that in mind while we're moving. We ain't home yet. Any other questions?"

McCall looked around the small circle of his diminishing force. No one spoke.

"Okay, then, I want two men to rig up a litter for Sergeant Richardson. The rest of you gather up all the ammo you can carry. I hope we don't need it, but better safe than sorry."

The team members moved to their assigned tasks as McCall sat down next to Richardson and lit a cigarette. "How's the legs, Rich?"

"Well, JD, Jesse Owens ain't gonna have to worry about me breakin' his track records anymore."

McCall forced a grin as he leaned back against the rocks. JD McCall was tired. Not just physically, but emotionally as well. The needless death of Sergeant Brown—why hadn't he just shot Pepper and moved on? Maybe that was it. That was McCall's answer to everything. If it don't do what you want, you shoot it, you don't like something, you shoot it, you don't like someone, you shoot 'im. . . . Everything was so easy in Vietnam. You just shoot everything. Pretty soon it just doesn't matter anymore. That was why Brown was dead now. He hadn't been here long enough. But his inexperience had also killed Esswain.

As if reading JD's mind, Rich asked, "How about that guy Brown and the lieutenant?"

McCall's voice was sad and low as he answered, "Pepper got 'em both."

Richardson pounded his fist into the dirt. "This has been a damn expensive trip, JD."

"It sure as hell has. At least we sent those two bastards Salt and Pepper straight to hell this morning."

A heavy silence arose between the two men. Finally, Rich asked, "What's weighing so heavy on your mind there, boss?"

McCall crushed out his cigarette before he answered, "I was just thinking about our boy Thanh. We hurt him real bad out there this morning. He can't have more than ten or eleven people left, and he's not really sure how many folks we've got left. I believe that was why he held back and didn't commit his troops to the battle. He's no fool, Rich."

Richardson shifted his position to get a better look at McCall. "What d'you think he'll do now?"

"That's what bothers me, Rich. I'm just not sure. He's a professional who lost three-fourths of his command, and he's not sure of the force he's up against. Also, if I've read this map right, he's only fifteen to twenty miles from his home base. The professional thing to do would be to drop the whole fuckin' mess and head for home."

Richardson's face was serious as he said, "You mean write the whole thing off as a bad day at the office."

"You got it."

"OK, JD, that's the logical shit. Now, you tell me what you'd do if *you* were in Thanh's situation."

McCall answered without hesitation, "Hell, Rich. If anybody shot us up that fuckin' bad, I'd go after their ass with everything I had left."

Rich gave a low moan. "Man, I was afraid you were gonna say some shit like that! Where do ya think he'll try us?"

"It'll be before we get to the Z, you can bet your ass on it."

"Shit, JD, we ain't hardly got enough ass left to bet with."

The litter was ready and Rich didn't want to ask any more questions. He'd already gotten too many answers.

Placing his point man out front and flankers to the left and right, McCall gave the order to move out.

Thanh was becoming impatient—his trackers had been gone for an hour. Calling his squad leader, an old veteran named Thieu, the major was about to dispatch two more men to search out the trackers when they appeared out of the jungle. Their mission had been successful. They had found the Americans only a mile from the valley. They had counted a total of 11. One of them, a black soldier, had been placed on a litter, both of his legs heavily bandaged. The Americans were heading south in the direction of the DMZ. Thanh asked about the tall American with the bandaged hand. "Yes, he was there. This one was obviously the leader."

Thanh commended the two scouts on their excellent job and told them to get some rest. The squad would move in 30 minutes. Thanh sat and studied his map. His primary interest was the main route and the terrain that ran to the south from the Americans' position. The tall American was experienced—he had lured Thanh into a trap this morning with devastating effectiveness, and Thanh had no reason to think that he would get careless now. He calculated that the American unit was less than 18 miles from the DMZ. It was almost two in the afternoon. Carrying a wounded man on a stretcher through the dense jungle would slow them down considerably. There was no way they could possibly reach the DMZ before dark.

With his eyes still locked to the map, Thanh tried to put himself in the Americans' place—which route would Thanh take?

Looking away from the map, Thanh rubbed his tired eyes. This simple operation had become one of the toughest he had been on in years. The loss of his friend Salt still weighed heavily in his thoughts. He looked around at what remained of a 48-man unit. Counting himself, he had only 11 men left, and of that number, five were on their first operation—they were young and inexperienced. The Bien Cao operation was to have been a simple training mission for them, but it had become a matter of life or death. Only the squad leader, Thieu, had been with Thanh for many years. His experience would be invaluable.

Thanh knew he was breaking every rule that he had been taught in Moscow. He should be moving his remaining people back to the north and the safety of his headquarters. But then, those in Moscow did not understand the attitude of the Vietnamese high council in Hanoi. It had been Thanh who had persuaded the council to let Salt and Pepper join him in the field. There were those who would more than welcome the chance to hold him up to ridicule for his actions and for the loss of the two American deserters. The Green Beret leader did not realize that he had placed Thanh in a "have to" situation. Thanh's hopes of reassignment to Hanoi would depend on his ability to kill or capture these Green Berets, to drag the killer of Salt before the council in chains. That would quiet his enemies and save Thanh's reputation. If only he had more soldiers like Thieu.

Thanh turned back to the map. The key was the wounded American on the litter. The American leader was heading south. He had broken off his pursuit—that could only mean he was seriously worried about the wounded black soldier and was trying to get him back to the south as soon as possible. But Thanh knew that to carry a litter through these jungles without the use of trails was a long and tedious venture, and for a wounded man, time was an enemy in itself.

Tracing the terrain features on the map with his finger, Thanh found only one route that would provide a minimum amount of climbing and heavy jungle brush. He had studied the American leader this morning as he stood on the crest of the ridge. The man epitomized confidence and self-assurance. His total disregard for the firing going on around him as he stood there in the open said much about his character. It was these factors in the American's personality that would make him take chances that a lesser leader would not. True, the cold, uncaring way that he killed Salt momentarily lit a fire in Thanh's very soul. But there was something about this enemy that Thanh respected in a strange way. The man was a professional much like himself, and whether it be a French uniform or an American uniform, Thanh had always respected professionalism among warriors. In this world of modern warfare, computerized weapons, and guns that could kill from miles away, professional respect and honor among true warriors were becoming things of the past. This American leader would be a worthy opponent for Thanh.

Thieu approached the major and said, "Sir, we are ready to go whenever you are."

His thoughts interrupted, Thanh said, "Thank you, Thieu. Please gather the men around so that I may speak to them."

"Yes, sir."

As the men stood around him, Thanh could not help but notice how young so many of them were. He knew that the look of youth would soon disappear, and for some, this would be their last day on this earth.

He began, "Men, we have suffered a sad and terrible loss today. Many of our comrades have died in the struggle to free our country. Those that have committed this act of murder on our friends are seeking to flee to the south and safety. I do not intend for them to live to brag of their actions today. We shall intercept them before they reach the DMZ and destroy them. Then and only then shall we return to our home. Is there anyone who does not agree with my choice of action?"

There was no disagreement. Instead, there burst forth a wild cheer from the NVA soldiers. They were ready to fight to the death.

"Thieu, I believe our men are ready to go. Move them out."

Thieu saluted. "Yes, Commander."

As his troops filed past him, Thanh thought of the girl in his dream, the one with the long black hair who awaited him in Hanoi. As the last man passed, Thanh's vision drifted into unfulfilled memory. . . .

XV.

The overhanging clouds finally began to break up, allowing the sun to peer through every now and then. The heat and humidity made breathing hard. The team rotated the responsibility of carrying Richardson. The intensity of the heat and the weight of the litter sapped the strength of men already battle-weary. Jungle vines and thick brush were obstacles they had to fight every step of the way. Tired and dejected, Striker One fought the jungle for three hours now and covered barely three miles.

Hotujec dropped back to talk with McCall. "JD, we're makin' lousy time in this thick shit."

McCall wiped the sweat from his eyes. "Tell me something I don't know. How's Rich holding up?"

"He passes out off an' on. His legs are starting to swell pretty bad. It don't look good, JD."

McCall's web gear got tangled in some vines. Ripping the small vines from the tree, he said, "Fuckin' shit! Jeff, get up there and stop the team. Tell 'em to take a break in place. I wanna' look at this fuckin' map again. There's gotta be a better way through this crap!"

After halting the team, Hotujec rejoined McCall. "Jesus Christ, JD. I can't remember ever being this damn hot."

McCall didn't answer. He spread the map on the ground and scanned the terrain around him. To his right the hills were even steeper. To the left lay the Ho Chi Minh trail, the most traveled road in Vietnam.

During the day you hardly ever saw anything moving on it, but at night it became the Times Square of North Vietnam. McCall knew they had no chance of making the DMZ before dark; traveling at night was an open invitation for a shootout with the NVA. But he had to be close enough to the Z to link up with the Mike Force in the first hours of dawn. Leaning back on his rucksack, McCall asked Hotujec, "What d'you think, Jeff? Do we keep fighting this shit for two more days or do we try to run the parallel trails of the Ho Chi?"

Hotujec was stunned that JD had asked him his opinion. "Hell, JD, I don't know. That's why you're the man. I know one thing for damn sure, Rich is hurtin' real bad. The longer we take, the more chance he has of losin' his legs. We gotta pick up the pace."

"Goddammit, Jeff, I know that! That's why I'm askin' you."

Hotujec saw the pain in McCall's face as he spoke. He knew it was JD's hand bothering him again. "You better let me take a look at that hand, boss, it's . . ."

"Forget it—we've gotta figure a way out of this shit."

Jeff started to argue the point but decided against it. He had caught the foul-smelling odor of decaying flesh the moment he sat down next to McCall. Gangrene had set in. JD was going to lose his hand—if not his arm—and Jeff realized that McCall had already written it off. That was obvious by the tourniquet JD had tied tightly just below his elbow. Jeff Hotujec suddenly felt years older than he was. He wanted so desperately to do something for McCall, to make the swelling go away, the pain stop—anything—but he knew these were things that he could not do. Watching McCall going over the map, he asked, "JD, you got a cigarette?"

McCall looked up, a little puzzled at the question. "Hell, Jeff, you don't smoke."

"I think this is one hell of a good time to start."

For the first time today, McCall grinned as he tapped

a cigarette from the pack and passed it to Hotujec. Lighting one for himself, he passed the lighter over and leaned back. "OK, Jeff, I take it you're gettin' ready to lay some heavy shit on me, so let's hear it."

Taking a deep drag of the smoke, Hotujec coughed a couple of times before he said, "JD, I think you and Rich are a couple of fine motherfuckers."

"Okay, so you know about our kinky sex life. What are you trying to say?"

"Well, since you ask, I say we take the parallel trail and we move like hell. I'll take the point. If anything gets in my way I blow the shit out of it, which will alert you guys to trouble and you can break off and try another route."

McCall tapped the ashes from his cigarette and slowly looked up at Jeff. "So what you're sayin' is you want a chance to play fuckin' John Wayne?"

Hotujec laughed as he said, "You're fuckin' *a* right! Neither you nor Rich are in any shape to run the point, and I haven't done a damn thing but follow people around since I've been out here. I just think it's fuckin' time I earned my money for this team."

McCall could tell by the look in Jeff's eyes that he was serious, but JD had mixed feelings. He felt pride at being with a man such as Jeff Hotujec, but also fear of something happening to the kid. He had grown almost as close to Jeff as he was to Richardson. They were so close to getting out of here and home, he just didn't want to lose any more people, especially someone like Jeff. Hotujec sat quietly, watching McCall stare at the ground. McCall might not want to go along with his idea, but it was the only logical answer, and he knew it.

Slowly raising his head, McCall said, "What the hell you doin' sitting here? Thought you were gonna take the point and lead us out of here?"

Throwing the bad-tasting cigarette to the ground, Hotujec jumped to his feet, the grin covering his entire face. "You got it, boss! We're gettin' out of here, you can count on it!'' Grabbing his rifle, Jeff moved up the line telling the rest of the team to get ready to move out.

McCall watched as the young soldier with all the pride departed. It reminded him of another young guy that had come to Nam so many years ago, who now sat with a bandaged hand and a wounded friend. He hoped Jeff didn't stay in this fucked-up country as long as he had. It messed with your mind after a while. Like now, sitting there on the ground, knowing damn well that he was going to have to have his hand cut off if and when they did get back. Then what? Would they put him in prison for killing that asshole Nichols? Maybe a VA hospital for the mentally and physically dead of this damn war? Worse than that was the thought of returning home and nobody anywhere giving a fuck about where he'd been or what he'd done. Only time would tell. Right now getting Jeff, Rich, and the others out and back home was all that mattered to McCall. He'd worry about the other shit later . . . if there was a later.

Hotujec came running back down the line. "Well, I guess we're ready to go for it, JD.''

"OK, kid, let's start the music and see who wants to come out and dance.''

Jeff winked. "We're gonna make it, man. I can feel it.''

"You just keep your eyes wide open and watch your ass out there. One more thing, Jeff. Don't get so far ahead of us we can't help you out if you get in a bind, ya hear?''

With the smile still on his face, he slapped JD on the back and sprinted for the front of the column.

Thanh had placed his people in position and now sat patiently awaiting the arrival of the Americans. He had chosen a place along a trail that paralleled the Ho Chi Minh. The DMZ was only five miles farther south. To Thanh, this was the most logical route if one wanted to

make good time. It was the route he would have taken
if he were in the same situation. He also realized that
if he had guessed wrong and the Americans crossed
the DMZ somewhere else along the line, there would
not be another chance for an ambush. Once in the
south, the Americans would be safe. Thanh would
have to return to his headquarters in defeat. Explain-
ing the loss of Salt and Pepper was going to be hard
enough, but to have to tell the council that the killers
had also escaped was not a possibility he wanted to
dwell on at this moment. For now, all he could do
was wait and hope that he had made the right decision.

In his excitement, Hotujec had picked up the pace
and, unknowingly, was getting far ahead of McCall and
the team. The trail improved their time, but the litter
and the heat were still taking their toll on the team.
McCall figured they were within eight miles of the Z
when he gave the men a well-deserved break. At the
rate they were moving they should be within two miles
of the DMZ by dark.

Wiping the sweat from his forehead, McCall pulled
the NVA radio out of his rucksack, set the firebase
emergency freq, and tried calling any friendly station in
the range of the radio set. "Any station, any station,
this is Striker One, come in. Over." Minutes passed in
silence. "Mike Force, Mike Force, this is Striker One.
Come in. Over." No reply. Checking the radio for
damage, JD tried once more, "Mike Force, Mike
Force, this is Striker One. Come in." McCall told
himself they must be out of range. He'd try again when
they got closer to the Z. Hell, even if someone did
answer, it wouldn't do any good. It would be dark
pretty soon, and to try and bring a chopper in after
dark was asking to get killed. The NVA had 37mm
antiaircraft guns all along the zone, and those guys
prayed every night for some chopper jockey to try his
luck.

Getting his people back on their feet, McCall told them to move out. One of the young members of the Deliverance team dropped back to talk with JD. "How far do you figure we have to go, Sergeant McCall?"

McCall kept moving as he talked, "Seven or eight miles, kid. We should be pretty close by dark."

"Sarge, I can't believe we haven't run into any NVA on this damn trail."

McCall looked at the kid's boyish face—he couldn't be more than 19. "We've been damn lucky, kid. That's all it is—luck. And you better hope that luck stays with us a little longer."

"Right, Sarge." The kid moved on up, leaving McCall to his own thoughts. Right now those thoughts were of Jeff, and a major who might be waiting around the next bend.

The sweat ran down Hotujec's face and arms as he kept up the steady pace. The sun would be going down soon, and JD wanted to be as close to the DMZ as possible for link-up with the Mike Force. Jeff was going to see that they got there. He had only stopped twice. Both times he thought he saw movement ahead of him in the trees, but it turned out to be no more than shadows cast by the lowering sun. Keeping his finger on the trigger and his eyes on the trail, Jeff kept moving. Only two or three more miles and they'd have it made. . . .

The butt end of the AK-47 came out of the shadows. Hotujec caught only a glimpse of the dark-brown wood before it impacted with his skull. The Green Beret was knocked off his feet from the blow. Two NVA grabbed Jeff's body and pulled it from the trail and into the jungle. Thanh was informed of their good fortune and, within minutes, was leaning over Hotujec and gently slapping his face.

"Come on, wake up, wake up, you are not hurt bad. Wake up, Green Beret."

Hotujec's eyes slowly opened; they couldn't focus on the form that stood over him. He thought he heard words being spoken, but they were drowned out by the steady ringing in his ears. His eyes closed once more.

Pulling the canteen from Hotujec's pistol belt, Thanh poured the water over the American's face and repeated, "Wake up, wake up, American."

The water felt good on his face. Jeff opened his eyes once more. This time he could see that the figure above him was an NVA officer. Even now, his only thought was that he had let JD down. He had walked right into this like a rookie out of basic training.

Thanh smiled. "You have done a foolish thing, Green Beret. You have let yourself be captured. Do you understand what I am saying?"

Jeff's eyes had cleared by now and he recognized the NVA officer. It was the face he had seen a hundred times in the pictures back in Saigon. It was Thanh.

"Oh, I see you know who I am. That is good. You have been chasing me for some time. I am glad we finally get to meet face to face. Now, Green Beret, you will answer a few questions for me, yes?"

Hotujec did not look away from the major's stare. He didn't want to. Here, only inches from him sat the man that had cost so many people their lives and Hotujec couldn't do a damn thing about it. At least he could still talk. "Why don't you go fuck yourself, asshole!"

Thanh slapped him across the face. "Now that the introductions are over, you bastard, tell me how far back the others are."

Jeff could feel the warm blood running down his chin as he said, "Fat fuckin' chance, you motherfucker!"

Thanh slapped him again, harder this time. "You will not be so disrespectful in a few minutes, my young friend."

Hotujec slowly turned his head one way, then the other. He was trying to count the NVA that were standing around him. He was able to see three before Thanh slapped him again. Jeff didn't think about the pain of the blow, only of McCall and the team. JD had said Thanh couldn't have more than 10 or 11 people left. If Thanh had three with him, that only left six or seven hiding out there waiting for JD. Jeff had to keep Thanh here as long as he could. McCall would be coming any time now—if only he could hold out that long. . . .

Thanh pulled the long, slim knife from his boot and waved it in front of Hotujec's eyes. "I promise you, my friend, you will talk to me." Placing a gag in Hotujec's mouth, Thanh then tore open the American's shirt. He then pressed the knife along one of the ribs and carefully sliced the skin open. Wiping away some of the blood, he made another incision below the same rib. Hotujec tried to scream, but he was the only one who could hear the agony of that scream. The gag held back any noise.

Having completed his work like a dedicated surgeon, Thanh asked, "How far are they behind you? Nod your head if you are willing to answer and I shall stop this needless torture."

With tears welling up in his eyes, Hotujec shook his head.

Worried that the other Americans might be approaching at this very moment, Thanh became impatient. Shoving his fingers into the top incision, he forced his fingers out the bottom cut. Grasping the rib tightly in his hand, he broke it outward. Hotujec's eyes opened wide in disbelief. The pain sent shock waves to every nerve in his body.

Thanh wiped the blood from his hand on Jeff's shirt, then pulled the gag down from Jeff's mouth. "Are you ready to talk now? There is no need for more of this."

Jeff Hotujec never knew this kind of pain existed, but he was still conscious as he answered, "Why don't you go suck a dick, bitch!"

Thanh only laughed as he looked over at one of his men and said, "You go tell the others to be ready for the Americans. I am convinced they are coming this way." The soldier acknowledged the order and reluctantly departed.

Thanh then called Thieu over to his side. "Do you know what we have here, my friend? We have what the American Green Berets like to call a hard-core soldier." Flipping the knife in his hand, Thanh tapped the handle against the gleaming-white rib bone that protruded from Hotujec's side. Pain flashed in Jeff's eyes as he almost passed out from the gentle blow. "Yes, Thieu, these Green Berets are tough men, but they have no manners. Did you hear what he said to me only moments ago?"

Thieu's voice was bitter as he replied, "Yes, I heard, Commander."

"What would you do to a man who spoke to you in such a manner?"

"I would give that person what he wished upon me, sir."

Turning to Hotujec and leaning close so that he could look him in the eyes, he said, "Tell me what I want to know, American, or I shall turn you over to my men. Now, how far away are the others? How many are left? Talk to me, damn you!"

Seeing the look of hatred on the face of the man named Thieu, Jeff knew he was as good as dead. Thanh asked again, "Tell me what I must know."

Jeff's answer was soft and uncaring. "Fuck you." Then he spit in Thanh's face. Thieu kicked Jeff in the face, then slammed the rifle across the protruding rib, breaking it off.

Thanh wiped the spit from his face and stood up. "Do with him what you want, but, when you have finished, I want him placed in the center of the trail for the other Americans to find."

A sadistic grin appeared on Thieu's face. "Yes,

Commander. It shall be done." Thanh picked up his knife and walked away. Thieu turned to the other NVA soldier that was with him and handed him his rifle. Pulling a knife from his belt, he knelt next to Hotujec and cut away the buttons on the front of the American's pants. Jeff's senses were still reeling from the trauma of the rib being broken from his body. The boot to the face had broken out his front teeth and driven his jawbone out the side of his cheek. He no longer felt pain. He was beyond that. He felt hands on his crotch, but that didn't matter either. There was a stinging pain down there, then something soft was forced into his mouth. He didn't know what it was. He didn't care. Jeff Hotujec saw and felt only the white, cold snows of the Colorado mountains. He had just completed his second run down the slopes and walked into the lodge. There was a long-legged blonde with a cast on her leg. She had felt so very soft in his arms. The thought of her body made him smile as the darkness closed in around him. She had been so wonderfully soft to the touch, but she would only make love in the dark. . . .

Thieu wiped his bloody knife on his pants leg as he approached Major Thanh.

"It has been done as you asked, sir. I mean no disrespect, Major, but I thought we wished to surprise the Americans and ambush them. They will find the body of their comrade and know we are waiting for them."

Thanh spoke softly. There was sadness in his voice as he said, "Thieu, we have fought together for many years now. Have you not noticed the character of these Green Berets? They are unlike the other Americans that ravage and burn our beloved Vietnam. They are men of great courage. They are among the hardest-fighting men I have encountered for two wars. They are professional warriors, the same as you and I. For that reason I have great respect for this enemy. There is no

honor in what we have done to their comrade who now
lies on the trail, but such are the ways of war. Did you
not see how the young soldier died? No, my friend,
these are not just ordinary Americans, they are the best
their country has. By placing their fallen comrade on
the trail, I have offered their leader a challenge. It is an
honorable challenge among professionals. Do you now
understand?"

Thieu answered, "I do, Commander. But we have
young ones with no experience with us. Were it not for
that, I could see the reasons for this action."

"They must learn as we did, Thieu. The Green Beret
that we just killed was not much older than our young
men. Now prepare them for the fight. I know the tall
one that commands the Americans will accept our
challenge. The soldier's blood that flows through his
veins will not let him run away."

There was a tone of uncertainty in Thieu's voice as
he said, "I hope the major is right. Once they have
been warned of our presence, they could very easily
turn off the trail and escape across the border."

"Do not worry, Thieu. They will come soon enough.
Now, go."

Thieu nodded and went to prepare the team.

Gazing upon the body of Hotujec one last time,
Thanh slowly brought his hand up in a salute. "You
have brought honor to your unit, my young friend.
Now you have found peace and the eternal rest we all
shall find one day."

Lowering his arm, Thanh picked up his rifle and went
to await the arrival of the Americans. He knew the tall
one would be coming. . . .

McCall tried the radio again but still did not make
contact with the Mike Force. Pulling his URC-10 from
his web gear, he also tried to contact Jeff, but got no
answer. Either he had his radio off or he was in trouble.
JD was hoping it was just off. McCall sent two men

forward to attempt a link-up with Hotujec and tell the young trooper to wait for the rest of the team. The two men now came rushing up to McCall. They were both out of breath and pale.

Gasping for breath, one of them said, "JD, they . . . they got Hotujec! They cut him to pieces. . . . God-dammit, they cut his . . . his . . ." The soldier turned away from McCall and threw up beside the trail. He did not have to finish his statement. JD had been here a long time—he had seen more than his share of atrocities in this war.

Speaking to the other man, McCall asked, "Where was the body?"

Having caught his breath now, the man replied calmly, "They had him laid out right in the middle of the trail, JD."

Gathering the team around him, McCall said, "Gentlemen, Major Thanh has killed Sergeant Hotujec and right now is sitting somewhere down this trail waiting for us."

One soldier asked, "How do you know it's Thanh, Sarge?"

"Oh, it's him all right. That's why Jeff's body was left on the trail. Thanh's telling us he's between us and the DMZ. Jeff was a message, a challenge, if you will. He's giving us the option of running or going through him to get home."

Another asked, "Excuse me, JD, but why would this major tip us off that he was waiting down there when he could have just as easily blown our shit away in the next couple of miles?"

McCall glanced down at Richardson lying on the litter before answering. "Because we destroyed his command and killed Salt and Pepper. Thanh is a professional. You see, kid, there are a few of us still around who play the game by the rules. This has become a matter of honor for Thanh."

The kid kicked at the dirt with his boot as he said, "Jesus, JD, this is 1967. King Arthur and his boys have been out of style for a long time."

McCall quietly said, "Yeah, I know, kid, and it's a goddamn shame, too."

"So what you're sayin' is this NVA major is sitting down this trail waiting to ambush the hell out of us and he wants us to know about it, then just walk right into it. Is that about it?"

"That's it, man. He's daring us to walk down there and finish what we started," said McCall.

The group stood silent for a moment. No one knew what to say.

Richardson painfully pulled himself up on his elbows and said, "Well, what the fuck are we waiting for? Let's go on down there and kick his ass!"

All eyes were on Richardson as he finished. McCall could see the doubt in the eyes of his men.

McCall cleared his throat and said, "I know you guys risked a hell of a lot to come in here, and that this was not part of the deal. You got us out of a tight spot earlier. I want to thank you for that. Anybody that wants to can split off here and head southeast for the DMZ. It's your choice. I'll understand."

One of the men asked, "What d'you plan to do, Sarge?"

"I'm going to try to finish what we started. Thanh was part of the mission—still is, far as I'm concerned. I'm going to try to kill him. I owe Jeff that much. You guys make up your mind what you want to do. I'm not giving any orders anymore."

The group of volunteers looked at one another. No one moved, no one spoke. No one had to. The oldest member of the group said, "JD, like the old saying goes, 'The opera ain't over till the fat lady sings.' We're going with you. What're your orders?"

McCall could feel emotion rising within himself. This

was what made Special Forces *special*. It was not one man alone, but a team united as one.

Holding back the water welling up in his eyes, McCall said, "Thank you, men. We'll make our move in five minutes. Check your weapons; it's going to get pretty hot and furious down that trail."

Kneeling down next to Richardson, JD said, "Well, ol' buddy, I guess you finally get to make a decision without me tellin' you what to do."

Richardson said, "Just what the fuck ya' talkin' about, man?"

"Three facts, Rich. One, we know we're gonna get hit before we reach the Z. Two, you can't walk two feet without falling flat on your face, and laying on this litter you'll be as good as a dead fish in a barrel. Third, you dumb shit, I'd like to see somebody get out of this crap alive."

Richardson was up on both elbows trying to swing his badly swollen legs off the litter, but they wouldn't move. McCall watched his friend's effort but made no move to help. Rich knew it was useless. Falling back in exhaustion, his voice still had determination as he said, "Listen, asshole, you're not leavin' me here. I started this goddamn ball game with you and I'm gonna finish it one way or the other, you fuckin' got that?"

McCall stared at the ground and slowly flicked the dirt with his finger before he said, "Well, since you seem to feel so strong about it, I guess you can come along." A slight smile tugged at the corner of JD's mouth.

"You prick! You didn't have any fuckin' intention of leavin' me here. You just wanted to see if I could walk, didn't you, dick-breath?"

McCall stood up and disappeared into the jungle, returning a few minutes later with a Russian machine gun that one of the Deliverance team had been carrying.

"Here, you non-walkin' asshole. At least with this

you won't have to reload, and you might even be able to help us out."

McCall dropped the heavy weapon and ammo on Richardson's chest and walked away as Richardson laughed out loud and said, "You always were a softy, you big motherfucker. Thanks!"

XVI.

Colonel Davis had just finished his second pack of cigarettes. His cigars had run out hours ago. Crumpling the package, he threw it in the trashcan. The radio operator quietly placed another pack on the bank of radios that ran along one wall of the operations room.

"If you're out, sir, you can have mine."

"Thanks, Sergeant. I never have been very good at this waiting game."

Jess Baron walked into the room wearing a flight suit. "Sir, the choppers just put the Mike Force on the ground. They should be in position by last light. They're going to lay quiet till daylight, then try to make contact with McCall on the URC-10s." Baron paused a moment to pour himself a cup of coffee, then continued. "The Mike Force commander said that the last-minute in-flight change in coordinates would be no problem—they could still reach the target area."

Davis dropped his cigarette. "What change in coordinates, Jess?"

Baron's face went blank. "I . . . the change you called to the choppers, sir!"

Davis moved to the map. There was excitement in his words. "Show me where the Mike Force was put in!"

Baron threw his coffee in the trashcan, stood beside Davis, and pointed out the LZ the Mike Force had used going in. It was three clicks off the planned infil point. Baron was confused. Something was wrong, very wrong.

"Jess, do you care to tell me why you chose to divert from the original plan?" Davis's tone was not friendly.

Baron was startled. "I didn't change anything, sir. We received a call over the chopper frequency telling us to divert to another area. That LZ was the closest thing available. I just assumed the change came from you, sir."

"Did they use the correct call-signs, Jess?"

"Yes, sir! That was one of the reasons I figured it came from this headquarters. Hell, sir, the only people with that chopper frequency are the Mike Force, the commanders of the 101st, and the Marine unit at Camp Carroll. We gave it to them in case of an emergency, so we could scramble assistants if it was needed. But they've pulled all of their people back from the DMZ. They're just on standby at the firebase."

Worry deepened every line in Davis's face. "Well, somebody sure as hell diverted our choppers, and it wasn't us."

Baron suddenly slammed his fist into the plexiglass covering the map. "Goddammit! I should have realized!"

Grabbing the colonel's fist, Davis said, "What is it, Jess?"

"Thanh! The bastard speaks English. Somehow the bastard must have got his hands on our frequency."

Davis couldn't agree. "Jeff, that's impossible!"

"Well, who in the hell could it have been? McCall sure as hell won't tell us to get the fuck out of the area. It couldn't have been the 101st or the Marines—hell, they don't even know where that Mike Force went in."

Davis said, "I don't know, Jess. But whoever diverted those choppers had to be in that immediate area." Turning to the communications sergeant, Davis continued, "Get that Mike Force on the radio, now. I want to know their exact position."

"Yes, sir. Mike Charlie One, this is Demon Leader. Over."

The room was silent except for the steady hissing of the speakers on the wall. The call went out again, "Mike Charlie One, this is Demon Leader. Over."

The reply was loud and clear, "Demon Leader, this is Mike Charlie One. Over."

Davis took the mike from the sergeant. "Mike Charlie One, what is your location at this time? Over."

"Demon One, Charlie One. We are moving to assigned coordinates. Estimate twenty minutes out. Over."

Davis slowly rubbed the mike in his sweating hands. What if Jess was right? What if Thanh did have their frequency? Was he sending a Mike Force into an ambush and possible annihilation or to the rescue of a beleaguered Special Forces team? A decision had to be made and it had to be made now.

Davis now spoke slowly and clearly. "Charlie One, this is Demon. We have reason to believe our frequency has been compromised. Do not . . . I say again . . . *do not* go directly to the coordinates that were assigned. You will follow alternate plan Bravo and await further orders. Do you roger? Over."

"Roger, Demon. Understand. Will activate plan Bravo at this time. Anything further. Over."

"Negative, Charlie One. This is Demon, standing by. Out."

Davis handed the mike back to the sergeant and turned to Baron. The look in Davis's eyes was all that Baron needed. They were the eyes of a man searching for a sign of approval, a glint of recognition for a correct decision made.

They found neither. "Sir," Baron said, "you're sending the Mike Force three klicks away from the rendezvous point for link-up with Striker. They can't possibly pick up McCall on the URC-10s from that distance."

"What would you rather I do, Jess? Send over forty men into a possible trap? What if you're right? If Thanh is out there, he could be laying an ambush for our Mike Force. If Striker can make it to the DMZ, they should be able to contact one of our choppers. We'll send them up and down the slot all day if we have to. That's a hell of a lot safer than risking a whole damn Mike Force."

Baron knew that Davis's decision was final, that there was no point in arguing. Instead, Baron turned to the map. The Ho Chi Minh trail stood out in bright red. Baron's eyes were not focused on the red, but rather on the small lines that ran on each side of the main trail. One of those secondary lines ran straight to the rendezvous point.

Davis came up to Baron, "Dammit, Jess, we can still get to them in time if we have to!"

With his eyes still locked on that one trail, Baron answered, "Of course we can, sir." There was a tone of doubt in his voice.

McCall checked each member of the team before walking up to Rich. "Are you ready, Rich?"

"Ready as I ever will be, I guess. Ya know, JD, I think we ought to call it quits after this one."

McCall glanced at Richardson's swollen legs and then at his own rotting hand before he said, "I think you got a good point there, ol' buddy. You can sell pencils on street corners and I'll be there to sharpen 'em with my hook."

Richardson forced a smile, "Now, now, let's not be bitter. We were big boys when we got into this crap. It's a little late to be wishin' we were someplace else."

McCall nodded and said in a low, almost regretful tone, "Yeah, I guess you're right, Rich. We knew what we were getting into."

Richardson slapped the machine gun and, with tears welling up in his eyes, said, "Let's go, boss. The sun's goin' down and we still got work to do."

McCall wiped a tear from Rich's cheek. "I'm gonna get you home, Rich. I mean that."

"I never had a doubt, JD."

McCall rose to his feet and gave the order to move out as he took up the point position.

Thanh sat watching the sun slowly disappear behind the treetops. In less than an hour, darkness would fall over Vietnam. For some, it would be the last time they would ever see a sunset. Thanh sat patiently waiting. He placed a mental picture of the beauty around him in the back of his mind.

McCall moved slow and easy at the point. The fading sunlight cast shadows in all directions, making everything around JD appear to be moving. He strained his tired and weary eyes. Somewhere in this kaleidoscope of changing colors and shadows, death waited.

If Richardson had not been lying on the litter, he would have missed the movement to McCall's left. JD missed it. Blinking his eyes to make sure he wasn't seeing shadows, Rich stared at the spot where he was sure he had seen the leaves move ever so slightly.

There it was again. . . . It was a gun barrel. At that moment, everything seemed to happen at once. Rich yelled a warning to JD, then opened up with the machine gun. To Richardson, everything seemed to be happening in slow motion. The rounds from the machine gun tore leaves and vines apart. The leaves were tossed into the air only to be torn apart again by flashes from the NVA along the side of the trail. The front of the litter dropped to the ground, dumping Rich and the machine gun hard to the ground. Dirt popped and jumped all around him as bullets searched him out. Dragging himself off the trail and under cover, he saw the two litter-bearers lying in the middle of the trail. They were dead. Trying to straighten out the machine-gun's ammo belt, he felt the impact of the first round rip through his side. The second round tore through his right shoulder, knocking him onto his back. As the new pain raged through his body, Richardson whispered, "Oh, sweet Jesus."

McCall had spotted the ambush at the same moment Rich had yelled, but it was too late. Before JD could react, one bullet ripped through his right leg and a second passed through the bandaged hand, spinning him into the dirt. McCall fired into the flashes along the edge of the trail, two of his rounds catching one of the NVA square in the face. Another five rounds drove their way through the chest of another. Struggling to get to his feet, JD hobbled to the side of the trail, searching for some type of cover. He'd almost made it when a third round slammed under his left arm, tearing a large chunk of flesh from his side and driving McCall face-first into the dirt.

One of the Deliverance team had pulled the pin on a grenade but, before he could throw it, two rounds hit him in the stomach. In one last dying effort, he threw the grenade and screamed, "Fuck you!"

The explosion killed two NVA and added yet another sound to the ear-shattering opera of death that was being played in the last glimmer of sunlight.

It had been Thanh's shot that knocked McCall to the ground. As the battle continued to rage, Thanh stared at the tall American's body. This was not how he had wanted it to happen. He had hoped to capture the leader. He had wanted to talk with him, if only for a little while.

An explosion to his right brought Thanh back to reality. The battle was not over yet, and death still hovered above the jungle, waiting to claim the careless.

Thieu appeared at Thanh's side. Blood covered his right sleeve.

Thanh asked, "Is it bad, Thieu?"

"No, sir. The man who did this is dead now."

"Do you know how many are left?" asked Thanh.

"We have three pinned down on the other side of the

trail. They should not take long to dispose of. What of the leader?"

Thanh paused and looked in McCall's direction. He didn't feel the uplifting surge of victory he had thought he would. He answered, "He is dead. Come, let us end this madness once and for all." Both men departed to aid their comrades in the final battle.

Richardson could hear the firing to his right and left. The sounds seemed to be miles away. He tried to lock another belt of ammo into the machine gun, but it slipped from his hands. It didn't seem to matter anymore. He was tired, so very, very tired.

McCall spit the dirt from his mouth, leaving only the taste of blood. His body felt numb—in a way, that was a blessing. He knew he had been hit bad. For the first time in his life, McCall felt the urge to give up. It would be so easy; all he had to do was lie here in the dirt and let himself die. Who would really give a shit, anyway? The sounds of battle were still going on around him. Where was Rich? Was he still alive? Hell, he couldn't quit. He had made Rich a promise. That thought was enough to make McCall move his right hand forward. Instant pain shot its way into McCall's brain. His scream was covered by the rifle fire that cracked all around him.

Reaching deep inside himself for extra strength, McCall forced himself to slowly inch his way up onto his knees. Compared to the pain in his foul-smelling hand, the holes through his leg and underarm were nothing. He tried to think of Oklahoma, the ranch, the horses—anything to block out the pain. It had been his Chinese who had taught him how to ignore pain by centering thoughts on a pleasant experience or place. For now, at least, it was working.

Pulling the sweat-soaked bandanna from his forehead, McCall wrapped it tightly around his leg. The stinking odor from the hole in his hand brought a wave of nausea to his stomach, causing him to gag. He slowly reached for his rifle, then realized the futility of his act. "You dumb shit," he muttered, "you can't reload the damn thing anyway. Hell with it!"

Jerking the Magnum from its shoulder holster, he flipped the cylinder open. He had six rounds. It wasn't much, but then he didn't figure he was going to need any more than that. Struggling to his feet, McCall forced one foot in front of the other as he moved to the sound of the gunfire.

Richardson had regained consciousness. His eyes were focused on the machine gun and the belt of ammo. The rifle fire had all but died out. What few rounds he could still hear were coming from AK-47s. That could only mean that Thanh had won.

Slowly reaching for the machine gun, Richardson felt someone standing over him. Looking up, he saw the barrel of an AK-47 and the smiling face of an NVA holding it. Rich thought of Alabama, his mother, and the first girl he had ever made love to. Closing his eyes, he lowered his head and waited for the shot that would end his life. The shot was loud, but he didn't feel any pain. Opening his eyes, he saw the NVA lying next to him, a huge hole in the back of his head.

McCall slumped down next to Richardson. His breathing labored, he said, "I shoulda known!"

Richardson was half laughing, half crying. "What the hell you talkin' 'bout now, man?"

With his head lying on his arm, JD said, "You fuckin' niggers've gotta have your damn nap or you just ain't worth a shit the rest of the day."

Dragging himself up against a tree, Richardson looked at the blood-covered, torn body of his best friend. His eyes filled with tears. "Oh yeah, you honky shit, you probably been out gettin' laid while we took care of your light work for your white ass."

McCall painfully inched his way up beside Richardson and rested his head on the man's chest. "It's been a hell of a day, ain't it, man?"

Wiping the blood from JD's mouth and nose, Rich said, "Yeah, man, a good time was had by all." A moment passed. "Hey, JD, who fuckin' won?" Rich asked.

"Hell, Rich. Who fuckin' knows? . . . Have you seen any of the others?"

"Just the dead ones."

McCall's voice was soft and quiet. "How about Thanh? Did you see him?"

"No, man. They blew my ass out of that litter the minute I opened up on 'em."

McCall coughed. More blood flowed from his nose. Reaching in his pocket, he pulled out his pack of cigarettes. The act brought back the memory of Jeff asking for a cigarette earlier. McCall wished he could give him another one right now. He only had three cigarettes left in the pack. He decided he didn't really feel like smoking, and returned the pack to his blood-soaked shirt.

Richardson had been watching McCall. "JD, you sure look like shit, brother."

"I've seen you lookin' better, Rich."

Both men sat silently containing their pain and thinking of other things. They had got their ass kicked and they knew it. Neither one really wanted to talk about it right now.

Ten minutes had passed. There was no shooting. It had been quiet for what seemed like hours, but it had been only minutes. The last shot they heard had come from a Russian AK-47.

McCall was the first to break the silence. "Ya know, Rich. We really got us a problem here."

"Really? I thought it was pretty peaceful till you started yackin'."

"Ain't you just a little bit worried right now?"

"Hell, why should I be worried? You said you were gonna get me out of here, didn't ya?"

McCall had started to laugh, but it hurt too much. Raising his pounding head off Rich's chest, he said, "Yeah, I did say that, didn't I? Well, I guess we ought to get up off our lazy butts and get it done, then."

McCall found that saying it and doing it were two different things. As he started to move, his body screamed for him to stay put. It was a warning that McCall ignored as he pulled himself up using the limbs of the tree.

Richardson felt warm blood drip onto his face from JD's wounds.

"Oh, sit down, JD. We've had it. We can't go no place."

Every part of McCall's body hurt. "No way, mother! I'm takin' you home."

Before Rich could protest, McCall took a deep breath and, leaning over, grabbed Richardson under the arms and slung him over his shoulder all in one swift move, the weight driving McCall down on one knee. Richardson moaned in pain as McCall fought to regain his feet. Calling on all his reserve strength, JD pushed himself up. "I told you I was gonna take you home, and I mean it."

Richardson could not hear him. He had lost consciousness again. Gripping the .44 Magnum tight in his good hand, McCall began swaying and staggering down the center of the trail with a brother on his shoulder, five rounds in his Magnum and a determination to kill anything that got in his way.

Thanh stood over the body of the last man of the Deliverance force as he asked, "Thieu, are there any others left?"

"No, Commander. This was the last one."

"What of the black soldier on the litter?"

"He was killed in the opening part of the battle, sir," said Thieu.

Thanh's eyes met Thieu's. "What are our losses?"

Kicking the body of the dead American in frustration, Thieu answered, "There are but four of us left, sir."

Studying the body that lay before him, Thanh slowly shook his head. Not speaking to anyone in particular, he quietly said, "So many people dead to kill so few."

Thieu could not argue that point. "Do we go home now, Major?"

"Yes, old friend. Darkness will be here in a few minutes. Have the men rest for now. We will wait for the coolness of night to begin our journey home. At least it will not be a long walk in defeat. We have eliminated the Americans once and for . . ."

Before Thanh could finish, a deep, threatening voice said: "Not fuckin' likely, asshole!"

The four NVA in the middle of the trail were totally stunned to see the tall American with the blood-soaked fatigues standing less than five yards away. They had neither heard nor seen the man approach in the fading light. Now he stood before them with his black friend hanging over his shoulder and a huge pistol hanging loosely in the hand at his side. Thanh realized that his soldiers still had their rifles slung over their shoulders, and there was no doubt in his mind that the American could use the big gun.

Thanh said, "You are truly an incredible man, my friend. We thought you and your friend to be dead."

Never taking his eyes off the four men, McCall spit blood from his mouth as he said, "Not hardly, Major Thanh."

Thanh slowly moved his hand toward the holster at his side. "So, Green Beret, what do we do now?"

McCall grinned. "Well, Major, I could ask you and your boys to drop them guns and surrender, but I don't really think you're gonna wanna do that. That guy beside you don't seem too thrilled by the idea already," he added, referring to the look on Thieu's face.

Thanh's fingers reached the snap of his holster. "I

would be more than happy to make you and your friend the same offer, but I also feel that your answer would be—how do you Americans say? Oh yes, 'No fucking way,' I believe is the term."

McCall had watched Thanh's hand, and he hadn't missed the slow sliding of NVA hands up their rifle slings. McCall said, "Well, since there ain't anybody wantin' to surrender, I guess we'll just have to shoot it out, Major."

Thanh nodded, then said, "I'm afraid so. But I will allow you the opportunity to put your friend down if you like."

McCall's answer was calm. "No, thanks, Major, me and Rich are real close. He's been out for the last ten minutes anyway. You kill him, he'll never know the difference."

The NVA soldiers inched away from Thanh, working the slings off their shoulders. Quietly unsnapping his holster, Thanh asked, "Are you ready to die, my friend?"

McCall screamed, "Start the ball, motherfuckers!"

The NVA all moved at once. Thanh's pistol never cleared the holster as McCall swung the heavy-barreled Magnum up and blew a hole through his side, knocking him off his feet.

Thieu had been faster. Dropping to one knee, he let the sling fall free and fired at the same time as McCall. Thieu's shot tore through JD's leg just below the knee and sent him crashing to the ground. Firing as he fell, McCall's hit Thieu in the right side of the chest, knocking him six feet backward and into the brush. The youngest of the two remaining NVA was pointing his rifle at McCall and trying desperately to squeeze the trigger, but the rifle wouldn't fire; the safety was still on. Pushing Richardson off his body, McCall fired. The young soldier's head exploded, blood and brains splattering into the face of the last NVA. The man screamed in horror and rage as he fired wildly at McCall lying on

the ground. McCall wiped the flying dirt from his eyes
as the bullets hit all around him. The NVA stopped
firing. He was out of ammunition. Throwing the rifle
down, he stared at McCall with pleading eyes, then
turned and ran. McCall gave him three steps before the
Magnum exploded a final time. The hollowpoint bullet
hit the soldier between the shoulder blades, sending
him spreadeagled into the air. He was dead before he
hit the ground.

The entire action had taken less than two minutes.
McCall lowered his head onto his outstretched arms.
God, he felt so tired. The sound of the slide going back
on a pistol sent a chill down his back. Looking up, he
saw Thanh trying to force a round into the chamber of
his pistol. Getting to his knees, McCall slowly raised
the Magnum and said, "Don't do it, Major."

Thanh looked down the barrel of the gun, then at
McCall. Dropping the pistol to the ground, he said,
"Of course you are right, it would be useless to even
try."

McCall lowered his weapon, dragged himself over to
the edge of the trail, and sat across from Thanh.
Reaching into his shirt, he brought out the pack of
cigarettes, lit one, and leaned back, letting the smoke
drift slowly from between his lips.

Thanh now pulled himself over to the body of Thieu.
Resting his head on the man's lifeless legs, he also lit a
cigarette before saying, "What is your name, Green
Beret?" Thanh coughed. Blood mixed with the cigarette smoke in his mouth.

"McCall . . . JD McCall."

Lowering the cigarette, Thanh smiled wryly. "Of
course. I should have known. I have heard many stories
about you, Sergeant McCall. But this shows you how
reliable our Russian comrades' intelligence reports are.
They reported you killed over a year ago. I . . . " He
coughed again. More blood.

McCall asked, "How bad is it?"

Thanh's breathing was becoming harder as he answered, "Oh, you did not miss, JD McCall. I am just taking my time about dying, that is all. Tell me something, my friend. Why have you stayed in my country so long?"

"Somebody had to be here, Thanh. It might as well be me."

"Oh no, McCall. You stay because you like it. There is nothing as exciting in life as war, and you, my friend, need that excitement."

McCall gave a low moan as he shifted his stiffening legs. "Well, Major, I think I'm about all excited out." The tone of voice changed. "Why'd you have to do that to Hotujec?"

Thanh asked, "Who? . . . Oh, he must have been the young man walking point for you. I had to ask him questions. He never did answer any of them, though. He was very courageous to the end. I had nothing to do with that other business. You must remember, Sergeant McCall, you killed many of my men, and they too had friends. Now, tell me why you did not take the one we call Salt back as a prisoner?"

"He was a traitor to his country. He killed his own country's soldiers. If I had taken him back, some bleeding-heart lawyer would have put him in a nut ward somewhere for six months, then they'd let him walk. That wouldn't be right. No, sir, not right at all."

"So you became his judge, jury, and executioner?"

"Damn right I did. Hell, Thanh, we *are* judge and jury out here, you know that."

"That is true, McCall. Sometimes it is not easy, but it must be done. Will you go home after this?"

Looking at his mangled hand, McCall said, "Yeah! They'll send me home this time, but not before they cut this hand off. Then they'll give me a couple of medals and a few bucks each month so I can crawl in a bottle somewhere and never have to sober up."

Thanh's voice was getting weaker. "I am sorry about your hand, McCall. Even more, I am sorry that your country would treat such a warrior as you in such a manner. It is truly a sad thing."

McCall could tell that this man he had tried so hard to kill really meant what he had just said. It gave him a strange feeling.

Vietnamese voices carried through the darkness. Both men were silent, listening. There came a faint sound of metal clanking against metal; it was an NVA patrol moving on the trail next to them.

McCall expected Thanh to start yelling at any second. If he did they could hang it up. He only had one round left in the Magnum and, at this point, he was so tired he didn't care. Thanh watched in amazement as McCall strained to lift the heavy gun and point it in the direction of the voices. Thanh had fought with and against brave men in his many years of war, but he had never met such a man as this.

As the voices faded away, McCall asked, "Why didn't you yell, Thanh? They could have got you to an aid station or something."

Thanh's voice was broken as he said, "No . . . Mc . . . McCall, this was our . . . battle. You won. . . . I will respect that. You must understand, McCall, we do not have the modern medical equipment that you have. But even without these things . . . my people will one day walk the streets of Saigon and my country will truly be one. Make no mistake of this, Sergeant . . . McCall. We have fought long and hard for that day, and we shall fight for as long as it takes, so in the end we will win."

McCall asked, "Why can't you work it out with the people in Saigon?"

"Come now, McCall, you have been here long enough to know why. They want to talk as long as we have other powers controlling our country. But the Americans' time here will end soon, and it will not be because of men like us. Your departure from this land will be brought on by your own people in the United States. They are not as patient as we are, but then they have never had to fight four hundred years for their freedom. You will see. One day it will happen."

For McCall this conversation was an awakening. He had never thought of the NVA as anything other than the bad guys in a bad movie. But there was no doubt in his mind that Thanh believed what he said. JD asked, "Do you really believe that the President of the United States would spend all these American lives just so he could lose a war? Mister, we ain't never lost a war."

"You may be right, McCall. I do not know your president, but I do know the American people. They want things done quickly, so that they may get on with other things. They will grow tired of seeing this war in their homes every day, week after week. Already your young men leave their country so that they will not have to serve in your army. So you see, my friend, the erosion has already begun. All we have to do now is keep fighting and wait."

McCall searched for some reply to Thanh's remarks, but he couldn't find one. What was worse, he had a gut feeling the man was right. He had to say something, so he asked, "So, you're tellin' me this whole fuckin' mess is for nothing. Is that what you're telling me, Major?"

"No, Sergeant McCall. This has all served some small purpose in the realm of things that are to be. We may never know how much our actions today affected the outcome of those things, but I do believe there was reason for us to be here in this time and place. To believe otherwise would be insane. A man must know his life was taken for a purpose."

Richardson started to come around. McCall moved next to him, gently placed his hand over Rich's mouth, and whispered, "Rich, keep quiet, there are NVA patrols moving around out here. Can you hear me, Rich?"

Richardson nodded. McCall removed his hand. Rich asked, "What the hell happened, man? Where are we?"

"You passed out on me, buddy."

"Where the hell are we?"

"Not far from the DMZ, Rich. We'll make it."

Thanh's voice came out of the darkness. "Sergeant McCall, is your friend better?"

"Holy shit, who the hell is that?" asked Rich in a startled tone.

McCall placed his hand on Rich's shoulder. "Relax, man, that's Major Thanh."

"Say what!"

"It's a long story. I'll explain it when we get out of here. Now lay back and get some rest. We're gonna pull out about four in the morning."

"But, JD, Thanh? What . . . Oh hell. . . ."

"Just get some rest, Rich, I've got everything covered. Now, go to sleep."

"Sure, boss, sure." Richardson drifted off into semiconsciousness.

McCall loosened the tourniquets on Rich's legs. The wounds were swelling more each hour. Only the coolness of the night was holding back the spread of infection.

Each movement caused unbelievable pain. McCall had been able to stop his bleeding while listening to Thanh, but it was going to be a long night. The new wounds would be bad by morning. Searching his pockets for morphine, he remembered it was gone. Jeff had been carrying the full packet. McCall knew that without the drug he would never be able to carry Richardson the last few miles. Moving back to his position against the tree, McCall leaned back exhausted. He wouldn't leave Rich, he knew that for sure.

Thanh watched McCall and his friend as they talked. Waiting until JD was back, Thanh said, "I see that you care much for your friend, Sergeant McCall. I find that very honorable. You are indeed a man of many qualities. Would you please come over here for a moment?" McCall reached for the Magnum. "You will not need that, McCall."

"Let's just say it will make me feel better, Major."

"As you wish, but I assure you it is not necessary."

Thanh smiled to himself as he heard the double clicking of the hammer on the .44. McCall moved closer.

"What do you want, Thanh?"

Thanh didn't speak. Instead, he reached out to McCall and placed something in his shirt pocket. "You will have need of that, my friend. I am proud to have met you, JD McCall. It is too bad it had to be under these conditions. I feel we could have become friends. When you . . . return home . . . you remember my . . . words. . . . Good-bye, my friend." Thanh's chest rose and fell twice. Then his eyes closed. Major Thanh was dead.

After feeling for a pulse, McCall laid the major's head gently on the ground and moved back to the other side of the trail. The short distance took his breath away. The pain coursed through his body. Reaching in his shirt pocket, McCall withdrew two tubes of morphine. Holding them tightly, he stared into the darkness at the lifeless form of Thanh and asked himself, "Why?"

Checking the seals on the tubes to make sure they hadn't been tampered with, McCall broke one and, sticking it in the vein, forced half the fluid into his arm. Relief came in seconds. Taking the pin from his teeth, he replaced it in the tube. He knew the medics back at CCN would be screaming their heads off if they'd seen him do that. But, hell, they weren't out here shot all to shit. He was.

Relief brought with it the realization of how tired he really was. McCall couldn't remember when he last slept. It felt like days ago. He didn't release the hammer on the Magnum before closing his weary eyes. If he could just sleep for 30 minutes—just 30 minutes, that was all he wanted. What if another NVA squad came by? For now it didn't matter. McCall was asleep.

* * *

Richardson woke up at about three in the morning. McCall lay next to him sound asleep. Looking at his watch, Rich remembered JD had said they would start moving at four. He saw no reason to wake McCall now. He'd wait until four. Lying back, Rich stared at the stars that blinked between the leaves of the trees. It helped take his mind off the pain in his legs. He wondered what it was like back in Alabama. He wondered what his mom was doing. More than likely she was trying to keep the younger kids out of the kitchen and away from the apple pies she always fixed on the weekends. This was a weekend, wasn't it? He had no idea anymore. Mom would always make a big deal out of trying to save her apple pies. She'd chase the kids around the kitchen with a broom, never hittin' anybody but puttin' on one hell of a good show. This would go on for a while until one of the kids grabbed a pie and made it out the back door with the rest of the mob scurrying after him. 'Course, Rich knew Mom always made an extra pie just for that weekend chase. He loved that old woman and, thanks to the guy next to him, he still had a chance to tell her that. He might not be able to run around the kitchen anymore, but at least he could hold her tight and talk about the night he laid in Nam and thought of her. Had McCall said something about Thanh? He couldn't remember. He must have dreamed it.

At four in the morning, Rich reached over and touched JD lightly on the forehead. Leaning close to his ear, he whispered, "Wake up, JD. It's time to go home."

McCall brushed the fingers from his forehead.

"Come on, JD. Wake up."

McCall slowly opened his eyes. The attempt to sit up reminded him that he had been shot all to hell.

Rich could see the pain in JD's face. "Are you okay, boss?"

McCall held the scream in as he sat up and asked, "How long you been awake?"

"Since about three. Thought I'd let you rest, man. You need it."

McCall rubbed the sleep from his eyes. His body wanted more sleep, but there wasn't time. McCall knew it was going to take them a while to get to the rendezvous point, and he wanted to cover as much ground as he could while it was still cool.

Rich asked, "Did you say some shit about Thanh, or was that just a nightmare?"

"Told ya, don't worry about it. I'll tell ya all about it when we're home. And I mean home! Not CCN, not Vietnam, I mean home for good!"

Richardson looked into JD's eyes. "You really mean it, man. Home! You sayin' we're really through with all this shit for good?"

"You damn right I mean it. We're gonna go home and start a business together, play golf on Sundays, and eat at fuckin' McDonald's every damn day. We're gonna be just like everybody else, Rich."

Richardson reached up and pulled the big man close to him. His voice was filled with emotion. "God, I love you, you dumb bastard."

Pulling away, McCall pushed a laugh forward as he said, "Hell, man, we ain't been out here long enough for you to be turnin' gay on me."

"Fuck ya, McCall."

"I don't think so, Rich. My ass is about the only fuckin' thing that don't hurt right now."

Richardson started to say something in return, but McCall never gave him the chance. Grabbing the front of Rich's shirt, he pulled him up on his shoulders. McCall almost collapsed from the weight on his pain-filled, damaged body. His legs wobbled and threatened to go out from under him. Grabbing for his shirt pocket, JD found the half-used tube of morphine.

Shoving the needle into his arm, he squeezed the last drops of the precious drug into his body. Richardson's weight suddenly felt like nothing at all. The pain was still there, but it wasn't so bad. Casting one last look of thanks in Thanh's direction, McCall headed for the DMZ—and home.

XVII.

The Mike Force reported the sounds of gunfire in the general direction of Striker One's rendezvous point. Colonel Davis paced the floor of the operations room as Baron read the report. Once finished, Baron said, "Sir, I honestly believe this report confirms that survivors of Striker and Deliverance are trying to reach the rendezvous point. They'll be expecting a Mike Force that is not there. Sir, please, we have to move that force into position for rescue and cover fire if it's needed."

Davis spoke as he continued to pace the floor. "And what if it's a trap to draw our people into that area? Striker One and the Deliverance team have become expendable, Colonel. I think it's time you realize that point. I don't like it any more than you, but there it is. I will not risk the lives of over forty men on guesswork. If we have confirmation that they are at the link-up point then we'll take action, but not until then. Do you understand, Colonel?"

"Yes, sir. Do I have your permission to release two more of our choppers to run the slot along the DMZ?"

"My God, Colonel, we gave ten men a job that would have been close to impossible for fifty, yet you still believe McCall's people or Esswain and the Deliverance team could have survived. I would like to remind you that Lieutenant Esswain went in there with two operational radios, and we have not heard a word from them since the jump. That alone should tell you something, Jess."

With the anger rising in his voice, Baron said, "Dammit, sir, I picked these people because they were the best. *I* picked them and I think I should at least have the chance to confirm they're fuckin' dead."

Davis looked at his watch, then at the colonel. "It is oh-five-hundred Colonel. I will give you seven hours to locate any survivors from either of the two teams. At exactly thirteen hundred hours I will recall the Mike Force and report to Saigon Command that the mission has failed. I am sorry, Jess, but I have no choice."

"That's all I'm asking for, sir, just a chance."

"You have seven hours, Jess."

Baron left Davis and headed for the air-operations shed. He wanted those choppers in the air at sunrise.

Looking at the horizon, McCall could see the gray line of approaching dawn. In another 30 minutes he would be standing at the edge of the DMZ. JD McCall had reached the limit of his endurance. The morphine would begin wearing off soon, and his wounds had reopened from the weight of Richardson. McCall had made it this far on a wonder drug, pure guts, and determination. But even these things could not repair his torn and weary body. Staggering to keep on his feet, he kept repeating the same thing over and over, "One foot forward, one step home. One foot forward, one step home. . . ."

At 0545 hours, the first chopper lifted off, followed by two more. Baron watched as they disappeared beyond the range of mountains. The orders to the pilots had been simple—stay on station and search for Striker One. Monitor the radio at all times, and return only to refuel. The colonel had given him seven hours, and Baron intended to utilize every minute of it.

There was no doubt in McCall's mind that he was at

the DMZ. There was no other place like it on earth.
Heavy fog floated a few feet above the ground. Under
that fog were thousands of bomb craters filled with
stagnant water that spread a foul odor over the entire
area. The trees stood gray and barren, the work of a
new chemical they called Agent Orange. There was no
color in this place. It was only fitting it was called a no
man's land.

Richardson was just coming to as McCall gently lay
him against a mound of dirt at the edge of a bomb
crater. Dropping next to him, McCall leaned back,
exhausted.

"You did it, JD. You got us here," Richardson said in
a weak voice.

"I told you I'd get you out, Rich." Pulling the
URC-10 from his pants-leg pocket, McCall switched the
radio on and began to call, "Any station. Any station.
This is . . . Striker One. Over."

Richardson asked, "What happened to the NVA
radio, JD?"

"It was either carry you or the radio. Which one
would you have picked?"

"Oh. Sorry I asked."

McCall put the small radio to his ear. There was
nothing but a steady rush of static coming through the
speaker.

"Any station. Any station. This is Striker One.
Striker One. Come in. Over."

There was no reply. Lowering the radio to his side,
McCall looked at Rich and said, "Well, partner, we
gave it one hell of a good run for the money."

Richardson heard the disappointment in McCall's
voice.

"Maybe they're just runnin' a little late, JD. You
know how the army is."

Passing the radio to Rich, McCall lay back against
the crater and let his eyes fill up with the morning sky.
He had never seen it so blue. Here and there a small

cloud of pure white floated gently through the calm blue.

Rich continued to call, but no one answered. Looking at the desolate terrain around him, JD thought of how ironic it was that he had struggled so hard to get to this place to die. The silence of the radio caused him more pain than all the bullets the NVA had fired through his body. With the silence went his hope.

Richardson switched the radio to the beeper position and placed it at the top of the mound. If they were in range, any aircraft could pick up the signal and home in on it. But it would have to be soon. The batteries couldn't last more than another hour. Looking over at McCall, Rich watched his chest rise and fall under the bloodstained shirt. JD was asleep.

In the operations shed, Baron keyed the mike and called the lead chopper.

"Black Bandit, this is Demon Two. Have you spotted anything yet? Over."

"Demon Two, this is Black Bandit. Negative contact. We are swinging back around and will shift our pattern more to the northern sector. Over."

Baron's eyes swept over the map as he answered, "Roger, Bandit. Try to stay as low as possible and watch for any signal from the ground. They may not have any radio communication equipment left. Over."

"Roger, Demon Two. We copy. Bandit, out."

Colonel Baron had just replaced the mike when another voice came on the radio.

"Who . . . ver . . . charge . . . f . . . those damn chop . . . out of her . . . we are . . . out."

Davis entered just as the unknown caller began his transmission.

He said, "Jess, who the hell was that?"

Grabbing the mike again, Baron yelled, "Station calling. Station calling. Identify yourself. Over." There was no reply.

Baron pressed the switch again. "Mike Charlie One, this is Demon. Did you copy last transmission? Over."

The Mike Force commander replied, "Roger, Demon. We copied. It was not, I say again, it was not this station. Is it possible the bad guys are using one of our radios, and do you want us to check it out? That joker has to be out here somewhere. He was talkin' about the choppers, but his set is breakin' up real bad. You want us to try and pinpoint the source? Over."

Baron turned to Davis. "What d'you say, sir? We've got 'em out there, we might as well use 'em."

Davis hesitated; he was trying to weigh the advantages against the disadvantages. If the Mike Force was hit in an ambush, they were going to need every chopper they had to pull them out, and three of those were already out somewhere on the search for Striker. They would have to return, refuel, then get back to the area. In that amount of time, Davis realized he could lose half of his Mike Force. But what if McCall or any members of Striker made it to the DMZ? They would be waiting for a rescue team and choppers to get them out.

Baron stood silently holding the mike in his hand. The Mike Force commander repeated his question.

Davis looked frustrated. "Dammit, Jess. You better hope someone from Striker One made it to the DMZ! Tell Charlie One to move for the original link-up point, and for God's sake be careful. We still don't know who's on that frequency."

Baron grinned. "Thank you, sir."

The Mike Force commander rogered the message and departed for the area immediately. The radio operator had been listening to the tense conversation going on in the room, and now he sat tapping his pencil on the desk. There was something bothering him; he just couldn't put his finger on it. Then it hit him like a bolt out of the blue. His voice echoed around the room. "Oh, dammit!"

Surprised by the outburst, both Baron and Davis turned at the same time and watched as the commo sergeant moved to the map. Davis asked, "What is it, Sergeant?"

"Hell, sir. I'm supposed to be an expert at this shit. I should have realized this sooner."

Baron asked impatiently, "What are you talking about, man?"

Pointing to the planned pickup point, then to the location of their headquarters, he said, "Sir, that station that keeps coming up can't be Charlie! Striker didn't have anything but URC-10s for the past forty-eight hours. Even if Charlie got their hands on the things, they couldn't transmit this far, and, besides, that damn radio doesn't even work on the frequency we're using with the choppers. So how can it be the bad guys with Striker's radios?"

Davis said, "Well, then, who the hell's on that freq?"

Baron glanced at the map once more. "Sergeant, get me the commander of the First Marine Div . . ." Before he could finish, the lead chopper came up on the radio, loud and clear. "Demon Two, this is Bandit. We've got a beeper signal. It is extremely weak, but it is definitely a beeper on the emergency frequency. Estimate coordinates at Papa Kilo two seven nine, five six four. Over."

Davis muttered, "My God. . . ."

Baron was on the radio again. There was excitement in his voice.

"Mike Charlie One, did you copy chopper's last? Over."

The Mike Force commander sounded as excited as Baron. "Roger, Demon. We are heading for that location at this time. Have choppers ready for pickup. Charlie One, out."

Baron relayed the message to the chopper. "Black Bandit leader, this is Demon. Head for that signal but do not, I say again, do not try to land until Charlie

One has secured your LZ. Over."

"Roger, Demon. Understand. Bandit, out."

The commo sergeant noted the text of the radio transmissions in his log, then asked Baron, "Excuse me, sir, you want me to contact someone?"

Baron could not remember ever feeling as good as he did now. He said, "Never mind, Sergeant. Colonel Davis and I are going to step next door for a cup of coffee. Let us know the minute Charlie One is in the pickup area."

The two officers left the room and headed for the mess hall. Everything was working out well for a change. . . .

Richardson painfully pushed himself up into a sitting position. The sound was still a long way off, but it was a sound he would recognize anywhere. It was a chopper. Gently shaking JD, he said, "Wake up, JD. Wake up. It's a goddamn chopper, brother. Wake up."

McCall's eyes opened to face the bright morning sun. "What the hell you want, Rich?"

"Listen, man, you hear it? That's a chopper, baby. We're out of here."

McCall shook his head, trying to clear it. It was a chopper, that was for damn sure. It was east of them. Still a long way off, but coming their way. The sound sparked new life into McCall. "Rich, give me that radio, quick."

Pressing the switch, JD said, "Chopper, chopper, this is Striker One, Striker One. Come in. Over."

Both beleaguered Green Berets held their breath, praying for an answer. It came. "Striker One, Striker One, this is Black Bandit leader. I have you weak but readable. Leave your beeper on until we have you in sight. Do you copy? Over."

"You got it, Bandit Leader. You just bring that sweet fuckin' bird right on in here. We've been trying to figure out who's going to kiss you first."

"No problem, guys. You just sit tight. We're comin'

to take you home. Charlie One is the friend you were
expecting to meet. He is coming your way at this time.
He should be less than a mile from you now. They will
secure the LZ for us. I'll give you another call in a few
minutes. Bandit, out."

Richardson reached over and grasped JD's good
hand. "You did it, man. You got me out."

McCall lay back. "No, Rich, it wasn't just me. It was
a lot of people. A lot of damn good people on both
sides."

The commo sergeant sent for Colonels Davis and
Baron the minute Bandit Leader confirmed radio contact.

Baron hurried to the radio, grabbed the mike, and
said, "Bandit Leader, this is Demon Two. Have you
been able to confirm ID of survivors? Over."

"Negative, Demon. Contact was weak. Stand by, we
will try again. Break. Striker One, Striker One. This is
Bandit. Over."

The sergeant reminded the officers that they would
only be able to monitor the chopper's side of the
conversation.

"Striker One, this is Bandit. You're coming in much
better now. Our higher-ups request identification of
Striker personnel for pickup. Over."

Baron and Davis stared at the speaker on the wall.

"Roger, Striker, I copy. Out."

"Break . . . Demon, Bandit. Over."

"Roger, Bandit. Go!"

"Demon, we have two personnel for pickup. I say
again, two personnel. ID as follows: McCall, J.D. and
Richardson, Abraham L. How copy? Over."

Baron lowered his head and said, "We roger, Bandit.
Over."

"Uh, Demon, McCall said to tell you mission was
complete. All three appointments were kept, whatever

in the hell that means. Over."

"Thank you, Bandit. Demon, out."

Davis had a look of total disbelief on his face as he whispered, "All three—they got all three of the bastards. You know what this means, Jess?"

Baron was not cheering anything right now. All he could think of were the losses. Eight of the original 10 were dead. All of Esswain and Smith's people were dead. That was another 20. Salt and Pepper, Thanh, all the dead in the photos. The number was staggering. But at least McCall and Richardson had made it. That was some consolation.

The radio conversation between the Mike Force and the chopper had begun.

"Charlie One, this is Bandit Leader. What is your ETA to LZ? Over."

"Bandit, we are less than ten minutes away at this time. Over."

"Roger, Charlie One. We will be standing by on station. Give us a call when you're set to go. Bandit, out."

No sooner had the chopper pilot said, "out," than the unknown station they had monitored earlier came on the air again. As the static broke across the radio, everyone in the room strained to hear each word.

"If you have operat . . . in . . . coordinat . . . clear through ou . . . quarters, repeat you mus . . . cle . . . arters . . . confirm . . . ver."

The tension in the room mounted as Baron's eyes searched every face and asked, "Did anyone understand that?"

No one had.

Baron slammed his fist on the desk. "Dammit! Who the hell is that?"

The question was forgotten as Charlie One came on the radio. "Demon, this is Charlie One. We have Striker in sight. They are four hundred yards across from us. We have established radio contact with them and are now securing the area for Bandit to come in. Advise that you have medical personnel standing by. These guys look like they went through a meat grinder. Do you copy? Over."

Baron's eyes went back to the map. Davis caught the look of confusion in those eyes. "What is it, Jess? What's wrong?"

Before he could answer, the speaker came alive again.

"Demon Two, this is Bandit. We have spotted Striker and are awaiting call from Charlie One that we are secure. From the looks of your people down there, we better not take too long. Do you copy? Over."

The commo sergeant shifted nervously in his chair as he spoke. "Sir, you have to answer."

There was something wrong. Baron could feel it. But things were going so fast now. It was something that someone had said only a few days ago. At the time it had seemed unimportant, just a minor thing. But now every fiber of his being screamed for him to remember.

"Demon, this is Charlie One. We have secured the LZ. Over."

There was only silence as Baron stood motionless, gripping the mike.

"Demon, this is Bandit. Are you able to copy, Charlie One? Over."

The unknown station came up to add to the confusion in the operations shed.

"Bandit Leade . . . his . . . you confirm what area yo . . . need clea . . . confirm all . . . we . . . confir . . . ove . . ."

"Charlie One, this is Bandit. Could you copy that?"

"Negative, Bandit. What's happened to Demon Two? Over."

"No idea, Charlie One. Are you ready for us to come in? Over."

"Roger. We're just waiting for confirmation from Demon Two. Over."

Baron was standing motionless as if in a daze, his mind overwhelmed with a premonition of impending doom.

Davis grabbed the mike from his hands. "Jess, what the hell is wrong with you? Speak to me, man."

"I don't know, sir. It's something about those broken transmissions."

"Hell, Jess, we are ready to pull McCall and Richardson out of that hellhole. Do you want me to take control of this operation or do you want to do it?"

"Sorry, sir."

Handing the mike back to Baron, Davis watched him closely.

Baron's hands were wet with perspiration, his heart pounded, and a small voice inside him kept screaming, "No!" He took a deep breath and then spoke into the microphone. "Charlie One, Bandit, this is Demon. Get those choppers in there fast. I want Striker out of there now."

McCall and Richardson had been monitoring the conversation between the chopper and the Mike Force. Taking a final puff from his last cigarette, McCall flipped it into the crater and said, "These boys sure do get excited over small shit, don't they?"

Richardson tried to laugh, but the pain was really starting to get to him. He was beginning to feel like he was going to pass out any minute.

"Striker One, this is Bandit Leader. We're coming in to get you. ETA, three minutes. Be standing by. Bandit, out."

McCall gave out with a laugh as he looked over at Rich. "Well, you heard the man. He wants you *standing* by. Hell, man, we only got one good leg out of four. But we'll make do, won't we, partner?"

"You got it, boss."

Hooking the radio onto what was left of his web gear, McCall forced himself to his feet. His whole body felt like one large exposed nerve. Shaking his head, he cleared his eyes. The pain was unbelievable. Reaching down for Richardson, the two men locked arms as JD pulled him up.

"JD, if you don't mind, I think I'd like to try an' walk this last hundred feet."

"You sure you can make it, Rich?"

"Well, ya might have to drag me a few feet, but I'd sure like to try."

McCall smiled at him. "Hell, you just wanna use it for a war story when you're sittin' around drinkin', don't ya?"

Rich forced a grin and said, "Come on, JD, let's go home."

Richardson had moved only a few feet when the bullet ripped through his throat. A second round slammed into his chest, knocking him out of McCall's grasp. The lifeless form of Richardson crumpled into the dirt beside the crater.

McCall screamed as loud as he could, "No! No! Goddammit, not now!" Trying to move his pain-ridden body over to Richardson, tears flowed from his eyes as his screams dropped to only a confused mutter. "No! God, not now."

The choppers were less than a quarter of a mile away. The sound of the blades echoed throughout the dead world of the DMZ.

The first bullet struck him in the back and tore through his chest, the impact spinning him like a top in the loose dirt. The final round blew away the right side of his face—but even in death McCall and Richardson were together, for as his body dropped to the ground, his lifeless hand dropped across that of his friend.

The choppers swung in low over the DMZ and headed for the LZ.

"Striker One, this is Bandit. Over." There was no answer.

The doorgunner pressed his throat mike and said, "Sir, I thought I saw two bodies back there."

"Roger. We'll swing around and make another pass. Keep your eyes open."

The room of the operations shed was as quiet as a church. They had heard Bandit's last transmission. Baron sat rubbing his eyes. It couldn't be, not now. Not when they had been so close. Davis stared out the window, not wanting to believe what he had just heard.

The radio crackled again and came to life, only this time the voice was low. "Demon, this is Bandit Leader. We have two confirmed bodies, both American."

The pilot paused for a moment, then said in an emotional voice, "We will recover the bodies. Sorry, Colonel. Bandit, out."

Baron wiped the moisture from his eyes and joined Davis at the window. The older man had tears running down his cheeks. In a choked voice, and without looking at Baron, he said, "McCall told me before they left that if things didn't turn out right on this one, we shouldn't feel bad. He said people like him and Richardson and Doc Hawkins were like the wind—they were only here for a little while, then they moved on to another place and time."

The reverent attitude of the moment was broken by the booming voice of a Marine colonel who had burst into the room. He was arguing with one of the guards.

"Don't tell me I can't fucking come in here, sonny. I'm a damn Marine Colonel. Now get the hell out of my way."

The guard pulled his gun and was aiming it at the man when Davis intervened.

"That's all right, Sergeant. You can go."

Replacing his pistol, the guard saluted and turned smartly to leave, but not before he looked the Marine colonel straight in the eye and whispered, "You're one lucky asshole, Colonel." Smiling, he walked out and closed the door.

Davis asked, "What do you want here, Colonel?"

The man was a typical Marine, his voice loud and boastful. "I see why you Special Forces people have a problem with discipline, Colonel. Do you realize that guard of yours called me an asshole?"

Davis was not in the mood for formalities. "I'll ask you one more time, *asshole*. What do you want?"

The Marine officer was only momentarily stunned by the remark. Quickly regaining his composure, he said, "I felt that since I am the commander of the Third Marine Division in this area I should bring you the good news personally. Colonel, we Marines have done what all your Special Forces heroes could not do. One of our sniper teams just nailed that fuckin' Salt and Pepper team in the DMZ. Now, what do you have to say to that?" Placing his fists on his hips, the colonel waited for an answer.

The communications sergeant broke his pencil in half and, lowering his head, whispered, "Oh, my God!"

Baron and Davis stared at the colonel. There were no words. What could be said now that would change anything?

The Marine colonel was confused. This was not the reaction he had envisioned he would receive.

Colonel Davis placed his beret on his head and, without looking at the Marine, said, "You'll have to excuse me now, Colonel. I have two Medal of Honor winners coming in on a chopper."

Baron pulled his beret from his pants-leg pocket and started to follow Davis. The Marine colonel stopped him and said, "Jesus, Colonel, why didn't you guys say something? You know, I've never met a Medal of Honor winner. Would you mind if I came along?"

A sadistic look came over Baron's face as he carefully and proudly fit his beret to his head. Then he said,

"No, Colonel. As a matter of fact, I think you, more than anyone else in this compound, should be there to meet these two heroes when they arrive."

The door closed behind the two officers as the commo sergeant entered his last note to the log. 0845 hours. Confirmed. Striker One *Down*.